Richard stared at the face before him for a long moment, then removed Janine's hand from his and kissed her palm. His moist, tender mouth on her skin sent shivers through Janine, touching every part of her body. She felt weak at the knees.

"Richard..." she was drawn to say, while holding her breath, unsure where this was headed, if anywhere. Or nowhere. But she was too swept up in the moment to think rationally. She sensed they both were.

Setting down their wineglasses, Richard cupped Janine's cheeks and slowly, deliberately, brought his mouth down to hers. Their lips brushed softly as if testing the waters for warmth and invitation. For a moment Janine felt as if they were frozen in time, caught between the past, present and future in an inescapable black hole. They began to kiss passionately with a desperation that came with need, each releasing pent-up emotions that had been stored so long, it was almost forgotten they existed. Their mouths opened and pressed tightly together, as if to keep all the positive energy within from escaping, powering between them like steam in an engine.

They stayed that way for seemingly hours, but in fact it was only minutes. Then abruptly Richard pulled away, leaving Janine slightly off balance and feeling cold.

Love
ONCE AGAIN

DEVON VAUGHN ARCHER

ARABESQUE®

LOVE ONCE AGAIN

ISBN 1-58314-679-2

www.kimanipress.com

Printed in U.S.A.

Dedication

To sweet H. Loraine, my pride and joy, Marjah Aljean, the greatest mother in the world, and Jackie, the best sister a fellow could have!

Also to the fans that have come to appreciate my romance novels and keep me going, in conjuring up new and exciting love stories.

Acknowledgments

After being one of the first male authors to write for Arabesque, I am excited about making the jump to Harlequin and Kimani Press to carry on the tradition with my second Arabesque contemporary romance.

Love Once Again is sure to please my current fans and bring me new ones among Harlequin readers.

Many thanks go to my wonderful editor, Linda Gill, who brought me into the Arabesque family of authors and now the Harlequin community of wonderful writers, where I expect us both to enjoy a long career.

I would also like to express gratitude to Demetria Lucas, for her role in signing me on with Arabesque as a male author and continuing to support at Harlequin.

As the most important person in my world, and a lady who knows something about romance, thank you, Ms. H. Loraine, for your role in bringing this latest masterpiece to life and inspiring me for future ones.

Finally, the Man upstairs is greatly loved and appreciated for making it possible for me to become a successful writer and the many other blessings to come my way.

I look forward to the future and all its rewards.

Chapter 1

She had never even heard of Richard Lowrey before, as incredible as it now seemed to Janine. She was still barely able to believe it, the memories flooding her mind like a tidal wave, filling it with glee, contentment, optimism and even some regrets. Not until the day that was to inexorably change her life forever...

It began as a typical busy day in the life of an East Coast senior editor for the large African-American book publisher, Callister-Reynolds, Inc. The namesakes of the publisher, Earl Callister and Paul Reynolds, had been pioneers in African-American illustrated and visual books since the early 1960s. Four decades later, they had been sold twice, gone public, and were one step away from bankruptcy. Needless to say, the company had seen more than its share of ups and downs. Currently it was up, as there was suddenly a strong interest in professionally written and produced black fine arts, travel and coffee-table books.

Janine Henderson had only worked for Callister-Reynolds—located in the heart of New York City—for three months now, having previously been a senior editor for a Boston trade house. Two years earlier she had divorced the father of her seven-year-old daughter after tiring of his cheating ways and of his blaming it on her inadequacies. It was the best thing she had ever done.

Till the day she met Richard Lowrey.

She had barely acquainted herself with Callister-Reynolds's current list when Janine was told to familiarize herself with their backlist of titles and authors. It turned out that Richard Lowrey was prominent in the latter category. His beautifully photographed and written books exploring Africa, the Caribbean, and black America had almost single-handedly put Callister-Reynolds on the map—and had turned him into a renowned bestselling author. He was well regarded by many as an authority on unique worldwide travel experiences and hidden treasures within lands, places and spaces occupied largely by people of color.

At that point Richard Lowrey might just as well have been the man from Mars or on the moon, as far as Janine's knowledge of him was concerned. She hadn't been a real fan of fine arts and travel books and was treading relatively new ground professionally, as well.

That was when the vice president and executive editor of the publisher, Dennis DeMetris, who had summoned her to his office, literally dropped Richard Lowrey's latest book on her lap. Janine picked up the soft-cover edition titled *Autumn in Zimbabwe*.

"What's this?" she asked, batting her large amber eyes at him, while feeling some tightness in her light-brown-skinned, high-cheeked face.

Dennis was a tall, thin man in his early sixties with somewhat of a stoop. He had a remarkably full head of Afroish curly gray hair and a similar goatee that made him look like something akin to the devil, or perhaps an African-American version of Kentucky Fried Chicken's Colonel Sanders. Deeply lined coal eyes regarded Janine beneath wire-rimmed silver glasses.

"A masterpiece," he said simply, as if it should have been obvious.

Janine glanced at the cover. At the bottom read: "Photographed and written by Richard E. Lowrey." She found herself wondering what the "E" stood for. Edward? Edmond? Elliot? Elias?

She studied the black-and-white photograph that filled the cover nicely, as if taken specifically for that purpose. It was of a dark-haired, dark-skinned boy, maybe nine or ten. He was standing in the middle of what looked like an African village, guffawing, as if his funny bone had been tickled nonstop. In the backdrop what looked to be candelabra trees were parted almost magically to show a glimpse of a river. The foreground had a portion of an old and rusting bicycle, as if purely for effect.

"There are more magnificent pictures inside," Dennis said proudly. "But save that for later...."

Janine favored Dennis's face. It was permanently crinkled above the brow and along his cheeks in deep irregular lines. Only now, there were temporary folds between his eyes reflecting his present state of mind.

"Is there a problem?" She dreaded to ask.

It suddenly occurred to Janine that she had yet to have her three-month review. Though she had done her job sufficiently—it was actually a series of jobs, some that had very little to do with editing—her confidence was not as such that she felt any real sense of security in the ever-changing, ever-downsizing marketplace.

That old *last to get hired, first to get fired* adage drummed in her head.

Dennis seemed to ponder the question for a moment or two, as if still trying to decide. He removed his glasses rather dramatically, and said, "Yeah, there's a problem all right…and his name is *Richard Lowrey*—"

Janine once again peeked at the book and back at Dennis. "Richard…Lowrey?" she found herself repeating, as though duty-bound.

Dennis chewed on the part of his glasses that fit around his ear. "He's *disappeared*—"

A thin brow involuntarily raised, and once again Janine found herself sounding like a parrot. "Disappeared? As in *vanished*…?"

Dennis sat on the well-worn, soft black leather chair beside her. He put his glasses back on, as if feeling naked without them.

"In a manner of speaking," he indicated calmly. "The man has developed what I would call a terminal and very costly case of writer's block. *Autumn in Zimbabwe* was published *three* long years ago."

That explained, in part, why she wasn't familiar with the title. In the publishing world, three years was like an eternity. Ancient history. Without fresh exposure, even the hottest authors could turn cold as ice.

It still didn't explain the mystery that was unfolding about Richard E. Lowrey.

"So what happened to him?" Janine asked on cue, her interest admittedly piqued.

Dennis's face darkened as surely as if someone had

dumped soot on it. "Lowrey's wife and daughter were killed in a car accident," he said almost resentfully. "Occurred on the same day we sent him his copies of *Autumn in Zimbabwe*. Which also happens to be the *last* manuscript we've received from the man, though we still have him under contract for two more books."

Janine couldn't begin to relate to the sense of loss, despair and emptiness Richard Lowrey must have gone through in having his family taken away from him so suddenly and tragically. As a result, he had apparently shut off completely from that which he must have dearly loved at one time—his stunning photography and writing. But coming off a disillusioning divorce from a cheating husband at thirty-six years of age, and as a result being left to raise a child alone had left Janine with a certain sense of bitterness and loss in her own right, along with lingering feelings of frustration, resentment and betrayal.

On the other hand, Janine also felt as if she could empathize with Richard Lowrey on some sort of spiritual, emotional and perhaps physical level as well. *Any* separation could be numbing and seem as if one had slipped into a dark, desolate hole with little chance of ever coming back to the surface.

This is surely how Richard Lowrey must feel these days, she thought.

"We don't want to see Lowrey's promising career go up in smoke," Dennis said matter-of-factly. "And we certainly don't want to lose the rather substantial advance we paid him for the books he still owes us. There was a clause in his contract for nondelivery to this effect. The man sure as hell can't have it both ways…though he seems to think so—"

"Well, has anyone tried talking to him?" Janine asked, in what seemed like a reasonable question. *Or am I missing something here?*

Dennis waved his hand in the air as if swatting a fly. "Calls have gone unanswered…voice mails unacknowledged," he responded bitterly, shaking his head. "Mail has been returned unopened as if there was no one at the other end to receive it. It's been frustrating as hell, to say the least."

Janine stiffened. "I'm sorry," she told him, not quite sure where this was going or even why she was sorry. She had a feeling she was about to find out on both counts.

"Everyone's sorry," Dennis grumbled, rolling his eyes. "But that won't solve our little problem, will it?"

Janine did not respond as she assumed the question was rhetorical. Even then she didn't exactly consider it *her* problem…not yet, anyway.

Dennis furrowed his brows and said bluntly, "We think Lowrey's grieved long enough—assuming that's what's behind his lack of production. Now it's time for the man to honor his commitment to this publisher—"

Janine swallowed the lump in her throat. Courageously, she asked thoughtfully, "Can anyone really determine how long is *long enough* to grieve for another?"

She recalled that her father had been dead for more than twenty years and her mother had still grieved for him right up until the day she died. And, if true to herself, Janine had to admit that she, too, was still grieving somewhat for the man she had once thought would be her lifelong marriage partner. In reality, she decided, her sorrow might have been more for the fear of being alone, albeit due to circumstances that left her with no other sensible choice.

Dennis dismissed her words the way one might a gabby in-law's, and, looking Janine straight in the eye, said flatly, "I want you to pay Mr. Lowrey a visit—"

Janine's jaw dropped. She suddenly felt as if she had been

backed into a corner—like a trapped rat—in which there was no way out. But she tried to escape nonetheless.

"Dennis, I'm not sure I'm the right person to get Richard Lowrey to cooperate or whatever you want to call it." Not to mention there was nothing in her duties, as Janine understood them, that included visiting and nurturing wayward authors. "Isn't this something the attorneys ought to be handling?"

The frown deepened above Dennis's hard gaze. "Absolutely not!" he stated firmly. "We're not looking for a legal battle here—at least not yet—even if the terms in the contract Lowrey signed speak for themselves. What we really want is to get the man back in the fold, doing what he does best and what's best for Callister-Reynolds. Plain and simple. The time is right and the market is ready to embrace his considerable talents again in book form."

Perhaps, Janine thought. She just wasn't nearly as confident or comfortable with the thought of intruding upon this man's personal life for professional gain. Even if it was in his best interests, as well.

"Are you sure this is really such a good idea, Dennis?" she asked uneasily. "Maybe he just needs a bit more time to get his house in order."

"But it's *our* house we're trying to get in order," the vice president of the company reminded her, with a solid edge to his voice. "Time is money and there are simply no more bits and pieces we can spare to Richard Lowrey—you know what I'm saying?"

Janine nodded, even if doubts still lingered like a nagging pain. *I can only hope that I feel better about this when all is said and done.*

Dennis seemed to sense her misgivings. "I assume you are still part of our *team,* Janine." He favored her a shrewd look. "Aren't you...?"

Janine nearly froze under the weight of his cold stare. She took it as a veiled threat that she was either to cooperate or consider her employment on the ropes, if not subject to termination altogether.

Even if her heart was definitely not in it, she was not foolish enough to put her job on the line by taking a stand against something that technically could have been part of the job description—insofar as doing *whatever* it took to keep the lines of communication and cooperation open between the publisher and writer.

Think positive, her aunt Josephine always said.

Easier said than done.

"Of course I'm part of the team," she uttered somewhat shakily, forcing a wavering smile with thin lips that suddenly felt dry and chapped. "Whatever you think is best, Dennis."

He grinned with clear satisfaction and scratched his goatee. "Good to know. I'm counting on you, Janine, to find a way to get this unreasonable brother to be reasonable. His next book is long overdue. We'd much rather have that in our possession than the upfront money we gave him—which we believe can be recouped quickly once we publish a new work by the talented, if not enigmatic, Richard Lowrey."

"I'll give it my best shot," Janine muttered lamely, while knowing full well that might not be enough. It had better be, she thought, fearing the repercussions should she fail.

"That's all we ever ask of our employees, Janine," Dennis said disingenuously. He rose to his feet, removing his glasses as if to signal the meeting had come to an end. "I'll have my secretary make the travel arrangements for you. Meanwhile I'd suggest you learn as much about Lowrey as you can. It might help with your bargaining power."

Bargaining power, Janine thought, as if this were a real-estate deal. Or perhaps like trying to whittle down the price of a new car. Or maybe tickets to see a popular recording artist.

Would Richard Lowrey be in any mood to bargain away the pain, grief and memories that surely gnawed at him like termites on wood, and that wouldn't go away?

She wondered if he could have somehow missed the clause in his contract that stated the advance on his next two books was based upon satisfactory completion and delivery of manuscripts he agreed to write and the photographs to accompany them. Surely Richard Lowrey, an established and successful writer, had no intention of keeping what he hadn't rightfully earned? This would only be asking for trouble, no matter his other difficulties in life.

For her part, Janine knew there was really only one vital question she had to concern herself with at the moment: *Can I succeed where others have failed in getting to this man?* The thought left her unsettled, to say the least.

Janine stood up, hoping that her legs didn't somehow give out from underneath her. At five-seven and a half, she was nearly five inches shorter than Dennis. Self-consciously, she hand smoothed a wrinkle on the skirt of her Belldini tailored navy suit, which fit nicely on a slender frame. Two-inch matching heels brought her closer to Dennis's height. Her long, thick, naturally curly jet-black hair was hidden away inside the bun, as she often wore it on the job.

Dennis surveyed her in an appreciative, nonsexual slant of the head. "By the way," he said, as if were truly an afterthought, "Richard lives in Pebble Beach, California. Ever been there?"

Janine shook her head. "The closest was Los Angeles," she informed him.

Janine had been nine years old when her parents had taken her to Hollywood on a vacation, thinly disguised as visiting long-lost and all-but-forgotten relatives. All she could seem to remember of the trip was her father driving around—seemingly in circles—in a rented red convertible while they looked for homes of movie stars—if not the actual stars themselves. Pebble Beach had not even been on the map in her young mind, though she had heard since how picturesque the area was. Not to mention it was probably way too expensive a place to live on an editor's salary, she thought enviously.

"Then you've got a treat coming," Dennis said as though doing her a great favor. "They tell me it's like paradise on earth there, and then some." He narrowed his eyes tellingly. "What you choose to do on your own time out there is your business. Just remember, *my* business before *your* pleasure."

Janine raised a brow. She couldn't help but wonder what his definition of *pleasure* was. Several possibilities crossed her mind: the scenery, the sun, the sea and the sand.

Or, she mused uneasily, *Richard E. Lowrey.*

"I don't think I'll have much trouble remembering that," she murmured.

As far as Janine was concerned, she wanted only to go to California, get the job done, for better or worse, and return to New York.

And her daughter.

The last thing she wanted or needed was to mix business with pleasure, especially where it concerned the missing-in-action author.

Or so she thought.

Chapter 2

Janine lived with her daughter, Lisa, and their cat, Murphy, in a renovated, rent-controlled apartment in Manhattan. It was much, much smaller than the house they had in Boston, but more livable and in better surroundings. There were two bedrooms and a bathroom, a kitchen with an eating area, and a cozy living room. The floors were maple hardwood and the walls an off-white color.

In spite of having to get used to tighter spaces, Janine could hardly complain, all things considered. At least she didn't have to worry about another woman spending time in her bedroom.

In my bed.

Her ex-husband, John, had done his best, or so it seemed, to make her actually feel a sense of contentment being alone. She was in no hurry to become seriously involved again, much less share a residence with a man. "Trust" was a word Janine feared she no longer knew the meaning of in a relationship. It went right along with other terms that had pretty much gone out the window in her life: faithfulness, honesty, commitment and respect.

It would be a long time, if ever, before she was foolish enough to let her guard down with another man. Janine was steadfast in that thought as she prepared the dining-room table for dinner. Yes, there had been the occasional blind date based on the good intentions of a friend or coworker. But she had shut them off like a faucet before leading them on or vice versa, afraid of being hurt again and opening herself up to more deep wounds that never went away completely.

It was these very real feelings that strengthened the bond between Janine and Lisa. For, in the absence of a significant other, she was able to give her daughter her undivided attention. Lisa sometimes took full advantage of this, but she loved her for it. Janine could not imagine what she would do without her little shining star to dote on and spoil with unbridled adoration.

They sat at a square vintage oak table bought at a garage sale in almost perfect condition, save for a few nicks on the sides and corners. A sausage pizza was in the center of the table, still hot from the oven.

Janine took a slice and watched her daughter do the same. Lisa bit off more than she could chew, as usual, but that didn't stop her from putting forth the effort, giggling heartily as if it was the funniest thing to have the crust, cheese and sausage spilling out of her mouth.

Janine couldn't help but laugh, too. "Uh, let's try not to eat so much at once, *please,* sweet pea," she said, using the nickname that her own mother had given her when she was a little girl.

"Okay," Lisa mumbled, and immediately sank her teeth

into a smaller piece of pizza, strings of cheese dripping down her chin and onto the table like spiderwebs.

Janine handed her a napkin. "That's a little better, I think," she chuckled, grateful that Lisa was at least able to actually get some of it into her stomach.

Janine watched her daughter admiringly. Lisa had the best of her parents' features. She had Janine's long, curly, thick dark hair, high cheekbones and naturally slim build. Her nose was also like her mother's—small and refined—as was her mouth, which was thin and had a natural cheery curve to it. Lisa's inquisitive sable eyes and fine chocolate-colored skin were inherited from her father. The result was a beautiful little girl who meant the world to Janine.

For some reason, it made her think of Richard E. Lowrey. Surely his little girl had meant every bit as much to him. Not to mention his wife. They were taken away from him through no fault of their own and it certainly was not something he could have prevented. The thought of losing Lisa to a premature death at such a young age gave Janine the chills. She could not envision a life without her—Lisa was her heart and soul and the one ray of light in her life.

My little angel, and so much more, Janine thought, her eyes welling with tears.

Richard Lowrey had had the misfortune of a double tragedy of the heart. It had apparently fallen short of healing even after three long years of separation from his loved ones. Now she had to intrude upon his sustained and heartfelt grief and try to bring him back to the world that had continued without him. It was a daunting task, to say the least. One she hardly felt qualified for, but which had been thrust upon her, much like a doctor of education being asked to perform surgery on a heart patient.

She didn't look forward to it, yet accepted the challenge, given there was little choice in the matter. Her fervent hope was that at the end of the day Richard Lowrey would agree to write and photograph two books for Callister-Reynolds without compromising that which had stood in his way—the love, loyalty, longing and devastating loss he had experienced.

Central Park meant many things to many people in the Big Apple. To Janine it was a place to take her daughter when the weather was nice and the birds were singing spiritedly. It was also where she tried to jog at least three evenings a week, having taken up running in college and maintaining the regimen ever since. In addition to the obvious physical and cardiovascular benefits, it made her feel good about herself and the mental energy required to stick with the program when at times she would rather be doing almost anything else.

Janine ran that evening with Flora McDougal. Flora was an editorial director and longtime employee at Callister-Reynolds—and probably her closest friend there, even though they did little socializing outside of girl talk, running and an occasional lunch or after-work drink. Neither seemed to have the time or energy for much else.

At fifty, Flora had the tight, lean, healthy body of a woman ten years younger. Her bleached orange-blond hair was in tight curls like a lamb and contrasted sharply with her glossy ebony skin and neon-green Adidas jogging suit. Twice divorced, she was now living with a man fifteen years her junior and she was proud of it.

"Heard Dennis the black Menace is sending you across the country to do his dirty work," Flora said, her breathing a bit labored.

Janine tried to downplay it. "I guess he felt someone had

to talk to Mr. Lowrey," she said in earnest. "It appears there were no volunteers." *Present company included,* she thought.

"Good luck, girl," Flora said, eyeing her beneath fake lashes with some skepticism. "You're gonna need it."

"Sounds ominous." Janine gave a nervous chuckle.

Flora sucked in a deep breath. "If you want the truth, Richard Lowrey seems to be lost in his own little world—unwilling to let anyone get inside it, near as I can tell. He's one hell of a good photographer—probably the best I've seen at bringing virtually anything he sets his lens on to life. But he's become a royal pain in the ass since the accident. The man's all but abandoned his once-promising career and, so far, nothing we've done has been able to snap him out of his guilt trip."

"Guilt trip?" Janine lifted her thinly arched brows. "You mean because of the death of his wife and child?"

"No, honey," Flora said with a catch to her voice. "You see, Richard was driving the car when it happened,"

Janine suddenly felt a stab at her lungs as she took in air while willing her legs to keep moving against stiff resistance.

"That's terrible!" she gasped. "What happened?" *Maybe I really don't want to know,* a voice in her head said, even as Janine recognized that it was important that she find out exactly what and *whom* she was up against.

"Lost control of the car in bad weather," Flora said matter-of-factly. "Went over an embankment. His wife and daughter drowned. A real tragedy, but just an unfortunate accident. Could have happened to anyone at any time." She paused. "But it's hard trying to convince someone of that when he walked away without a scratch and they didn't make it out of the water alive."

Suddenly Janine's task seemed that much more formidable.

To carry around that sort of self-blame like a toxin must be unbearable. No one should have to experience such a tragedy.

"Maybe Richard has reached a point of acceptance and is ready to get on with his life," she suggested, and thought hopefully: *As well as his photography and writing.*

"And maybe a sista will occupy the White House before we both kick the bucket," scoffed Flora. "I don't think so! Honestly, I'd say your chance of getting Richard Lowrey to even give you the time of day—much less assurances of living up to his contract with Callister-Reynolds—is slim to none, honey." She sighed thoughtfully. "But hey, what do I know? I'm just an editorial director sticking her nose where it doesn't belong. Could be that Mr. Lowrey's run out of reasons for staying in virtual seclusion for three years now."

Flora sped up and Janine managed to keep pace. She found herself somewhat resentful that her efforts to reach out to Richard Lowrey were being summarily dismissed before she'd even had a chance to put them into action.

Is that a reflection of her lack of faith in me in this assignment? Janine could only wonder. *Or Dennis DeMetris's?*

More likely, it was the fact that Richard Lowrey's uncooperative stance thus far had had a ripple effect and negative impact throughout Callister-Reynolds—infecting even Flora.

"Well, someone has to at least *try* to get to the man," Janine said defensively. "I may not be crazy about being the one—in fact, far from it—but Dennis asked me to and I've accepted it as a worthy, if not particularly desirable, opportunity to maybe somehow make a difference to all parties concerned."

Flora began to slow down, causing Janine to follow suit. The older woman wiped her wet brow with the back of her hand.

"I'm sorry, girl," Flora said, frowning. "Been having some trouble with my boy toy lately and took it out on someone more my size. You know I really do want you to succeed in trying to lure Richard back to us to do what he does better than anyone. After all, with a two-and-a-half-percent stake in the company, I have a lot riding on this." She sighed. "But not as much as DeMetris. He was responsible for giving Richard the mega contract before they lost some steam in this new competitive environment. Now he has to either convince Richard to be reasonable and complete his part of the bargain or face a potentially ugly court fight. Callister-Reynolds would almost certainly win, but at what price? Unfavorable press— maybe even looking like they're picking on one of the few successful nonfiction African-American authors—and perhaps most of all, missing out on the much-needed sales and credibility having him back on our list would bring. It's not just about earning back the advance—it's about bringing in the business that can help us keep getting paychecks. Not an enviable position to be in."

The stakes seemed to keep rising like the tide and Janine felt as if she had been placed squarely in the middle of a war zone, uncertain of its outcome or if she would be standing once the dust settled. Maybe she would be doing more harm than good by encroaching on his sorrow and self-imposed solitude.

Janine's thoughts turned to Callister-Reynolds—or, more specifically, to Dennis DeMetris.

Would Dennis have to answer to the shareholders if there was nothing more to show for the money and time invested in Richard and his incredible literary and photographic skills beyond that already accomplished?

If her employer lost this tug-of-war, there was a good chance that she would be the first to face the proverbial chopping block. Worse was that she could wind up being the scapegoat should things end poorly.

"Looks as if I have my work cut out for me." Janine made no bones about it as she caught her breath. Before Flora could respond, she said cleverly, "It appears as if we *both* need a shot of adrenaline, girlfriend, if we're going to finish this run and still be standing."

On that note Janine once again picked up the pace and Flora, smiling tenderly, came after her, seemingly determined to match her step-for-step. Janine enjoyed the friendly competition and workout, even if her mind was very much elsewhere.

Chapter 3

Janine spent the next two days at her computer, digging up anything and everything she could find on the Internet about Richard Lowrey and the tragedy that had turned his life upside down and his career inside out. She found herself riveted and saddened at the same time. Richard had been a prizewinning photographer early in his career, catapulting him to fame and fortune through sheer natural talent, choice assignments and bestselling books.

He had been thirty-five at the time his wife, Kassandra, thirty-four, and his seven-year-old daughter, Sheena, were killed in the car accident. Richard had been the driver of the Mercedes that went out of control on a rain-slick coastal road, miraculously suffering only minor injuries. The cause of the accident had been listed as weather related, with mechanical failure also playing a role.

Richard blamed himself for what had happened and, according to published reports, had gone into a deep and sustained depression. At the height of his career he had given up everything he'd worked for as an African-American success story—unable or unwilling to continue his brilliant photography and authorship.

Janine felt for this man, as she would for anyone who had gone through such a nightmarish ordeal. Sometimes it seemed as if life could be much too cruel for any normal person to cope with, let alone one who might have been pushed to the limit. Yet she knew that coping was something everyone had to do when facing life's struggles and unexpected twists and turns—no matter how traumatic the ordeal.

At least Janine believed this was true in theory. In reality, she was well aware that some people never recovered from the type of gut-wrenching pain that all too often seemed never ending and all-encompassing.

Janine wondered if Richard E. Lowrey was such a person. She could only hope that all was not lost with this man, that he was walking the line between despair and hope, regret and acceptance, the past and a future.

She had been assigned the job of bringing the man back into focus with the real world. Or at least the world of Callister-Reynolds, where he was contractually obliged to give them two more books with the option to contract for at least two more.

Janine did not like her task, but she knew she had to try for Richard Lowrey's sake and perhaps his sanity. And maybe, she mused, even for her own peace of mind, as well.

On the Internet Janine found information on Richard's books. She focused on excerpts from one title in particular: *New Guinea in Pictures*. Like *Autumn in Zimbabwe,* there was ample evidence of his talent in the artful way in which he managed to capture the most simple and extraordinary things on film. And his gifted prose in writing about the sights and scenes was almost as mesmerizing and entertaining. It gave Janine a whole new appreciation for visual books.

Or at least Richard Lowrey's books.

She clicked on a page with his photograph. Richard Lowrey was pictured in a full-length shot. A caption indicated that it had been taken five years ago. Wearing a dark double-breasted suit, he appeared as a sturdily built, tall man with an oak-colored complexion. His dark hair was closely cropped and showed a few flecks of premature gray, surrounding ruggedly handsome features. Deep-set eyes were a cross between gray and coal with thick, curved brows above. A medium-depth mustache tapered evenly at the corners of his wide mouth, which carried a smile that somehow seemed in-genuous, as though he felt that life was something to embrace and treasure.

Janine couldn't help but think that between Richard's ob-viously good looks and skills behind the camera, his wife had been fortunate to have him—even if only for a short time. She wondered what toll the terrible tragedy had taken on his ap-pearance over the years. It was obvious that the man's mind-set had definitely taken a beating. Usually mental and physical strain went hand in hand. Was that the case here?

Janine made arrangements for Lisa to stay with her ex-husband in Boston, not knowing how long she would be on her West-Coast mission. He had not fought for joint custody, apparently not wanting the responsibility of being a part-time dad, which would interfere with his burgeoning law practice and love life. Instead, they mutually agreed that Lisa would spend part of her summers with him, some holidays and some weekends when there weren't other things Janine had planned for their daughter. Whatever she may have thought of John as a husband, she had never doubted that he adored Lisa—even if he didn't always show it through attention and his time.

By the time Janine boarded the plane, she had already begun to miss her little pride and joy. She could only imagine how hard it would be to watch Lisa grow up and go off to college. Not to mention becoming her own woman with a career, husband and her own kids—leaving little room in Lisa's life for her devoted mother.

Sadly, Janine thought, Richard Lowrey would be forever deprived of those stages of development and progress in his daughter's life.

Chapter 4

Janine arrived at San Francisco International Airport at 11:00 a.m. It was the first week of July and the place was jam-packed with people coming and going as they took full advantage of the summertime. She rented a car and began the seventy-mile drive to Monterey/Pebble Beach.

There was no specific plan as to what to say to Richard Lowrey, or what not to say, for that matter. *I just know I have to say something.* She had thought about phoning him in advance, but given that this strategy had clearly failed in the past, it seemed futile to try and warn him of her arrival.

It seemed best to simply play things by ear. Ideally, she would speak with Richard, get some sort of timetable as to when they could expect his next book—or at least a commitment that he would begin working on it, if he hadn't already—and be back on her way to New York in a matter of days, if not hours.

But Janine wasn't counting on things running that smoothly. They rarely did. Especially when dealing with strong emotions and delicate subject matters.

Richard E. Lowrey lived in the Del Monte Forest, a private resort community in Pebble Beach known for its natural scenic beauty and the famed 17-Mile Drive. Janine was in awe, like an only child surrounded by toys on Christmas Day, as she drove through the pine forests and groves of Monterey cypress. A solitary deer stood off to the side of the road, staring at the traffic the way people might watch monkeys in a cage.

Suddenly the ocean came into view like a giant mural. It was absolutely stunning in its crystal bed of blue. Billows of foamy waves surged toward the shore as if on a mission to merge the two. The coastline itself was seemingly miles of pristine white sand that the sun's bright rays settled on, as if enthralled by its beauty. On rocks and in the water offshore was an array of fascinating aquatic life, including sea otters, seals and sea lions—all wonderfully wrapped up in their own existence for all the world to ponder.

Janine pulled into the parking lot of the Pebble Beach Inn. After checking in, she went up to her room and unpacked the week's worth of clothing she'd brought just in case she needed it. *Yeah, right,* she thought. *Dream on, girl.* Once upon a time she had, in fact, dreamt of coming to such a place with John. Now she was happy to be there without him.

That was what divorce did to you, Janine told herself bitterly. Made you dismiss old feelings as though they never existed in the first place, and replace them with something more comfortable and less painful.

After freshening up and changing clothes, Janine headed out to stretch her legs, not yet ready to face the man she had traveled clear across the country to confront. She ended up at a place called Pescadero Point, at the northern tip of Stillwater Cove and Carmel Bay. Bringing her camera along, she couldn't resist taking a few pictures of this unbelievable place to show Lisa and have for her own memories.

She must have used up nearly half the roll of film when Janine heard a strong and confident, low-pitched voice say, "*Pescadero* means *fisherman* in Spanish, in case you're wondering...."

She turned and looked straight into the dazzling eyes of Richard Lowrey, causing her knees to wobble. He looked somewhat different than the photograph on the computer. He was older, thinner and grayer—yet it was definitely the *same* man.

"Excuse me?" Janine managed, admittedly not well-versed in Spanish—in fact, she didn't speak the language at all—or used to being caught off guard.

Richard favored her with what appeared to be an amused smile on a slightly crooked jawline. "This spot you're standing on was once called Rancho Pescadero," he explained calmly. "It's the name of a Spanish land grant encompassing four thousand acres. Or basically the entire Del Monte Forest."

Whatever else was causing her stomach to churn like butter, Janine couldn't help but be impressed by the man and his knowledge of the locale.

"You sound like an authority," she remarked.

He gave a throaty chuckle, looking out at the water for a long moment before turning back to her. "Not really. When you've lived somewhere as long as I have here, you have plenty of time to memorize all the tourist brochures."

Janine smiled softly at his modesty, while studying the man she had come to see who had somehow found her first. She couldn't help but wonder if it was pure coincidence.

Maybe he had been tipped off and decided to be the aggressor in telling her where to go.

Or maybe this wasn't a planned meeting at all.

In person, Richard Lowrey was not the most handsome man she had ever laid eyes on. Yet his features were certainly arresting. He was at least six-three and his physique was lean and taut from top to bottom. His once thick head of hair had thinned somewhat and was now an even blend of gleaming black and silver, cut short. Murky gray eyes were speckled with gold and had soft bags beneath them, as though he'd been too long without rest. His nose was a tad wide but well suited to the contours of a sharply defined face. A wholesome mouth tended to slant downward, as if by design. Gone was the mustache, replaced by a slight shadow.

All in all, Janine felt that Richard Lowrey looked somewhat older than his thirty-eight years—perhaps a reflection of the terrible ordeal he had gone through. The richness of his complexion had darkened somewhat after years of living and working under the California sun. Instinctively, she pictured him as a man who spent a fair amount of time outdoors, as opposed to being locked up inside his house most of the time. This suggested he was not exactly living the life of a hermit, as was the common perception by those who thought they knew him.

A good sign, she thought, perusing his clothing. Unlike in the photo, he was dressed rather casually in a L.A. Lakers sweatshirt, well-worn black jeans and brown hiking boots. This somehow seemed more fitting for the photographer-author than if he were dressed in a Brooks Brothers suit.

Janine suddenly became aware that Richard was regarding her, as well—perhaps even more intently. A wave of self-consciousness swept over her like a gust of wind. She was never one to wear much makeup, especially when not going out for a social occasion. Her hair, haphazardly tied in a ponytail that fell just below her shoulders, was still limp and oily from the long plane ride. The baggy outfit—a roll-neck ecru sweater and dark green sweatpants—with creases still visible from her luggage—didn't help much either, and all but obscured what by most accounts was a nice and shapely figure.

Does it really matter if I'm not at my best?

Janine had her answer. The reality was that she had not come there to win Richard Lowrey's approval, physically speaking. Rather, her mission was something far more important for both of them. *Stay focused, girl,* she told herself determinedly.

"So, how long have you lived here?" Janine asked abruptly, breaking the spell that had momentarily seemed to engulf them. She decided that the best strategy was to somehow ease into getting Richard Lowrey to reveal more about himself and the issues that were so troubling to him, and grinding his career to a virtual halt.

"Ten years," he responded unevenly.

"That's a long time," Janine reflected. She marveled at the notion of living in such a place of natural beauty, though she was mindful that tragic circumstances for him had taken off some of the luster.

"It often seems like no time at all," Richard muttered pensively. "Time has a way of giving us all a false sense of security so that we lose sight of the things most precious to us."

It was clear to Janine that he was talking about his wife and daughter. A perfect opportunity to seize the moment. Yet, for some reason, she found herself unable to broach the subject that had been so painful to him, and, to a certain extent,

Callister-Reynolds. Much less tell him why she was there
and what she wanted from him. The setting, magnificent as
it was, somehow seemed all wrong for that.

Would it ever be right?

"I take it you're a visitor to these parts?" he inquired.

Janine avoided his eyes as they centered on her face like
charcoal-gray-tipped arrows.

"Yes," she responded. "I'm from New York."

He mused interestedly. "New York, huh? The Big Apple?"

"That's the one," she told him. "Ripe and red as can be."

He smiled and nodded. "Yeah, that's what they say.
Been there once or twice. Never particularly cared for the
place...not sure why..."

Janine was thoughtful. "It has its ups and downs," she said.
She would be the first to admit it. "But when all is said and
done, I find that the city works for me."

Richard pursed his lips. "Isn't that what's most important
when all is said and done?"

"Yes." Janine curved her mouth slightly at him. "I think
so." Along with living each and every day to the fullest, including using all the skills and talents that make you unique.
Such as taking pictures and writing about them. This was an
area in which he had fallen short in recent years. With any luck
that would all change soon.

But now was not the time to get into it, Janine concluded.
First she needed to better assess the situation. Ease her way
into her mission without scaring him off and possibly ending
her assignment prematurely.

"Well..." Janine showed a little teeth, hiding her nervousness. "I guess I'd better be getting back to my hotel."

"You're staying at the Pebble Beach Inn?"

Janine wondered if this was a lucky guess or simple deduction. She refused to rule out that he could have somehow been tipped off about her coming and, as such, knew all there was to know, right down to her accommodations.

But he'd given no indication of such.

Indeed, if Janine didn't know better, she would think that the man was simply bored—and maybe even glad to have a stranger to flirt with.

Speaking nonchalantly, she told him, "Yes, as a matter of fact, I am. So far no complaints," she added, as if to downplay her being there.

"Good to hear." Richard Lowrey regarded her as if wanting to say something, but thought otherwise. He gave her a friendly nod and said simply, "Enjoy the rest of your trip."

"I will, thank you." Janine walked away as though she were just a tourist, feeling as uncertain about her undertaking as ever.

Fighting back guilt and second thoughts, Janine again convinced herself that it wasn't really necessary to be forthcoming at this particular time and place. There would be ample opportunity to talk with him when the setting and mood were right.

And her legs were steadier.

This feeling seemed to be supported by the fact that when she turned around, Richard Lowrey had completely vanished, like a thief in the night.

Chapter 5

Richard Lowrey was still thinking about the nice-looking lady he had spoken to at Pescadero Point as he climbed the steep hill and made his way to the twisting walkway in front of his house. She had reminded him of his late wife, Kassandra, more than he cared to admit. Not so much in appearance, though there was a strong resemblance there, too. It was more in her confidence in character, the movement of her graceful body and the smoothness of her voice, almost melodious in its tone.

It had been a very long time since he'd even looked at another woman, much less been attracted to one. Not since Kassandra and his beautiful young daughter, Sheena, had been so abruptly taken away from him three years ago. No reason to start looking now, he told himself, as though warning against temptation, while entering the split-level house that overlooked the ocean.

No one could ever take the place of the great love of his life, Richard had decided obstinately the day he'd buried her.

It was his own damn fault that Kassandra wasn't with him today—and wouldn't be tomorrow or the day after. If he hadn't insisted like an idiot that they go out for dinner, that night of all nights, things might have been different. If the weather hadn't gone from bad to worse in a matter of minutes, they might have been able to make it through the storm. If the car had chosen to cooperate rather than fail him during that critical moment in time, he might have been able to negotiate the treacherous curves and slick road.

If he had been driving just a bit slower or his reflexes were just a bit faster…it might have made all the difference in the world in saving his wife and little girl instead of killing them. Part of him had died, too, for he had no real life to speak of without the two people who meant more to him than anyone.

If only…

Richard's dog, Kimble, ran up to him in the hallway, thrusting his paws up against his muscled thighs, as if they hadn't seen each other in years, rather than hours. He knelt and rubbed the ears of the cocker spaniel.

"I missed you, too, boy," he said affectionately. "What would we do without each other, huh?" *Or more, what the hell would I do without you?*

Richard hugged the dog, then watched him scamper away, following it into the kitchen. He took a beer from the refrigerator, opened it and took a long swig before feeding Kimble and retreating to the living room. He looked at framed pictures of Kassandra and Sheena sitting on the mantel as if to remind him that they would never walk in that front door again. The reality of that gnawed at him like a bloodthirsty demon trying to capture his soul.

He *deserved* the emptiness and purgatory he felt trapped in like a dark, desolate cave. When the light of his life had been prematurely lost, he found himself unable to take photographs or write about the stories they told as he had done for much of his adult life. To do so would be to act as if his life was somehow back to normal.... But it never would be normal again, he knew, no matter how hard he tried to pretend otherwise.

Richard's thoughts returned to the woman he had seen on 17-Mile Drive. He wondered why he was unable to get her out of his mind, as if she had become permanently attached to it. Was she that much like Kassandra that he wished she were her? Or maybe it was the lady herself who had intrigued him all on her own.

He found himself curious about the story of her life, realizing he knew virtually nothing about her. Of course, why would he? He probably shouldn't even go there, but something inside seemed to compel him to wonder about the woman. Like, exactly who she was. Why she was in town. And what made her tick.

She'd said she was from New York. The Big Apple. *Ripe and red as can be,* as she'd put it. He wondered if she had always lived there. She didn't really have a New York accent as far as he could tell. But what did he know about accents? His own had often been mistaken for everything from Midwestern to Southern to even Jamaican.

So she was a New Yorker, he thought again, wondering if she really liked living there as she indicated. Sometimes people said what they thought you wanted to hear. Or what they tried to convince themselves of. Maybe she was the type who liked anywhere she happened to live.

His own ties in New York City were limited to his longtime publisher, Callister-Reynolds, to which he owed two more books. *And they aren't about to let me forget it.* He wasn't mentally prepared to deliver one book, let alone two, for the time being, if ever. Nor could he return the generous advance he had been given. He had spent it a long time ago, paying off the mortgage on his house along with sustaining some heavy losses on good investments that had turned out to be not so good. Admittedly, he had boxed himself into a corner, with no way out at the moment that he could think of.

Once again Richard turned to more agreeable thoughts—the fine woman he had fortuitously run into at Pescadero Point, snapping pictures as though she had discovered a lost world. He couldn't help but wonder if she had come to Pebble Beach strictly for the joy of it. Or was it a business trip? Maybe it was both, he told himself. After all, the area certainly offered enough to bring in business travelers as well as those who wanted pure entertainment.

Was she here alone?

He knew of few who could truly appreciate visiting the magnificent Del Monte Forest on their own. Yet he noted that there was no ring on her finger, presumably indicating she was not married.

But that didn't mean a boyfriend or partner was not left waiting for her at the hotel while she scouted out the place, he thought.

What the hell am I doing? Richard scolded himself for expending precious thoughts on someone he was likely never to see again. He didn't even *want* to see her again, for that matter. He had his life here—if you could call it that—and she had hers in New York. Nothing could or should ever change that.

End of story.

Period.

He finished the beer and tried reading the paper. When that

failed he called his father, the best friend he'd ever had aside from Kassandra. But his answering machine came on with the usual gruff and laconic sound of his voice. "This is Henry. I'm not here. Leave a brief message and I'll get back to you. Bye."

Richard hung up without leaving a message. No reason to, he told himself. There was nothing in particular he wanted to say. Not to a machine, anyway.

Instead, he left the house and headed for nowhere, but ended up at the inn. By his calculations it was about dinner-time now. Maybe she had decided to try out the inn's restaurant instead of going elsewhere to eat.

On the spur and against all reason, Richard found himself in search of the as yet nameless woman who he couldn't seem to shake for the life of him. Admittedly, this was hardly his style and he could think of no good reason why he should bother looking for someone that he'd had only a brief encounter with. There were certainly no guarantees that she would be interested in company.

His company.

Have I lost my mind? Richard seriously wondered as he entered the restaurant. His answer was one of uncertainty.

Maybe, in some strange way, the lady in question could clear things up, one way or the other.

Chapter 6

Richard Lowrey was a twenty-four-year-old freelance photographer when he first met Kassandra Simone. It was during a shoot in Montego Bay, Jamaica, where he was on assignment. Kassandra was a Jamaican tour guide, working out of the hotel where he was staying. He knew there was something special about her from the moment she walked past him, with a group of British tourists close behind. She winked at him, flashed a ten-thousand-watt smile and said, "If you ever get bored with taking *dull* pictures, mon, you are always welcome to join us for some *real* fun."

"I'll keep that in mind," he told her, feeling the heat of the April day seemingly rise several degrees.

Richard found himself unable to remove his eyes from this beautiful slice of heaven as she stopped, facing him while entertaining her gathering. She was a combination of young versions of Jayne Kennedy and Vanessa Williams, and the dazzling Halle Berry, all wrapped in one. Only better, if that was possible.

Taking another look at her, he knew it was.

Tall like a fashion model, the Jamaican lady had a body that wouldn't quit—slender with just the right amount of curves and an enticingly nice chest. Long, honey-brown hair hung across her shoulders in dreadlocks. There was a natural twinkle in her big, coffee-colored eyes that were mesmerizing in their effect. Her face itself was heart-shaped with naturally high cheekbones and a few tiny moles spread about randomly. She was dressed similarly to those she led—white shorts, a light and fluffy blue short-sleeved blouse and sandals. Her long legs and arms were lean and appealing, showing only the slightest tan in her yellowish-brown complexion.

Richard watched spellbound as she and her companions left the hotel and began loading onto a bus. Acting impulsively, he paid for the tour at the front desk, scooped up his gear and scurried outside. He climbed aboard the bus just before it departed. He had no idea what the hell he was doing or where they were going. He only knew that he didn't want to let *her* out of his sight.

Baby, he thought, *for you, I'd go to the ends of the earth and back!*

She seemed pleased by his presence, beaming as if waiting for him all her life. "Glad you decided to come along for the ride."

He smiled back at her, knowing even then that he was falling in love, hard and fast. "How could I resist your offer of some *real fun?*"

Her thin mouth curved into an even wider smile and she extended a small hand with delicate fingers, the long nails polished a bright red. "My name's Kassandra Simone."

"Richard Lowrey." He took her hand and felt as if he could hold on to it forever. In fact, he just might have had she not taken it back, seemingly amused.

"Nice to meet you, Richard Lowrey," she said, sounding sincere. "So, where you from?"

"Los Angeles."

Her eyes expanded. "Ah, the city with all the stars. Are you one of them?"

"Afraid not," he said almost embarrassingly. "The only stars I know are in the sky."

She chuckled. "I hear you, mon. And what brings you to Jamaica? Please don't tell me it's the cheap drinks?"

Richard laughed. "Maybe I'm here to try my damnedest to win you over," he said boldly.

She blushed. "Quite the charmer, I see."

"Is it working?" He could only hope.

Kassandra actually seemed to contemplate the notion. "That remains to be seen. Ask me again after the tour is complete."

"You can count on it!"

She gave him a teasing look. "Just what I'm afraid of."

He settled into his seat as she walked away, wondering if he had died and gone to the pearly gates of heaven where Kassandra Simone was waiting to greet him with open arms and a welcome body.

Richard went through the motions as the tour moved into high gear, biding his time till he could spend some quality moments with the Montego Bay beauty. He took pictures as they visited Accompong with the Maroons, toured a banana and coffee plantation, and a renowned Jamaican beach with black rocks. But most of all, he photographed Kassandra Simone every chance he got. If by chance he never saw her again after this trip, he wanted something to remember her by. On the other hand, he hoped this impromptu photo session was only the beginning of their time together, with no end in sight.

That night, under the moonlight, he invited her to dinner.

She didn't bite the bait right away, saying, "On one condition...."

"You name it," Richard said, feeling butterflies in his stomach, hoping he hadn't just talked himself out of a date.

Kassandra licked her glossy lips. "Tell me what truly sets you apart from all the other visiting American men who like to hit on Jamaican women with corny pickup lines.?"

Richard couldn't help but give a little uneasy chuckle, even while his mind was working overtime to keep from blowing this. Finally he said coolly, even if his heart was beating like a drum, "What if I told you that you were the finest girl I've come across in some time...maybe ever, and I want to see what's inside that sweetness on the outside?"

Kassandra broke out into a chortle that was music to Richard's ears. At least he had her attention, for the time being.

"I love your style, Richard Lowrey," she said, still giggling, "corny and all. But I'm afraid you're going to have to do better than that...."

Knowing he was close to letting her slip through his fingers and into the arms of another man, Richard put his heart on his sleeve and, gazing into her eyes, said in earnest, "What if I told you you're looking at your future husband—as much as I'm looking at my future wife?"

She stood speechless, and Richard wondered if he had come on too strong, even if he meant every word, surprising himself.

Kassandra smiled at him naturally, if not with some hesitancy. "Slow down, mon. Why don't we see how dinner goes first, before planning our walk down the aisle? Agreed?"

"Most definitely," he said, trying hard to keep his enthusiasm and confidence in check.

Instinctively Richard knew this was the turning point of his life. What he didn't know was precisely where it would lead, or to what extent....

Chapter 7

She was sitting alone at a table by the window, seemingly deep in contemplation. Or perhaps she was waiting for someone. He watched her from afar, his ears catching the soft sounds of instrumental jazz piped into the restaurant. He had guessed correctly that she might be there at dinnertime, but Richard now questioned the wisdom of showing up himself as though by some force of nature. The last thing he wanted was for her to somehow misconstrue his presence as a pickup attempt.

Isn't that why I'm here, he had to ask himself, *to try and pick her up?*

If not, he could only wonder what he hoped to gain by having dinner with this woman from New York. *Beats the hell out of me,* a voice inside said, totally perplexed. That is, if she was even willing to depart from her previous plans, which surely didn't include him.

Richard feared that she would probably see through him—

looking in a window of his tortured soul. Worse yet was a sense of treading into dangerous territory where he didn't particularly wish to go. In spite of this foreboding, something inside compelled him to put one foot in front of the other and see where it led.

Making his way between the maze of tables and chairs, Richard found himself standing before her table. He studied the woman he'd come to see like he used to scrutinize a town or place he intended to photograph. Damn. She reminded him so much of Kass, with maybe a dash or two of Beyonce, Halle, and Alicia Keys. She had untied the long, luminous charcoal-colored hair so that it spread invitingly across her shoulders, as if calling out to him to touch. In spite of the same loose clothing she'd worn at Pescadero Point, he could tell that she had an ideally small frame with curves only where they should be.

He noted that she was so preoccupied with her menu—as if it offered some cuisine out of this world—that she was not aware of his presence.

He said in an unsteady voice, "Hello, again...."

She looked up, startled, as though expecting anyone to be standing there but him.

Recovering quickly, she uttered, straining to produce a convincing smile, "Oh, hi."

Where do I go from here? he asked himself, uncertain.

After a moment or two of feeling like an idiot, Richard asked hesitantly, "Mind if I join you?" Then, having second thoughts, as if rejecting the first ones, he said, "Look, I didn't mean to butt in on your private party—"

"It's all right," she told him almost eagerly, and offered a more radiant smile to that effect. "I'm alone. I was just about to order dinner. You're welcome to join me, if you like."

He weighed the notion, before deciding he had gone too far to back away now. And, frankly, he didn't want to.

Sitting across from her, he introduced himself. "My name's Richard Lowrey."

"Hi, Richard," she said easily enough. "I'm Janine Henderson."

She gave him a curious look and stuck out her hand. He shook it and was immediately taken by its almost perfect fit inside his own hand. There was a slight tremble of her palm and soft fingers, making him wonder if she was as nervous as he was. This was somehow reassuring to him.

"Nice to meet you, Janine," he said sincerely.

She flashed pearly, straight white teeth his way. "Same here, Richard—and for the second time today."

And this time was not by accident, Richard thought, shocking himself that he would seek out this woman.

He smiled back at her, then said, "If you haven't already ordered and want to try something special, I would suggest the curry goat, served with brown rice, turnip greens and biscuits."

Janine cocked a thin brow. "Why not? I've never had goat before, curry or otherwise. Maybe I'll find out just what I've been missing." She closed her menu and looked over it at him. "You must come here often."

"Only when I tire of my own cooking," Richard responded dryly. "Which usually isn't the case." He tried to remember the last time he'd cooked anything that didn't have "microwave" on the box. Eating alone hardly seemed worth the effort.

"I see," Janine hummed. "A man who's not a chef who can *actually* cook. Now, *that's* a concept."

He met her probing eyes as she chuckled appreciatively, and kept a straight face when he suggested forwardly, "Maybe I actually am a chef. Or maybe you've just met the wrong men."

She seemed to ponder the notion. "Maybe...."

Richard could tell by Janine's revealing facial expression that he had touched a raw nerve in her. And it had nothing to do with cooking. It appeared men had hurt her badly in the past. Or perhaps one man in particular, he deduced.

It made Richard consider his own deep hurt that still burned in him like an all-consuming, never-ending flame. Favoring the fine lady across from him, he wondered if he was somehow trampling on Kassandra's grave and her memory by having dinner with this New York woman who seemed to have almost materialized out of nowhere.

They ordered, then neither seemed to know what to say to the other, as if a lid had been put on speech. For his part, Richard had been out of the practice of dating—if you could call this that—for so long, he was afraid he might say the wrong thing. Hell, he wasn't even sure what the right thing to say to a woman was these days.

It was Janine who finally spoke up as though a light had gone on in her head. "So, what do you do when you aren't hanging around Pescadero Point or eating goat at the inn, Richard?"

He contemplated the question. Lately he had found himself unable to do much of anything, aside from meditating, fishing, walking Kimble and reflecting sadly on days lost forever.

"I'm a photographer," he said as if it were a foreign word to him.

"What do you photograph?" she asked with a curious catch to her voice.

"Everything and anything," Richard responded, thinking back. "Whatever seems fascinating enough to belong in a picture."

"Interesting." Janine paused, eyeing him carefully. "You

know, it would be nice to see some of your work while I'm in town—if that's possible."

Evidently she hadn't heard of him, giving Richard both a sense of surprise and relief. His photography had led to an award for the best photograph of the year. That resulted in his writing a series of visual books on places around the world where black folks lived, worked and had colorful histories, often extending for generations. Each book, with its unique insight through photographs and words, was more successful than the last. With it came more attention, fame and fortune than he ever wanted or needed.

That was when disaster had struck like lightning or a ten on the Richter scale, taking away those most dear to him and all but ending his career, in effect. He'd suddenly found himself less and less interested in anything having to do with photography—that included taking pictures for books.

Though feeling an attraction to Janine Henderson—more than he had to any woman since Kassandra—Richard wasn't sure he was ready to share any of his photographs at the moment with her or anyone else. It was something that no longer seemed right after losing Kass and Sheena.

"Tell me about *your* work?" He evaded the delicate subject as though it were a knife aimed straight at his heart. The more he thought about it, the more it seemed that Janine's interest in his photography was largely for the sake of conversation and not to be taken literally. Which, in this case, was probably for the best.

She regarded him thoughtfully. "I'm an editor."

"Oh…." He had guessed she could be an interior designer. A teacher. An attorney. A model. Or maybe even an investment banker. But, for some reason, he hadn't considered that she would be in the publishing business.

As if she could read his mind, Janine said with a slightly uncomfortable half grin, "What? You have something against editors?"

"Not at all," Richard responded quickly, though he suspected one or two might have a beef against him. Or worse.

"Well, that's good," she said, feigning a sigh of relief, "because I don't have anything against photographers, either."

An amused, if unsteady, smile formed on his lips. "Then I guess we'll get along great." He had not yet decided if this was something to look forward to. Or avoid like the plague.

By the time the food arrived, Richard began to question why he felt so comfortable with Janine. He wondered if it was because she eerily reminded him so much of Kassandra. Or maybe there was more to it than that. Maybe he was starting to lose his mind. Could be that he'd become so lonely that the first woman to cause him to give a second glance since Kass's death was somehow suddenly the reincarnation of his beloved wife.

Another thought occurred to Richard as he eyed Janine Henderson. So attractive, charming and seemingly full of life, along with a little mystery about her, he could not deny that she had piqued his interest all on her own.

"So how long are you going to be in town, Janine?" he asked casually.

She pondered the question as if the fate of the universe rested on her answer. "Not sure, really," she said tentatively. "Probably a week or so. It just depends on..." Her words trailed off thoughtfully.

Open-ended trip, Richard mused curiously, wondering if the length depended on how much it was worth her while to stay longer. Interesting, he had to admit. Obviously she was not in a great hurry to get back home to someone special in her life, something he could relate to.

"Are you here on vacation?" he asked while slicing goat marinated in curry sauce. "Or is it a business and pleasure thing?" He hoped he wasn't getting too personal. But then again....

"Business and pleasure," Janine answered with a quiver of her lower lip, then moved her fork nervously across the plate.

Richard contemplated that for a moment or two. Obviously, he decided, she wasn't that interested in coming to this area. Still, it made him think about his own life. It had been a long time since he had conducted any career business to speak of. And even longer since he'd known any real pleasure.

What type of pleasure has brought her to Pebble Beach?

"Do you have family?" Janine intruded upon his thoughts with casual interest over a glass of chardonnay.

Richard was about to respond with the routine sad truth, but instead found himself saying tersely, "No. Not really." He sighed, thinking that there hadn't been any family in three years, aside from his father. He couldn't even begin to describe the loneliness and sense of detachment he felt. "How about you?"

"I have a seven-year-old daughter," she told him proudly, meeting his gaze. "Her name's Lisa."

"Lisa, huh? That was my grandmother's name." He favored her with a brief smile, pondering the irony of it.

"That's amazing," remarked Janine of the coincidence.

"Yeah, it is. I loved my grandmother. She was always there for me."

Richard thought about his own daughter. Sheena would be ten now, had it not been for the accident. The realization that it was he who had deprived her of living a full life and having her own children and grandchildren someday broke his heart in a thousand places. He would have loved to be a grandfather. And for Kassandra to be a grandmother. But they would never experience that multigenerational pleasure that so many people took for granted. It just wasn't meant to be, he thought lamentably.

"You married?" The question seemed to come to his mind totally out of the blue.

"Divorced." Janine's pensive eyes betrayed her regret.

"Sorry to hear that."

"Don't be," she said bravely. "They say it happens in at least half the marriages, if the statistics are to be believed." She sighed. "I guess the deck is stacked against half of us from the very start."

Richard wondered if the same were true in separations by death. Perhaps the cards truly were, in effect, laid out like on a poker table so that his family's fate had been signed, sealed and delivered well before they'd ever gone out that fateful night. There might not have been a thing he could have done to prevent the terrible tragedy. That still didn't stop him from thinking otherwise and hating himself for it.

He fixed his eyes on Janine, wanting to tell her the truth— that his beloved wife and child were dead and buried, safe from the cruelties of this world. But he couldn't. It was as if it was his private connection with them from beyond the grave, providing a strange kind of solace. And he did not wish to share it with a stranger. Not even one so fine.

Surprising himself, Richard realized that he didn't want to see the lady's company come to an end. Not this day, anyhow.

"If you don't have other plans tomorrow afternoon, Janine," he ventured forth, trying to keep his voice steady, "I could probably borrow my father's boat and take you on a better sightseeing tour of the region than you could ever get by doing the 17-Mile Drive, designated assembly-line tour."

He half expected Janine to say she was busy with her business or pleasure and that would be that. After all, she no more owed him her precious time away from home than vice versa. Besides, Richard thought, maybe he had already gone way too far in befriending someone that he had no chance of ever developing anything serious with, given that they lived on opposite sides of the country. And he had no desire whatsoever to try and replace his beloved Kassandra, as she was irreplaceable.

But Janine, not privy to his reservations, flashed him an agreeable smile and said enthusiastically, "That sounds nice. I'd love to go on a boat tour of the area, Richard."

Chapter 8

The small reddish-orange brick house stood a block away from Fisherman's Wharf in Monterey. In the dark of night, a half moon smiled from above, surrounded by a multitude of barely visible stars. Richard scaled the cobblestone steps only to find his father waiting for him at the door, as if he had a sixth sense.

"Hi, Pops." Richard gave him a boyish, crooked grin.

"Hi back at you," he responded in a gravelly voice, the result of a lifelong smoking habit.

Henry Lowrey looked a lot like Richard, only older, an inch shorter and a bit thicker around the midsection. His features were more weathered due to time and years of working on the railways under the hot sun. The sixty-six-year-old retired engineer had been a widower for the past ten years. His wife had died after a long bout with breast cancer. Feeling alone and bored, Henry had moved to Monterey from San Diego three years ago to be closer to his only child.

Richard appreciated his father's support and friendship more than he could ever say. Henry had been his Rock of Gibraltar at the lowest ebb of his life, when nothing seemed to matter. If not for his old man's listening ear, words of wisdom and quiet understanding, Richard was certain he could not have survived his ordeal or maintained some semblance of sanity and purpose in life.

"Kinda late, isn't it, son?" Henry favored him with a curious stare and grizzled eyes, heavily bagged beneath.

"Yeah," Richard mumbled guiltily, "it is. And I'm sorry. I should have called first—"

"It's all right. You know you're welcome here anytime." Henry opened the screen door. "C'mon in."

He moved aside and Richard stepped into a tiny, low-lit living room. The sparse furnishings consisted of a fawn-colored couch, glass coffee table and a reddish-purple leather recliner that Henry had managed to hold on to since Richard was a boy. A portable TV sat on a stand in the corner. On the mantel was a photograph of Henry, his wife, Marjah, and Richard. It was taken when Richard was twenty and a senior at San Diego State. Back then the world was much different for father and son. Neither could have anticipated the cruel fate that life sometimes brought, as if being cursed by the Grim Reaper himself.

There was the smell of raw fish in the air, not surprisingly, since Henry spent much of his time these days out on the water fishing and making good use of his boat.

"You want something to eat?" Henry asked, scratching his pate above a receding hairline of backward-combed thinning white hair intermixed with a few black strands atop, as if hanging on for dear life. "I got some fresh salmon in the fridge and what's left of yesterday's potato salad."

Richard waved him off. "Nah. Already ate."

Henry raised a bushy black brow at him, as if sensing there was something more to the visit. "So what's up?"

Richard crossed his feet awkwardly, hands in pockets as though in search of some spare change. The truth was that he wasn't sure what the hell was up. Only that he had to see this through, aware there were no guarantees either way.

"Need to borrow your boat, Dad," he said with a catch to his voice.

Henry had purchased the boat a year ago and Richard had taken it out solo from time to time when he needed to do some soul-searching or spend some quiet time remembering those he missed seemingly more with each day.

"Tonight?" Henry wondered out loud.

"Tomorrow afternoon."

"Oh. No problem." He shrugged. "I wasn't planning to take it out then."

"Good." Richard stared blankly at the wall, as if it were a portal to another dimension.

Noticing his preoccupation, Henry said, "You could have phoned to ask for the boat. Something troubling you, son?"

Richard met his father's gaze squarely, paused, then said, "I met a woman...."

Henry reacted with shock. "A *woman?* When? Where? *Who?*"

"Today—out at Pescadero Point." Richard recalled their initial chance meeting, followed by the chance he took that she might be in the inn's restaurant, and how everything seemed to flow so easily between them. "I invited her for a ride in the bay." He shrugged. "Nothing special." He tried to convince his father, if not himself.

Henry ran his hand along the rough edges of his chin and

grinned. "I'm really happy for you, Richard. I was beginning to think you'd never even look at another woman again—much less date one."

"It's not a date," Richard insisted, not quite sure in his mind what the hell to call it. Just being hospitable to a nice woman who seemed to need a friend as much as he did, he supposed. "She's just in town for a week, if that." He looked down, almost embarrassed, and up again. "When I first saw her, Dad…she reminded me so much of Kass—"

Henry rested a callused hand on Richard's shoulder. "You don't have to explain that. Certainly not to me, son. It's only natural that you would be attracted to someone like her. Kassandra was a good woman all the way through."

Richard's eyes glazed over. "She was more than that. Kass was my life. I don't know how the hell I've survived this long without her. I'm not looking for a replacement."

"No one's saying you have to," Henry responded emotionally. "I know Kassandra can never be replaced in your heart any more than your mother can be replaced in mine. But it's about time you moved on with your life, Richard. So maybe this woman isn't the one in the long run. If not, you'll know. Doesn't mean there isn't a right woman out there waiting for you somewhere."

"I had the right woman for me," Richard muttered painfully. "The *only* woman for me—Kassandra. Now she's gone, *forever.*"

Henry grimaced. "Dammit, Richard! Don't torture yourself like this. Don't let life pass you by. It's the only one you'll ever have. Kassandra wouldn't have wanted you to throw it away. I think you know that. Keep your options open. Whatever happens will happen, including with this new lady."

Richard forced a weak but accepting smile. He understood

that, as always, his father was only trying to help in the best way he knew how. He just wasn't sure he wanted or needed advice where it concerned moving on with his life, as if the past had never existed. Or should no longer be a factor in determining his future. As far as he was concerned, he didn't have much of a life without Kassandra and Sheena. And he preferred it that way.

"I'm going to go now," Richard said with a sigh. "Thanks for the boat. I'll pick it up around one."

Henry nodded, his eyes bulging perceptively at his son. "You know where to find it."

Richard left, appreciative that his old man never pressed things, allowing him to make his own choices when all was said and done. No matter how difficult or unsatisfying. Even if a choice had him falling flat on his face.

He looked up at the stars, which now seemed to be glowing brightly, and wondered which one represented Kassandra in the heavens. And which one was Sheena.

They were both watching over him now like guardian angels, he knew intuitively. Less certain in Richard's mind was if they approved of the path he had taken. Or chastised him for living too much in the past at the expense of a future that didn't include them.

He wondered if it was possible to become romantically interested in someone else, while at the same time mourning the loss of the only woman he had ever loved.

The very notion seemed to shake Richard from head to toe.

Chapter 9

The first time Janine suspected that John had been unfaithful was when she was pregnant with Lisa. It had been a difficult pregnancy and she found herself in bed more than out of it. John had just been made a partner in his law firm at the age of thirty-one. This meant more pay, more prestige and more time away from home—which, in and of itself, usually was cause for warning bells.

Only, Janine had failed to hear them till it was too late. Her heart had been broken and her faith shattered.

Janine had met John Henderson when she was twenty-two and right out of college with a degree in journalism. He was three years older and already an established attorney in civil litigation. It was hardly love at first sight. At least not for her. John was not particularly good-looking or in the best shape, but he had a gentle appeal about him, along with a sharp wit and a confidence Janine had not known in other men she had dated, or, for that matter, possessed herself.

When he asked her to marry him a year later, Janine said yes, truly believing she was in love and loved by him. All she ever really wanted in a man was someone who could love and respect her. Someone to make all the misgivings she had about marriage, loyalty and true soul mates go away. She trusted that John was such a man. Only, it became apparent all too soon to Janine that what they had was more of a sexual attraction, and less of an all-consuming love match. Even the sex itself was fleeting, as John's appetite for her gradually declined to the point of almost no intimacy at all. Less than a year into the marriage, their mutual interests suddenly became separate interests altogether.

By the time Janine was pregnant five years later, they were rarely intimate, save for the times one or the other had a need that brought them together if only for a night. One such time led to the birth of their daughter.

Even with separate lives and occasional sex, Janine had chosen to believe that John was still staying true to his marital vows, as she was. That was until the day she went to wash the sheets and found a spent condom tucked under a pillow like a child's tooth waiting for the Tooth Fairy.

The pain Janine felt was that of indescribable anger and, when she looked back, naiveté and stupidity on her part in expecting more from John. She wondered if his betrayal was just a natural man thing or only applied to the men in *her* life. After all, her own father had done the same thing to her mother, leaving her devastated and heartbroken. It almost seemed natural, as if some genetic predisposition, that Janine would suffer a similar fate and humiliation.

She confronted John that evening with the unmistakable evidence of his infidelity.

He made no attempt to deny it or suggest it wasn't what she thought. Instead, he said, wearing a smirk that had almost come with the territory over time, "I needed someone, baby, okay? And since you weren't able, or even willing, I found someone else."

"You *bastard!*" Janine wailed, her ears not believing the cruelty and selfishness of the words she was hearing from him. "How could you—while I'm carrying your child? And in our *own* house, John, for heaven's sake!"

John, who at six-two had put on quite a few pounds while losing much of his hair over the course of their marriage, shrugged it off as if dismissing a gnat from his shoulder. "Let's not be so damn melodramatic, Janine. You had to have seen this coming. The pregnancy has nothing to do with it. Or maybe it has *everything* to do with it."

She glared at him. "What's that supposed to mean? Are you blaming *me* or the child we're both responsible for creating for somehow causing you to disrespect me like this?"

John's dark-skinned face creased in several places. "No…I'm not saying that," he stammered uneasily.

All Janine could think of in that dizzying moment was that she would be left raising their child alone. The thought terrified her. *I can't do this by myself!* The last thing she wanted was to be a single mom, left to pick up the pieces from a failed marriage. But she could see the writing on the wall as plain as the nose on her face.

"Do you want a divorce?" she asked with dread. "Is that what this is all about?"

John had always been a practical man when it came to his own best interests. This was no different. He flashed her a twisted smile, and said in earnest, "I don't want to lose you, baby. Or our kid. Now, how would that look if the new partner in the firm couldn't even keep his own house in order?"

"You tell me," Janine challenged him, suddenly feeling more of what had been a decided imbalance of power. She wondered if she should use his desire to put up a false front for professional purposes to try and hold on to him. The thought quickly subsided. She wasn't that shallow or desperate to want someone who didn't want to be with her.

John placed his large hands on Janine's shoulders, as if to weigh her down. "I'm sorry, Janine," he offered lamely. "I'm just a man. I made a mistake. A dumb-assed one. It'll never happen again, baby, I swear it."

Though deep down she knew with every fiber in her body that this was merely a continuation of lies he would build like a pyramid till caught red-handed again, Janine did not want to see this marriage end. She desperately wanted to give their child every opportunity to be raised by a mother and a father. They both owed their child a life that included the comfort and security of a whole family.

Another side of Janine feared divorce the way people once feared bubonic plague. She did not want the stigma or hardships associated with single motherhood. It would perhaps be even more difficult being the product of a broken home. She wouldn't wish that on her worst enemy, much less her own child.

And maybe, somewhere deep down, she hoped that she and John could still build a real marriage together as husband and wife. So she ignored her instincts and self-respect, and essentially gave John a free ride to do as he pleased, at her expense and that of their relationship.

To Janine's deep regret he took full advantage of it, and then some. And he would do so until she finally woke up and smelled the roses—wilting as rapidly as they were.

Chapter 10

The night was quiet and on the cool side as Janine sat in her room at the Pebble Beach Inn. Her assignment concerning Richard Lowrey had thus far not gone according to plan. As if there had ever been a true plan of action.

Why didn't I tell him who I am? Janine asked herself, as if talking to a person she didn't know.

She came up with a number of excuses that seemed legitimate enough. The time had not seemed appropriate.

Or maybe it was because she was waiting for him to reveal more about himself and his tragedy first. At which time she would've readily admitted her true reason for being there, while hoping she hadn't overplayed her hand—or underplayed it.

Why on earth did I accept the man's offer to take a boat tour? Janine had to admit it was because she had unexpectedly found herself enjoying Richard Lowrey's company as a man. Maybe a little too much.

She definitely was curious about his motives in asking her to go out on the boat and was flattered that he had asked her out on something akin to a date, if not a romantic one. Or at least, she assumed it was not romance that Richard had in mind....

Lately she had been far too busy at work and home to spend much time thinking about socializing of any kind. And romance was definitely something that Janine didn't see in the cards for the foreseeable future. Certainly not while on Dennis's version of a working vacation. Yes, Richard was nice enough and fairly easy to talk to, but the line had to be drawn there. Her past failures and reluctance to open herself up to men, and possibly more hurt, had not changed in one day.

To Janine this outing with Richard Lowrey was for professional purposes in gaining more insight into this man of multiple, if neglected, talents. She could then use these insights to try and convince him to photograph and write the two books remaining on his contract with Callister-Reynolds.

Then everyone could walk away happy, she thought, knowing that the term "happy" didn't necessarily have the same meaning for all parties concerned.

Even in bed that night, Janine continued to contemplate her objectives and mixed feelings where they concerned Richard, before falling asleep. She awoke early the next morning to the phone ringing. Without time to adjust to the bright sunlight filtering through the open curtains like a high-beam flashlight, she reached across to the night table and grabbed the receiver.

Dennis DeMetris was on the other end of the line. "How was your flight?" he asked routinely, as if he really didn't give a damn.

"Pretty turbulent," Janine said just for effect. "But I made it in one piece."

He cut right to the chase. "Did you have a chance to talk to Lowrey yet?"

Her response came without preamble, while yawning. "I'm meeting with him today." At least officially, she thought.

"Good. It would be nice if we could have the brother on board for our spring list."

"I wouldn't get my hopes up just yet," Janine warned responsibly. "I have no idea what his state of mind will be when confronted." He seemed sane enough. But that was under casual, nonthreatening time together. Under pressure it could be a whole different ball game.

The same could be true for not-too-subtle coercion. Were the situation reversed, Janine imagined her own reaction would be pretty shaky at best.

"Take all the time you need, Janine," Dennis said with an edge to his voice, suggesting that she really needed to wrap things up sooner rather than later, "to get him to come around or give us back the advance—if it should come to that. Just don't take too long!"

Janine understood that there was a limit to how much he or the publisher was willing to spend to put her up in Pebble Beach to try and convince Richard to uphold the terms of his contract or face the consequences.

She felt like a pawn in a game where everyone could win or lose. Including her. And most definitely Richard Lowrey, though Janine wondered if he could ever really feel like a winner again. She hated having to make up the rules as she went along. But there seemed to be no other way, short of putting herself and her employer at a disadvantage, and perhaps costing them plenty in the short and long runs. Her hope was that she didn't get in too far over her head.

After telling Dennis she would be in touch, Janine dialed

John's apartment. Following the divorce, they had sold the house. She had a strong suspicion that he had already been using this apartment on the side for his sexual liaisons while they were married. Only now, he had decided to make it his official residence.

A woman answered the phone with a terse, "Yes?"

Janine sucked in her breath. "May I speak to John?"

"He's not here," she responded snidely. "Who is this?"

Janine bit her lower lip, somehow feeling like the other woman, after the fact. She had considered leaving Lisa and Murphy with a babysitter. But as she had no definite timetable for returning to New York, it seemed more reasonable to have them stay with John in Boston, even if it meant intruding on his bachelor life. And apparently the woman or women he was cavorting with these days.

Janine began to have second thoughts about the wisdom of her decision. "I'm his ex-wife," she told her tartly. "Is my daughter there?"

The woman made a strange noise into the phone that Janine took as sarcastic in tone. Finally she said, "Just a minute...."

Janine felt herself steaming. She had actually hoped John might want to spend the extra time afforded him with his daughter. She should have known better. *Damn him.* Obviously he was more than content with his normal visitation schedule and to allow strangers to care for Lisa.

Janine wondered if the one who answered the phone was his latest girlfriend. She tried to picture her ex actually hiring a sitter—he could certainly afford it. But that was beside the point. Lisa needed her father. Not strangers. Or a strange woman.

Janine could only ponder what type of effect this might have on Lisa and her time spent away from home and her mother.

"Mommy!" Lisa chimed enthusiastically into the phone.

"How's my sweet pea?" Janine asked, lighting up in hearing her daughter's voice.

"I'm doing great!" she declared. "Bernadette and I are getting ready to go out for raspberry ice cream."

How nice, Janine thought sardonically. The bimbo actually had a name.

"Miss me, honey?" she asked hopefully.

"Yeah!" Lisa boomed. "So does Murphy."

"Well, I miss you, too," Janine told her affectionately. "And Murphy."

"When are you coming home?"

Janine sat up in bed. "I'm not sure, honey," it pained her to say. "Real soon, I promise."

Lisa seemed to hide her disappointment. "Will you bring me back a present?"

"You can count on it," Janine responded, feeling guilty for having ever left her in the first place, though she was sure Lisa understood it was strictly for the job and that she was not abandoning her. "So who's Bernadette?" she had to ask.

"Daddy's new girlfriend," Lisa said with all the innocence and easy acceptance of a seven-year-old.

"I see." Janine wondered what constituted *new* with him. She could well imagine the last six months qualifying. Or the past month. She wouldn't even put it past John and his relatively new life of freedom from commitment to have a girlfriend of the week. Or weekend. Or even day.

Oh, hell, Janine cursed, realizing that these thoughts sounded as though they were coming from a bitter and miserable ex-wife, jealous that her ex asshole husband had someone—anyone—and she didn't. This couldn't be further from the truth, she told herself flatly. They were legally divorced now. He was free to be with whomever he chose, not needing her blessing. All she asked was for John to be there for his daughter—especially when he was supposed to be.

The fact that she had remained single and without a man in her life had been a personal choice for Janine. Even if it had everything to do with the man she divorced and his betrayal of what she thought marriage was supposed to be all about.

"Can you put Bernadette back on the phone, sweet pea?" she asked.

"Okay," Lisa said. "Bye."

"Bye-bye, baby." Janine made a kissing noise into the phone. "Talk to you soon."

A moment later Bernadette uttered in a somewhat loud, breathy tone of voice, "Hi."

"Hi," Janine responded tersely, wondering if she had been listening in on the conversation all along. "Would you ask John to give me a call as soon as he can?"

There was a moment of silence, as if Bernadette was wondering for what reason, before she uttered, "Sure. No problem."

Janine gave her the number at the hotel without expounding on the nature of the call. Somehow it didn't seem appropriate to say that she wanted to chide him for leaving Lisa with his girlfriend rather than spending time with her himself.

Janine hung up, immediately regretting how she must have come across. Maybe she was being a bit unfair to John to expect that he would drop everything on a dime to be with his daughter, whom she had packed up and sent his way with little notice. He had his own life, which didn't always include Lisa, and she had to respect that.

This did little to ease Janine's yearning to be with her daughter instead of across the country in California trying to recapture a reluctant photographer. There was something about being the mother of a young, precious child that made it difficult to ever want to be apart from her for any length of time, no matter the circumstances.

Janine showered and prepared for her afternoon outing with Richard. Strangely, she found herself excited about the prospect, almost as though it was a real date with an eligible, talented, fascinating, nice-looking man. Even if those adjectives aptly described Richard Lowrey, she had to keep in mind that this boating excursion was just a means to an end. One that, for better or worse, they might not see eye to eye on....

Chapter 11

The dark green Ford Bronco pulled up in front of the Pebble Beach Inn. Richard tilted his head away from the steering wheel and waved as Janine approached. She waved back awkwardly. They had agreed—or she had—that he would drive them to where the boat was docked, rather than meeting there. It only made sense, even if the close proximity in his car might make her just a bit uncomfortable.

"Hello," Richard said in a pleasing voice, a mixture of deep baritone and a smooth, comfortable West Coast inflection.

"Good afternoon," Janine responded brightly, fastening her seat belt. She immediately got a whiff of his cologne, which she recognized as Paco Rabanne. It suited him, she thought agreeably.

Richard was casual in a maroon polo shirt and pair of navy chinos, both fitting nicely on his tight body, along with those same brown boots he'd worn yesterday. Only, now they had a fresh shine to them. For her part, Janine was dressed for comfort, wearing a blue oxford shirt, tan khakis and flats. She had also brought a light jacket. Her hair was in a loose ponytail, mainly to keep it out of her face on the boat.

"Looks like the weather will cooperate with us," said Richard, gazing through the windshield as they pulled away from the curb.

It was sunny without a cloud in the sky, something that Janine luxuriated in, taking her sunglasses from her purse and putting them on.

"I guess it never rains in California," she quipped, alluding to the Tony, Toni, Tone song.

He chuckled. "Yeah, well, sometimes that's the problem. The farmers can't make much of a living when the rain won't come and water their crops before they wither and die. Tends to have a ripple effect out here."

"That's often a problem in the Midwest, too," she noted reflectively.

Richard cocked a straight brow her way. "You from the Midwest?"

"Detroit," Janine said proudly. "My parents moved to New York when I was eleven." She wet her lips, seizing the moment to get him to open up more about himself. "How about you—has California always been your home?"

"My dad worked the railways in the Deep South and West," he said. "We must have lived in eight different states between Mississippi and California by the time I turned eighteen."

"Is that what made you want to become a photographer?" Janine inquired.

He flashed her an uneasy gaze. "You mean, all the travel?"

"Yes. And the different and diverse scenery from state to state."

Richard looked back at the road. "Yeah. I think that probably had something to do with it. My folks bought me a camera when I was six or seven years old and talked me into using it. Ever since then, I knew I wanted to take pictures—ones that conveyed the beauty of life and death…."

His voice trailed off and Janine sensed that he was thinking about his late wife and daughter. And probably the significant and unfortunate changes their deaths had brought about in his life. Including the effect it had on his photography and writing career.

"I'm sure with that type of devotion, you're quite good at what you do," she offered, hoping to encourage him to talk about his photography in particular, and perhaps the inadvertent life-altering event that had taken away the will to continue his passion.

"Used to be," he muttered broodingly. "Not sure I'm good at much of anything these days."

"And why is that?" She stared somberly at his profile, wishing this wasn't so hard.

Richard was silent for a moment as he ran a thumb across the bridge of his nose. "Long story," he said evasively. "Maybe I'll tell you about it sometime if you're still around…."

Janine wondered if that was some sort of cryptic invitation to stay in Pebble Beach longer than she had intended. More likely, she decided, it was merely a figure of speech, telling her in effect: *Mind your own business, lady.*

On the other hand, Janine thought, perhaps he really was willing to speak candidly about the issues weighing on his mind if she made herself available to him. This could be just what he needed to turn his life around. And what she needed to successfully accomplish her assignment. Surely Dennis wouldn't quibble with a few extra days on the expense account, if it meant delivering the prized author to Callister-Reynolds's doorstep.

Another side of Janine couldn't help but wonder if Richard's words were prompted more by an attraction to her as a woman, rather than as someone with whom to get things off his chest. *Not that this is so bad,* she thought. At least it would show that he hadn't totally shut himself off from flirtatious overtures and romance.

Either way, Janine did not wish to get caught up in dangerous thinking. What was most important was that she use this slight crack in the man's armor to try and establish a dialogue with him that could lead to reestablishing a mutually beneficial relationship between photographer and publisher.

They approached the shiny white-and-blue motorboat named the *Marjah1*.

"It was named after my mother, Marjah," Richard explained. "My old man wanted a way to keep her alive after her death—at least for as long as he was around."

"How sweet and sentimental," Janine cadenced, imagining how much love they must have shared till the very end. Despite the fact she knew the truth about Richard's past, it was painfully obvious to her that he once had a loving marriage in his own right that had been taken away from him by circumstances beyond his control.

She wondered if it was possible that he could ever experience such pure love with anyone again. This made Janine muse about the prospect of knowing such love and deep commitment in her own life for the first time. She knew now that what she'd had with John had never really been the type of all-consuming love and passionate relationship fairy tales were made of. He had woken her up to the harsh realities of many modern-day marriages that were anything but a fantasy.

Though she had been stung badly once, Janine still clung to the hope that her soul mate might actually exist out there somewhere. Finding him was another story altogether, she thought wistfully, an eye on Richard as they boarded the midsize boat.

They took off in Monterey Bay and headed out into the crystal-blue waters of the Pacific Ocean. On deck in a picnic basket was some cheese, crackers, cookies, two glasses and a bottle of Pinot Noir.

"Seems like my father has been busy," said Richard, an almost embarrassed look spreading across his handsome face at the spread.

"Obviously he enjoys making your life a little easier," Janine said, smiling, and immediately went for the crackers and cheese.

Richard cleared his throat. "I'm not so sure about that. Sometimes I think he simply hangs around just to grate me."

"We should all be so lucky." Janine thought of her own parents. She would give anything if either of her parents were still around to offer her love, advice and assistance—even if they were overbearing at times, as most parents could be. Usually it was out of love, something she sensed was the case with Richard's father.

"I hear you," Richard agreed, opening up the package of chocolate-chip cookies and tossing one in his mouth.

A good start. Janine was beginning to warm up to the idea of this boat date and tour.

The boat made its way into Spanish Bay. In the distance were the San Gabilan Mountains, majestic in their beauty and backdrop.

"Juan Portola camped out here in 1769," Richard pointed out. "It was on his land expedition from Baja, California. On a return trip he found Monterey Bay."

Janine was once more awed as she stared out into the bay, thinking back to his earlier command of the area. "You really do know your stuff, don't you?"

Richard shrugged and flashed her a crooked smile. "Just enough to keep from making a fool out of myself."

"Oh, I don't think you have to worry about that," she assured him. "You're definitely not a fool." Indeed, she felt he was anything but.

Richard seemed to take that to heart while guiding them expertly into yet deeper waters.

Janine took pictures to show Lisa, certain she would be thoroughly captivated by the wonders of the Monterey Peninsula captured on film. Admittedly there was an ulterior motive as well in making use of her camera, a fairly inexpensive but capable 35mm. She hoped that by watching an amateur at work, it just might inspire Richard to want to put his professional skills behind the camera back in operation. And in the process, jump-start his career, leading to the fulfillment of his contract with Callister-Reynolds.

"So what type of business are you doing here?" queried Richard, a curious slant to his focused gray eyes. "If you don't mind my asking."

Janine felt color fill her cheeks. She didn't necessarily want to tell him a bold-faced lie. At the same time, she couldn't be too specific—at least, not till they were back on land and under conditions where it would be less traumatic…and safer.

"Oh, just some editorial-related work for my publisher," she told him nonchalantly. Which wasn't entirely untruthful.

Furthermore, Janine actually hoped that if she played her cards right, she might get to edit *his* books.

"I would have thought that in this age of the Internet, virtually all editorial work could be done on the computer," Richard remarked, studying her, "instead of having to fly across the country."

Janine felt her lower lip quiver. "Not quite true," she said in all honesty. "There are some things that still require old-fashioned travel and a hands-on approach."

"I suppose." He looked off into the distance and back at her. "Anyway, I can certainly think of worse places on the planet to do editorial work far away from home."

"So can I." She flashed him a gentle smile. Even then, Janine found herself missing her daughter and wishing she'd been able to bring Lisa with her.

"There's Point Joe." Richard pointed to a turbulent spot off the coast. "From the earliest days of sailing to the present, mariners have mistakenly believed Point Joe to be the entrance to Monterey Bay, and ended up shipwrecked on the rocks. Cargo ships such as the *Roderick Dhu* and the *Celia* have gone to their graves at Point Joe."

Janine took more pictures, again as taken with his knowledge of the surroundings as with the man himself. It was almost like being guided by a time traveler who had lived everything he described.

"Have you ever thought about writing a book about *this place?*" she asked innocently, finding it odd that he hadn't, as far as she knew. "With your photography skills and regional expertise, it seems like a natural thing to do."

Richard again stared out into the blue waters, as if hoping to discover a hidden island. Or perhaps to escape to one, Janine mused.

"Thought about it," he admitted. "Once. But the timing was never right…."

"Maybe now is the right time," she suggested boldly, deciding to go out on a limb. "Unless, of course, you're working on something else…?"

He glared at her suspiciously but quickly relaxed his features into a gentle gaze. "No," he said without preface. "Nothing."

When Richard seemed reluctant to say more, Janine did not press the issue. Or her luck. *Don't blow this, girl,* she warned herself. *Just let it happen.* She felt it had to come from him naturally if she was to have any chance of getting the man to resume his career. And his life.

Richard turned from her and steered the boat toward an old Monterey cypress. The trunk was bleached white by sea spray and the wind.

"It's called Ghost Tree," he noted somewhat eerily. "It was Robert Lewis Stevenson who said these trees were ghosts fleeing before the wind."

"Creepy," Janine uttered, clicking the camera. "I can only imagine how haunting it must look at night." She took more pictures.

Richard was watching her as he slowed the boat down. "You're pretty good with that," he said.

"Yeah, right," she said, batting her lashes wryly. "I'll probably win an award for these pictures—in my dreams." She chuckled at the absurdity of it. "But I do enjoy taking pictures when I travel."

He grinned. "Yeah, I can see that."

Janine suddenly pushed the camera toward him, deciding to act on impulse. "You want to give it a try? I think I can manage to steer the boat for a while. My daddy used to take me out in his boat every week during the summers when I was a little girl. Every now and then I'd talk him into letting me take the wheel. I nearly drove him crazy going around in circles, but we always made it back safe and sound."

Richard gave her an amused look and seemed poised to take the camera, lifting his arm mechanically, as though a robot. But he stopped hastily, putting the arm back to his side, and favored the water. "I don't think so," he said glumly. "Maybe some other time...."

Some other time? thought Janine disappointedly. She felt as if she had been *that* close to reaching him. Now she was back to square one.

Damn.

This was one tough man to crack, she mused, wishing there was a less painful way to do this.

Still, Janine felt there was hope. Could be that "maybe some other time" meant that he was planning to invite her back out again during the week. Or was it a polite way of avoiding the past as well as the future—both of which he was obviously still unable or unwilling to face?

What there was no getting around, Janine told herself mindfully, was that time was not on her side if she were to make this happen soon, if at all. She feared her chance to make some major headway had gone awry, much like the car that had plunged out of control, taking Richard's wife and daughter with it.

There was mostly silence between them for a stretch, though some of the spots of interest spoke for themselves, such as the lighthouse about twenty miles away that somehow looked much closer. Then there was the cypress tree that appeared as if it was rooted in bare rock, causing her to pause with amazement. The main attraction, Janine had come to realize, was perhaps the Del Monte Forest itself, with its acres and acres of native pines, shrubs and an assortment of wildlife to admire from practically every vantage point.

Richard slowed the boat down before bringing it to a complete stop. They were seemingly in the middle of the blissful ocean, unburdened by life ashore.

Richard filled their glasses with wine. Handing Janine one, he said unevenly, "I'm afraid I haven't been completely honest with you…."

Janine felt her stomach tighten. "Oh?"

He met her gaze and hesitated before saying, "I told you yesterday that I had no family. Well, I do, did, sort of—" He sipped wine thoughtfully. "My wife and daughter were killed in a car accident three years ago."

"I'm so sorry," Janine said sincerely, hating that she had not been totally forthcoming with him, either. She bit back the urge to come clean right there and then, believing that he needed to get it off his chest even more. Tasting the wine, she asked coaxingly, "How did it happen?"

Richard turned his head toward the sea. "I killed them," he muttered culpably.

"You *killed* them?" Her brows shot up dramatically.

"More or less." He spoke weakly. "I was behind the wheel. If I hadn't practically insisted we go out that night in the rotten-assed weather, the brakes might not have failed."

Janine moved in front of Richard so he would have to look at her. "You couldn't have controlled the weather or malfunctioning brakes, Richard. Surely you must realize that."

"Maybe I couldn't have," he conceded, frowning, "or maybe I could have used better judgment before the fact."

"Richard, I don't think—"

"The bottom line is that I lived and they didn't. There's

something not quite right about that." He sighed. "They were my life. And just like that—" he snapped his fingers so hard that Janine jumped back "—they were gone for good, and there wasn't a damn thing I could do about it but be a man and take responsibility for what happened...."

Without intending to, Janine put a hand to Richard's wind-dried cheek, feeling his sorrow as though it were her own. "You can't blame yourself for an *accident*," she said *sotto voce*. "Accidents happen, agonizing and unpredictable as they are. I'm sure your wife and little girl would have wanted you to move on with your life and your work...."

Richard took Janine's hand while favoring her with the weight of teary eyes. "I'm not sure I can," he stated languidly. "Something is missing inside me. It's like it's been eaten away by a cancer and can't be easily put back. Whoever I was, whatever I was, I think died with them that night."

"Maybe not," Janine voiced hopefully, her hand wrapped in his as though in a warm blanket. "I think you're still very much alive...."

She wasn't sure what was happening. Only that something powerful stirred inside her as if she was miles away from shore and the real world had somehow made her lose all sense of perspective and reason. Yet she knew there was more to these feelings than the clear blue water that surrounded them like an island in the sun. She felt his pain merge with her own, as though they were kindred spirits in the disillusionment of life and separation.

More importantly, she saw Richard for perhaps the first time as a man rather than a grief-stricken photographer. A man she found herself attracted to as much for his looks as his character and heart.

Though this struck Janine as precarious under the circumstances, it also excited her in a way she hadn't been in a very long time. She found herself wanting the feeling to last as long as it could, knowing she was treading on uncharted territory with no certainty or expectation of where it might lead. Or where it might go from here....

Richard stared at her face for a long moment, then removed Janine's hand from his and kissed her palm. His soft, sexy mouth on her skin sent shivers through her, touching every part of her body. She felt weak at the knees.

"Richard..." she was drawn to say while holding her breath, unsure where this was headed, if anywhere. Or nowhere. But she was too swept up in the moment to think rationally. She sensed they both were.

Setting down their wineglasses, Richard cupped Janine's cheeks and slowly, deliberately, brought his mouth down to hers. Their lips brushed softly as if testing the waters for warmth and invitation. For a moment Janine felt as if they were frozen in time, caught between the past, present and future as if in an inescapable black hole. They began to kiss passionately with a desperation that came with need, each, it felt like, releasing pent-up emotions that had been stored so long so as to almost be forgotten. Their mouths opened and pressed tightly together, to keep all the positive energy within from escaping, powering between them like steam in an engine.

They stayed that way for what seemed like hours, but in fact it was only minutes. Then, abruptly, Richard pulled away, leaving Janine slightly off balance and feeling cold. With the back of his hand, he wiped his mouth as though it had been laced with poison.

"I think we'd better get back now," he said tonelessly, unable to meet Janine's glaring eyes.

"Uh, yes, you're probably right," she mumbled, practically speechless and suddenly feeling foolish and ashamed for letting her guard down and losing track of her purpose for being in his company. She backed off and stared at the endless sea, hearing the engine start and the skipper get on with the business of bringing them back to shore, seemingly not fast enough.

What have I done? Janine thought with dread, wondering if she had compromised her mission and cheapened herself in the process. She feared that by allowing Richard to kiss her, she had only used him as a momentary relief for her own lack of companionship and loneliness, and taken advantage of his susceptibility at this time in his life.

But it could just have easily been the other way around, she mused.

Clearly, Richard had wanted to kiss her, if only in his own moment of weakness before coming to his senses. He'd apparently decided that she was really nothing more than a poor substitute for the wife he'd lost. A person who just happened to be there at a time when he most needed someone to reach out to.

Both were guilty of playing to their emotions and the idyllic surroundings while away from the real world where they had their separate issues to deal with in their own ways.

Janine felt her head spinning but knew it was not due to the wine she'd had. No, it had more to do with the kiss. The man. The moment. The mission. The sudden vulnerability she felt in giving in to parts of herself that she preferred to keep hidden and safe from heartache and disappointment.

Determined to clear her head and regain the equilibrium she'd brought with her onto the boat, Janine felt her resolve stiffen. She could only hope that a brief distraction had not seriously jeopardized a settlement in the contractual dispute between Richard Lowrey and Callister-Reynolds.

Yet a part of Janine pondered if she could somehow end up losing far more in coming to Pebble Beach than the books long overdue by the complex photographer....

She mulled these thoughts over as they neared the shore in silence—and with those thoughts, reality, as if what had happened had been only a pleasant, though somewhat disturbing, dream.

Chapter 12

That first night they were together, Richard and Kassandra made love as if they had been lovers forever. They seemed to fit together like two birds of a feather, anticipating each other's every move and reacting to it in perfect and sensual harmony. It only affirmed what Richard already knew in his gut from the moment he had laid eyes on the Jamaican beauty. He was very much in love with this remarkable lady, as he'd never been before, and couldn't bear the thought of losing her to distance or some other lucky bastard.

"Come back to Los Angeles with me?" Richard asked her in bed. She was wrapped cozily in his arms as if she'd already become his girl.

Kassandra lifted her big, stunning brown eyes to him, as if she thought she must surely have misunderstood him. "What? Did you just ask me to move to L.A.?"

"Yeah, I did," he responded sincerely, eyes never leaving her face. "That's where you belong now."

"Are you *crazy*, mon—like, certifiably insane?" She wrinkled her nose. "A nice meal and a couple of good—I mean *great*—hours in the sack and you're ready to live together? Is that what you had in mind?"

"It's exactly what I had in mind—for the moment," Richard admitted, surprising himself with the warp speed their relationship was moving at. "There's something between us that I've never felt before with anyone, baby," he said, laying it out on the line. "Powerful. Magical. All-consuming. And, yes, maybe even a little crazy. Whatever you want to call it. I can feel it in my bones. I don't want to lose that feeling. Ever."

Kassandra tilted her head, causing her long dreadlocks to shift to the other side of her taut face. She reached down and grabbed him between the legs. "Sure this isn't what you feel between us?" she asked teasingly. "Or should I say, between *me?*"

She gave him a genuine smile, though he could see that her wit was filled with reservations.

He had no such reservations. Only hopeful anticipation that he could get her to come around to his way of thinking.

"It's much more than just sex," he insisted, "as fantastic as it was. You, me…we were meant to be together, Kassandra."

"Oh, we were," she scoffed, "were we?"

"Yes!" Richard rested his gaze on her, cuddling a bit tighter. "Call it fate, destiny or whatever, but it's true." Something told him to slow down just a bit before he scared the poor lady to death and away from him. "At least give us a try," he pleaded calmly. "I promise, you won't regret it."

Kassandra opened her mouth as if to let out air, then said, "You really are crazy, Richard Lowrey. You know that?"

Richard conceded that this was probably the craziest thing

he had ever suggested in his twenty-four years of life. But his instincts were almost never wrong. He knew that what he felt for Kassandra was as real as having her in his arms. As real as the earth and the moon.

The sand and the sea.

Man and woman.

He could only hope to get her to feel the same way about him at the end of the day and night…the morning, afternoon and evening…and everything in between…over and beyond…

For the rest of their lives.

"I'm crazy, all right, Kassandra," he told her. "Crazy as hell about *you*—"

She sat up, running a hand across his cheeks, then frowned. "I'm flattered, Richard. Truly. No one has ever said such beautiful things to me—and meant it. But I can't just leave my job. My family. My friends. My country."

Richard could hear his heart thumping and feel her slipping away. "Why not?" he asked bluntly. "People do it all the time, if the right reason is there. You can come back to visit anytime and as often as you like. I'll even come with you. I'm always up for a trip to paradise—especially if I'm with the main attraction."

Kassandra cast him a thoughtful look. "You're very sweet, Richard, but you're still asking an awful lot, mon." She paused. "On the other hand, I've always been a bit of an adventurer and risk-taker. So maybe I'll take a chance with you, Mr. California. I admit it certainly doesn't hurt one bit if the American photographer happens to be sexy as hell. Not to mention, one damned fantastic lover!"

Richard's pulse raced even more as the tide seemed to be shifting in his direction.

"So is that a yes I hear?" he asked, holding his breath and her at the same time.

She gave him a hard kiss on the mouth. "What do you think? Call me crazy, too…."

They made love again and seemed to drift to a faraway land where they made all the rules and pushed each other toward greater heights. Even when coming back down to earth, Richard felt as if he was still up there somewhere amongst the clouds, reveling in his own ecstasy and the promise of a great life with the most wonderful woman he'd ever met.

Sometimes, he believed, the best dreams merged with reality. This was one of those times. He hoped he got to spend the rest of his life waiting on this woman hand and foot.

A month later Kassandra packed up her bags and left Jamaica for Los Angeles, following a couple of short but meaningful visits.

Six months after that they were married.

To Richard, it seemed as though life could not get much better than that.

It never occurred to him that it wouldn't last for reasons neither could have anticipated.

Chapter 13

The sun had begun to set over the horizon and a cool breeze came in from the ocean. Richard dropped Janine off at the inn. He gave her a perfunctory kiss on the cheek and said goodbye, resisting any urge to accompany her in. There seemed to be no real point to it. She appeared to be in agreement that they leave this alone, making no attempt during the drive to continue or discuss what they had started on the boat.

And neither did he.

He drove off not knowing if they would ever see each other again. Or if it should matter.

What's up with you, man? Richard asked himself, drumming his fingers agitatedly on the steering wheel. *I was kissing her like she was my woman.* He wanted to believe there was little more to it than playing some sort of sick game with this person, because being in her company happened to remind him so much of the only woman he'd ever loved.

But he sensed it went deeper than that. Maybe he actually was starting to feel something for someone other than Kassandra that he never thought he could feel again: *affection and yearning*.

If that was true, Richard reflected, he believed it worked both ways. Janine had reacted to his touch, his mouth, his kiss, his smell, just as he had to hers.

With longing. Joy. Satisfaction.

Even a sense of urgency.

He hesitated to consider that there might have been more going on between them than either was willing to admit. This was not the time to go down that road.

Richard pulled the Bronco into the driveway of his house and sat there, pensive, uncertain. Even a little frightened.

All right, hell, a lot frightened, he mused. The unknown and its ramifications tended to make him ill at ease.

He thought about how he had literally frozen when Janine tried to hand him her camera, as if it were a live grenade. He had not so much as touched a camera since the night Kassandra and Sheena had died. It was as if his will to pursue what had once been his passion had disintegrated before his very eyes. After all, there seemed no point in carrying on with his life as if nothing had changed when it damn well had. For the worse.

Forever.

Now he began to wonder if forever was meant to be just that. Or maybe it was supposed to be something short of eternity. A short-term thing till the darkness began to subside.

Can I possibly begin my life over at this stage? a voice inside asked Richard, not at all certain he was ready for this.

Ready for Janine Henderson.

But he had to consider the new and very real prospect that there might indeed be changes for the better in store for him. Possibly involving a woman he barely knew.

Ever burdening Richard in this scenario was the idea of Kassandra viewing it as the ultimate betrayal if he were to ever love another. The thought left him feeling weak with guilt and reservations.

"How'd it go?" Henry's voice boomed over the phone.

Richard held the receiver to his ear, wondering just how to answer that. He didn't want to suggest overexuberance like he'd found his other half. Nor did he care to dismiss his time spent with Janine as something he could have done without. Or just an everyday event in the life and times of Richard Lowrey. Nothing could be further from the truth.

"She enjoyed the tour," came his simple and, overall, sincere response.

Henry, not too surprisingly to Richard, refused to leave it at that. "I never doubted she would. My question is how did you enjoy *her* company?"

An uneasiness gripped him like a vise. Richard had been nudged by Henry for the last couple of years to start dating again, which he had steadfastly refused to do. It was always too soon or too late. Not right or too wrong.

But now, for the first time since Kassandra's death, Richard was feeling something for someone else. And it scared the hell out of him.

It also captivated him.

"I enjoyed going out on the boat with her," he admitted. "She's a nice lady."

"And you're a *nice* man," Henry said with a catch to his voice.

Richard recognized that tone of his father's and his between-the-words insinuations. He'd heard it all before. Especially when Henry had something up his sleeve, usually involving matchmaking.

"Whatever you're thinking, Pops," he pressed, "don't. I'm not looking to get involved with Janine or anyone else. And even if I was, this would hardly be a match made in heaven since the lady lives on the other side of the country."

Henry coughed into the phone theatrically. "Have you forgotten so soon, son, that Kassandra lived way over in Jamaica before she became sweet on you and you on her? But that didn't stop you two from getting together once you set your mind to it."

"That was different," Richard said feebly.

"I don't think so, son. The way I see it, the only difference is that you don't have to go across the water to see this lady. As your old man and still-wise father, my advice is that if you like her you ought to go after the girl before she gets away for good."

Richard couldn't help but laugh. "It was only a boat tour, Dad," he said defensively, "for crying out loud. Don't try to put anything else into it in that devious head of yours."

"I'm not putting anything more into it than you are, Richard," Henry declared flatly. "You think I was born yesterday? When was the last time you took the boat out as a tour guide for a lady? Never, if my aging but sharp-as-a-knife memory serves me correctly. But, hey, listen, it's your life and I don't want to meddle, any more than I already have. Let me just say this one thing, then I'll shut up. If you care for this woman that I let you borrow my boat for, you owe it to yourself to see where it leads…even if it goes nowhere."

After hanging up, Richard pondered the notion, even when he wished he could run away and hide from whatever he was feeling. He seriously doubted he was truly ready to "see where it leads" with Janine, no matter the outcome. There were too many unresolved conflicts in his head and unhealed wounds in his heart. He was a mess. What woman would want that?

He also had to look at it from Janine's point of view, too. She'd given him no reason to believe she was even interested in a long-distance friendship. Much less a coast-to-coast romance with a broken-down, has-been photographer.

Opening up a can of worms would only lead to more misery and regrets.

Richard turned his eyes to the oil painting on his bedroom wall. It was a painting of Kassandra made from a photograph when she was thirty. Damn, he thought, she still looked so good. He felt he could almost touch her in touching the painting. It did wonders in capturing her Jamaican beauty and natural spark. Her soul and spirit, as well as the love they had for each other, as expressed in her sheer grace and blissful look of contentment.

That love would be demeaned should he pursue another, he feared.

"Would it, Kass?" Richard pondered out loud. "Would loving another take away from my love for you…our love for each other?"

Kassandra remained speechless but spoke through her eyes, which seemed to regard Richard astutely from every angle in which he stood or sat, as if forever keeping watch over her husband. Her beloved. The father of her child. The man who promised to forsake all others. And making sure he knew he would always be hers and no other's.

He took that to heart.

The following afternoon the phone rang as Richard was eating lunch. He answered it on the third ring.

"Richard. Hi! It's Janine."

Richard's tongue somehow stuck to the roof of his mouth, as if attached there, rendering him virtually speechless.

"I got your number from the directory," she said falteringly. "I hope I wasn't interrupting anything...."

"No, not at all," he said, trying to keep from showing just how glad he was to hear her voice. "What's up?"

Janine sighed. "The reason I'm calling is that I think I may have left my bracelet on the front seat of your car."

"Bracelet? Oh. Right." Richard hid his disappointment that the call hadn't been more social in nature. Not that he had any right to expect more than he had been willing to give in return. "If you want to hold on for a moment, I'll be happy to run out and check."

"Thank you," she said, a slight hopefulness to her tone.

Richard moved briskly through the kitchen, living room and out the door, nearly tripping over himself—uncertain if he wanted to find the bracelet—which would mean they'd have to see each other again. Why create a reason to see each other again if it wasn't meant to be?

There, half wedged into the seat cushion, was a silver tennis bracelet. Richard pulled it out, studied it for a moment or two and brought it in the house. He wondered how the bracelet had managed to slip from her wrist. Maybe Janine had removed the bracelet, he thought, deciding it made no difference. Except that as a result they would have to get back together at least once...as though fated to.

"It was just where you suspected," Richard told Janine, moving the bracelet between his fingers and imagining her wearing it. "Would you like me to bring it over to the inn?"

"Actually, I thought I might come by there to get it," she said hesitantly. "I should have no trouble finding the place. If that's all right with you?" Janine added with anticipation in her voice. "I'd love to take the opportunity to see some of your photography...."

Richard's initial instinct was to reject the offer outright, preferring instead to come to her…not wanting to open up his life of photography like an old wound. But he knew that it might be misinterpreted.

Or perhaps, he considered, interpreted correctly.

He glanced at the bracelet in his hand. "That's fine."

"Will you be around tomorrow morning?"

"I'll be here."

"Great," Janine said positively. "Guess I'll see you then."

Chapter 14

Things came to a head between Janine and John for the final time the eighth year of their marriage. Well before that, they had drifted apart socially, emotionally and sexually. But Janine tried desperately to make it work, primarily for the sake of their daughter, who was nearly five years old.

Then came the visit that made it easier to go it alone rather than live a lie.

It was on a Friday night after Janine had put Lisa to bed. John was supposed to be out of town on a business trip. But she found out otherwise.

Janine opened the front door to find a woman, perhaps ten years her junior, standing there. She was an attractive African-American with a curly burgundy bob, big burnt-almond eyes that seemed to look through her, not at her, way too much makeup and a shapely, top-heavy figure—all of which, for some reason, told Janine right then that she had cause to be concerned. She wore a navy designer suit and matching heels, making them the same height.

"Janine?" the woman asked, as if in doubt.

"Yes," Janine answered cautiously, feeling self-conscious in her terry-cloth robe, nightgown and bare feet.

"My name is Monica. I need to talk to you. Can I come in?" In a conspiratorial undertone, she leaned forward and said, "It has to do with John."

Janine suddenly felt as if a nerve had been pinched. A small part of her thought that the woman was there to say John had been in a terrible accident or was otherwise in some sort of distress. Had that been the case, at least she could have dealt with it accordingly.

But, as she didn't take the maroon-haired woman to be a police officer or government official, it seemed Monica's reasons for coming to the house—uninvited and after 9:00 p.m.—were entirely personal.

Janine invited her in, eager to get to the bottom of this visit. As Monica walked past her, Janine got a whiff of her perfume, recognizing it as Chanel No. 5, John's favorite.

The two women stood toe to toe at the foot of the living room before Monica said in a wavering yet strong voice, "I don't quite know how to tell you this...so I guess I'll just come right out and say it. I've been having an affair with your husband for the past year."

Janine sucked in her emotions, the shock needing time to register. She wondered if in some pathetic way Monica had expected to be congratulated for stealing her husband away. Or maybe she was actually hoping they would come to blows.

Janine kept her options open, saying with feigned skepticism, "Oh, really...?"

She knew this would compel her husband's latest mistress

to finish what she had started, even as Janine was already
reeling from the expectation of what would come next.

"I'm in love with John," Monica uttered flatly. "And *he*
loves *me!*"

"My husband's at a conference in Washington, D.C.,"
Janine stated in denial, as if that had anything to do with it.
Or somehow exonerated him from guilt.

Or from being in love with this bitch with the big boobs.

Monica countered by saying, "No, he isn't, I'm sorry to
say. John's at a log cabin in upstate New York right now. He's
waiting for me...."

Janine reverberated from the blow, as if struck by a firm
right hook. Or as if she'd run into the side of a door. Instinctively she knew that Monica was telling the truth, but she still
tried to reject this and her own insecurities, as if the whole
scenario would somehow seem like a nightmare that would
go away.

She glared at the woman. "I think you'd better leave."

Monica flashed her an equally frosty look. "I work in his
law firm," she said, as if to impress Janine. "John and I hit it
off right away. We knew how we felt about each other and
nothing's happened to change that. The only problem is that
he's been dragging his feet in asking *you* for a divorce."

Janine batted her lashes with vexation. "Is that what he told
you?" She hated the thought of being John's *only problem* in
breaking up their marriage to be with someone else. *What a
fool I've been!*

"It's not that 'having his cake and eating it, too' thing,"
Monica stressed confidently, a hand now on her hip. "What
it boils down to is John's afraid of losing his daughter and
being taken to the cleaners by you!"

Janine's nostrils flared. No matter how despicable she

found her unfaithful husband's behavior, deep down she knew she would never try to keep John from Lisa, or take away his parental rights. It would not be fair to Lisa.

As for taking him to the cleaners, Janine had no intention of bankrupting the two-timing bastard. She only wanted what was her fair share of the life they'd built together. Not a penny more or less. Aside from child support and a property settlement, she didn't even want alimony from him. It would only be something else to bind her to a man with whom, given the situation, she wanted as few strings attached to as possible.

But she wasn't about to tell his whore that.

"Just get the hell out of my house." She spoke quietly yet firmly, leveling her gaze at Monica. All the while Janine fought back tears aching to come pouring out like an overflowing river that had gone over its banks. She added with a note of finality, "When you see John, tell him not to bother to come back from wherever he's holed up. I'm through fighting a lost cause over his sorry ass."

Monica started to say something, thought better and left, the smug look of satisfaction spreading across her face like a rash that wasn't ready to go away anytime soon.

When John showed up the next day, his wrinkled clothing and awkward demeanor said it all. Even his body smelled of sex and the perfume Monica had worn last night.

"I never meant for you to find out this way, baby," he slurred insincerely.

Janine bought none of his lies. Not anymore. "Like hell you didn't! And don't call me *baby!*" she blared painfully, having sent Lisa over to a neighbor's house in expectation of this confrontation. "You knew exactly what your *Miss Burgundy Thang* came here to say. Only, you didn't have the balls to tell me yourself. You've made a fool out of me for the last time, John!"

He reacted this time not with remorse, but with cold, hard brutality. "If you want to blame anyone, Janine, blame yourself! I can't even remember the last time we made love, and I don't mean just sex—though that, too, has been suffering big-time!"

Her eyes burned at him like piercing rays of light. "Don't you dare try to turn this around on me, you bastard! Is that what you think your whore's been spreading her legs to give you—*love?*"

Janine shivered before her husband. The truth was that any type of sexual relation between them had been rare in recent memory—ever since she'd learned of his first infidelity. Now she realized that probably wasn't the first time, after all. And certainly wouldn't be the last. Once an asshole, always an asshole.

Janine should have seen this coming. But no, she chose to wear blinders in denial of the writing that had been on the wall for some time now. *I'm such an idiot—like so many other women who want so much to believe in their men, they can see no wrong, even when it's staring them right in the face.*

No more.

Enough was enough.

She had more respect for herself than to put up with this crap.

But this newfound determination and the truth behind it did not set her free, Janine realized, wiping away bitter tears. It would take a lot more time and distance before that could come about, if it ever did.

Right now all she knew was that this was not the man she'd fallen in love with and married. Or maybe it was and she had chosen to ignore the signs from the very beginning.

Janine winced from the pain that hurt as badly as if she'd broken every bone in her body.

"She makes me happy," John said weakly, as if that somehow made it all right.

"Then you can have her!" Janine retorted, fluttering her lashes wildly. "And she can have your sorry ass! I just want you to leave me the hell alone."

A wave of resignation swept over John's face, followed by smugness. "If that's what you want."

"No, it's what *you* want, John!" she blasted. "It's what you've always wanted—to be single again and play the field. So go to your mistress and let her deal with you. I've had enough."

He ran a large hand across his balding head. "What about Lisa?"

"As far as she will know, Mommy and Daddy just decided to live apart," Janine told him sadly. Someday, when the time was right, they would tell her everything. "My daughter will stay with me! You can see her whenever you like. And don't worry about me bad-mouthing you—she doesn't need that kind of bitterness in her life. Besides, I'm sure she'll find out what an asshole you are all on her own."

He seemed satisfied with that and made no effort this time at a half-baked reconciliation.

John moved out that day and Janine's life was to change forever. Not even her soon-to-be ex-husband's upcoming romantic misfortunes could even the score for the betrayal and emptiness she felt inside when she thought of him. Things between John and Monica suddenly soured when she was no longer the other woman. Rather than feel some sense of elation or self-satisfaction, Janine pitied her.

And the many who would follow.

But Janine had her own life to worry about. Along with that of her daughter. She wanted only to bring Lisa up in the best environment possible.

A relationship was the furthest thing from Janine's mind at the time. She seriously doubted that she could ever find the type of man she sought in the first place—one of trust, faithfulness, integrity, commitment and respect.

But something deep inside Janine wanted to try to keep the door open to the slightest possibility.

Just in case such a man existed.

Chapter 15

John was already up when John phoned her at eight in the morning—11:00 a.m. in Boston.

"You wanted me to call you," he said disinterestedly.

Janine swallowed hard. "I wish you would've told me you weren't going to be around with Lisa there," she snapped. "Your girlfriends are poor substitutes for her *real* parent."

"I had to work," John responded unapologetically. "Besides, I'm doing you a favor, remember?" He grunted. "Maybe you should stay closer to home for your assignments in the future. Then you won't have to get pissed about who's taking care of Lisa."

"Forgive me for thinking you wanted to spend the extra time with her," Janine retorted. "Maybe I'll just bring her with me the next time." She hated placing Lisa in the middle of their squabbles. Or worse, letting John get to her at a time when they were thousands of miles apart, figuratively and literally. She took a breath and said, trying to keep the peace, "Look, I know you care about our daughter, John. All Lisa wants when she comes to Boston is to spend as much time as possible with her daddy. Is that asking too much?"

"No, it isn't," John said, then muttered something unintelligible into the phone. "Look, I have to go," he said. "Let me know when you get back and I'll bring Lisa home."

He hung up and Janine realized for perhaps the first time that they really had nothing left to say to each other outside of that concerning Lisa. She wondered if maybe it was better this way for people who were divorced. Keep it short, simple, unemotional. They didn't even have to pretend to like each other, or make halfhearted attempts to journey down memory lane and discover where it all went wrong, and how they might have changed things for the better. Whatever they once had—for better or worse, she knew—was now a thing of the past.

Over and done with.

And there was no turning back the clock.

Two hours later, Janine reluctantly phoned Richard.

It was an assignment she was beginning to dread more and more. The Richard Lowrey she had come to know without fully divulging who she was had begun to grow on Janine like vines on an old stately mansion. She sensed she was growing on him as well, though he was clearly fighting the chains that bound him to the past like a prisoner held for the crimes he'd committed.

For Janine it was the exact opposite. She felt largely unshackled from John and had absolutely no desire to rekindle anything with him. But moving into a new relationship was fraught with anxieties, uncertainties and pitfalls. This was especially true when it involved conflicting interests and a seemingly hopeless set of factors that stood in the way like a brick wall.

Janine found herself wondering if there was any chance that she and Richard might actually reconcile their differences and points of view. It was where they went from there that left her unsettled.

She had no illusions of seriously getting together with the troubled photographer and author, but knew she wanted to see him again both as a woman and as an employee of Callister-Reynolds. Yet Janine feared that she'd run out of serendipitous excuses to meet with him and might not have another chance. So she had slipped the bracelet off following the boat tour and stuck it between the seats, making sure it would be easy to find if he looked for it.

Now, as she drove to Richard's house, Janine questioned if her objectivity had been compromised beyond repair. Her mouth still ached from his kiss and her heart still raced from his touch. But he had pulled back from both, as if he had committed a mortal sin. And she was his temptress.

She was left to wonder if Richard would ever allow himself to feel anything lasting for another.

I can't compete with a ghost. Janine wasn't sure she even wanted to try. She wasn't ready to step into something without much of a future, with far too much of a horrible past.

Also troubling to Janine was how her personal feelings for Richard might impact the real purpose she had for being in Pebble Beach....

These thoughts drifted aside and prickles of nervousness crept about Janine's skin as she pulled into the driveway right behind Richard's Bronco. He was already standing at the door, waving.

Janine waved back uneasily. Looking beyond him, she

couldn't help but think that, everything else aside, the man had some impressive digs to go along with breathtaking surroundings. She could get used to this real fast.

Which somehow made her want to slow down and take a deep breath.

Don't get too carried away with the man or his surroundings, girl, she warned herself.

But that was easier said than done.

The house itself was fabulous by any standard of measurement, Janine thought as she approached it. The gray stone exterior had a reddish-orange tiled roof. Mullioned windows lined the front, bordered by brown shutters. The house was embedded in granite rock and on an elevated slope facing the ocean. Pine trees and high shrubbery surrounded it like an emerald fortress. She could only imagine what the inside looked like.

Moments later Janine stood face-to-face with Richard, each studying the other like gladiators ready to do battle. Or perhaps like two people acknowledging—through eye contact and posture—a physical and sexual attraction to one another that would not go away easily. If at all.

Janine willed herself to calm down and keep control of the situation before it controlled her completely and helplessly. She walked inside, feeling the heat emanating from Richard's body warming her as she brushed against him.

"Your bracelet," he said stiffly in the living room.

"Thank you." Janine started to take it with trembling fingers, only to have Richard move the bracelet just beyond her reach.

"Let me put it on you." A grin curved his mouth. "It's the least I can do." Effortlessly, he proceeded to wrap the bracelet around her wrist and latch it—watching Janine all the while as though unable to take his eyes off her.

Even as she shuddered from the closeness of their bodies and the intoxication of his scent—Calvin Klein's Obsession—Janine took a quick sweep of the large room where they stood. It had a dark flowery green sofa and love seat and an almond coffee table. There was plush olive carpeting that matched the drapes across a large bay window. A stereo system and big-screen TV filled an entertainment cabinet along one wall. On other walls were framed photographs of people and places. They were obviously taken by Richard himself, she thought.

Janine's focus then centered on the man of the house. He was dressed in a short-sleeved, button-down solid brown shirt and dark, pleated slacks. His closely cropped hair looked freshly washed and his gray eyes were angled down on her. She was beginning to feel hot under their intensity, when out of the corner of her eye she saw a cocker spaniel, which did its best to hide behind Richard's long, hard legs.

"This is Kimble," he said. "He gets a little shy some-times—especially around pretty ladies…."

Janine blushed and knelt down to pet him, happy for the diversion. "Hi, Kimble. Don't worry," she promised, "I don't bite. Not usually, anyway."

The dog seemed to quickly warm up to Janine, licking the side of her face like a lollipop and putting its paws in her lap.

"I think he likes you," Richard chuckled. "To tell you the truth, I'm not surprised. Kimble's always been a good judge of character."

Somehow Janine couldn't help but think that Kimble liked anyone who was willing to show him kindness and attention.

She wondered if the same applied to his owner as she stood up and was again confronted by their close proximity—and its discomfort.

"Can I get you something to drink?" he asked tentatively.

"I've got wine, some beer, fresh lemonade, orange juice and, of course, water."

"Lemonade sounds good," Janine uttered, trying to steady herself under his intense scrutiny.

"I agree. Two lemonades coming up." Richard moved to the stereo. "Do you like jazz?"

She nodded agreeably. "Love it."

"Good. Then you'll love this."

Momentarily, the rich jazzy vocals of a woman filtered through the speakers as though live in concert.

"It's called 'Wave,'" Richard said, "as in a sweet one sweeping ashore from the ocean."

Janine recognized the lyrics, which somehow seemed appropriate given the romantic undercurrent of waves continually bouncing back and forth between them. Its deeply intimate, somewhat melancholy meaning didn't escape her. She wondered if the song reminded him of his late wife and what they'd meant to each other.

Or perhaps he was thinking more of the present.

"Sarah Vaughan," Janine voiced. The singer's breezy, distinct, commanding sound was hard to miss.

Richard nodded with a slight twinkle in his eye. "I'm impressed," he marveled. "You really *are* a fan of great jazz."

"It's the type of music anyone who understands anything at all about music and its roots would enjoy." Janine downplayed her own pleasure. "My mother collected everything she could get her hands on of Sarah Vaughan's and Ella Fitzgerald's music. I guess she passed her musical appreciation down to me."

"I can see that." Richard looked at her with pleasure, then disappeared into the kitchen.

Janine took a deep breath, deciding to play it cool and just see what happened. She walked up to a group of framed photographs occupying a wall. One was a black-and-white picture of a group of African women posing in front of a hut.

Another was a color photograph of a young African-American girl with striking thick brown hair that hung in curls. Her face was ablaze with a bright smile; she was obviously a natural in front of the camera.

"My daughter," said Richard, entering the room.

Janine regarded her again thoughtfully. "She's beautiful."

"Yeah. Just like her mother." His face darkened for an instant before he looked toward the picture of the women. "Took that one in Nigeria. All of the women had AIDS. Yet every one of them still had a zest for life like you couldn't imagine."

Janine favored the images in a new and sorrowful light, finding it ironic that the photographer had struggled with his own zest for living his life when faced with a comparable tragedy. She turned to Richard. "You're really very good."

He shrugged, handing her a chilled glass of lemonade. "Was, I suppose. Once upon a time."

"You never lose the skills," she challenged him, "do you?"

Richard put the glass to his lips pensively. "Nothing lasts forever. Skills come and go, especially if you stop using them."

"So why did you?" Janine made the question seem casual enough, even if she knew full well what had possessed him to throw away everything he ever learned about photography.

He looked away. "Guess I no longer wanted to do the things that I did after…"

"…your wife and child were killed?" Janine could read his thoughts as if her own.

Richard shifted his head so that their eyes locked. "Yes. It took something out of me, in effect killing my spirit."

Janine wasn't sure where she wanted to go from here. Caught between obligation, pity, understanding and a desire that was threatening to consume her like a blazing inferno, she painstakingly shifted her focus back to him.

"You must have really loved them," she found herself saying quite enviously, thinking about her love for Lisa. The answer was obvious.

Richard turned his eyes away again. "More than life itself." He sighed. "For a while there I honestly didn't think I could go on without them. I mean, who would, in my shoes—"

"But you did, Richard," Janine told him emphatically. "And you owe it to their memory to keep your unique talents alive."

He regarded her for a long moment, abruptly changing the subject. "I'm glad you came, Janine. Even if it was only to pick up your bracelet."

I'd hoped to look at some of your photographs, too, Janine thought to herself.

Something else was happening, though.

Her cheeks flushed and Janine felt the sexual energy between them gathering steam as if ready to explode. She also felt more than a bit peculiar, realizing that there were certain barriers standing in the way of anything that could come to pass. She was hesitatant to enter that realm, not knowing the outcome.

And perhaps fearing it as much as she'd feared anything.

"Richard…" Janine's voice faltered and she felt her defenses weakening.

"Janine…" he gasped.

He took her drink and set it and his own on the coffee table. Fixing her with those intriguing ashen eyes, Richard put a hand to Janine's chin, caressing it with his fingers. She quavered at his touch.

"It's been a long time since…" he indicated.

"I understand," Janine said knowingly. "It's been a long time for me, too."

Longer than I care to admit.

Not wanting it to be any longer than it had already been.

They read each other's eyes like a book, the message passing between them being that they had to do this. Damn the consequences. The past. The future. Misgivings. Second thoughts. They couldn't turn their backs to the vibes that had brought them to this moment like a powerful magnet. Both knew it was time to delve into the unknown. Throw caution to the wind. Explore their inner feelings that were much too powerful to ignore and let the chips fall where they may. Even as each recognized that it was just as likely that the chips could scatter in different directions and tear them apart as well as bring them closer together.

Not even such fear and uncertainty could overcome the strong physical attraction that Janine felt had existed between them from the very beginning. Its potency was evident perhaps from the moment their eyes first met, even if neither could have fathomed at the time what it would lead to.

Richard tilted his head and slowly brushed his lips against hers. The impact could be felt all the way to Janine's very core. He held her gaze again as if searching for any signs of reluctance.

There were none.

When their mouths met again it was Janine who took the lead.

The kiss started off gently and grew firmer with each moment they were pressed together. Lips open wide and flattened against each other, the kiss brought their tongues together in frenetic harmony and an almost desperate search for satisfaction. Two breaths became one as each responded to the demands of the other's torrid kisses.

Richard enveloped Janine in his arms and brought their bodies so close that their contours lined up to a perfect fit. They remained locked in that position for what seemed like a millennium, as though inseparable.

Overcome by Richard's raw presence and her own unbearable desire, Janine pulled away, her lips bruised from the passion of his. She looked into the steel corridors of Richard's hungry eyes, then sank to her knees and unzipped his pants, wanting to give him the release that would set him free. She took his full erection deep into her mouth, surrounding him in warm moisture and undivided attention. She felt his body shiver violently, even as her need to pleasure him and be pleasured by him grew inside her like a child.

It had, indeed, been far too long, she gasped within, feeling the fire of absence and the prospect of fulfillment.

Richard raised Janine up effortlessly, took her by the hand and led her to the couch. Meeting her gaze, he said raggedly, "It's my turn to take care of you…."

She gulped with anticipation as he lowered her onto the soft cushions, placing a hand beneath her skirt. His fingers caressed her most private area through the fabric of silk underwear, bringing about instant and relentless gratification.

Janine thought she was going to explode, biting her lip to keep from screaming out her satisfaction. She watched Richard fall to his knees and put his mouth between her legs, using his teeth to nudge aside her panties. He began to kiss her there.

"Richard…hmm…" Janine bit into her lip from the sensations his mouth evoked, but tried to move him away, not wanting to feel what she was feeling until he was inside her and they could experience it together. But like a man on a mission, Richard ignored her pleas, determined to finish what he'd started.

Janine felt her body levitate as an orgasm roared through her like a locomotive, a lingering moan escaping her lips. She grasped at Richard's shoulders, wanting him, needing him more than she'd ever wanted or needed anyone before. He responded, standing up, as if reading her mind as well as her body and knowing it was time.

Overcome with desire for this man, Janine began feverishly unbuttoning his shirt. He did the same to her blouse. Neither could seem to get the other's clothes off fast enough. Soon they were both naked and conscious of everything each had to offer, relishing this knowledge and the moment at hand.

With the mutual ache of a primordial need to be appeased, Janine held her breath as Richard slid easily between her legs and they began to make love to each other. It was hard and intense as both craved the other's body and the release that accompanied their unbridled passion.

The sex ended quickly, neither apologizing, for it was to be expected the first time they were together—merging desires that had gone untapped and unfulfilled.

The second time around came shortly thereafter. Only now, more familiar with one another, they were able to take things slower, and were more sensual and deliberate. Each took turns being on top, then sideways, falling on the floor, then back on the couch and even halfway between the two. Every move led to another like a game of chess, as if Janine and Richard were fully in tune with one another's sexual appetites, physical yearnings and mental longings.

In spite of being out of practice, Richard had proven to be a superb lover. Wrapped in his arms and legs, Janine's body reacted to him in ways it hadn't ever before. She wanted to believe that she had given him as much as he'd given her, as his satisfaction was every bit as important. She melted her mouth into his and hung on for dear life as they rode to glory and beyond.

When it ended, Janine felt a sense of extreme fulfillment, like she was floating on a cloud of contentment and wanting to do nothing but sleep and never wake up.

Yet she knew she must wake up and face the music.

Whatever it might be.

And wherever it might lead.

Chapter 16

Janine stirred and found that Richard was not beside her on the couch, where they had cuddled till falling asleep. Her first thought was that he had rolled off onto the floor, since there was little room to spare. When she didn't see him there, she suddenly realized that a blanket was covering her body. How long had she been sleeping like a baby? She was still naked and felt a flicker of self-consciousness wash over her.

After grabbing her clothes, which were stacked neatly on the love seat, Janine put them on. The smell of food infiltrated her nostrils like perfume. Without allowing herself to even consider the implications of having sex with the man she was supposed to be leading back to Callister-Reynolds, she followed the inviting scent into the kitchen.

Standing over the stove in a calf-length black robe was Richard. A man who could cook, Janine mused whimsically, as if from a different planet than the one she lived on. She cleared her throat, getting his attention.

He turned to her, a slight grin on his face. "Hey," he said as if they were now on a much more familiar level of communication. "Hope you're hungry."

"Starving," she admitted, wetting her lips at the thought of food.

"Good. I put together a little something... There's pork chops, fried tomatoes, baked potatoes, salad and wine."

Janine was overwhelmed. "I'm impressed. But why didn't you wake me? I could have helped."

"You still can," Richard responded succinctly. "The table needs to be set. The glasses and dishes are in that cabinet—" he pointed "—and the silverware's in the drawer below the microwave."

"Say no more," she told him happily.

Janine went about making up the table for two. It felt strangely alien to do so. *I certainly never expected this when setting off for Pebble Beach and Richard Lowrey,* a voice said inside with a mixture of amusement and nervousness. Not only was this an unfamiliar setting, but it had also been some time since she had set a table for anyone other than her and Lisa. The notion filled Janine with excitement and, at least temporarily, took her mind off other things. John seemed like little more than a distant memory at this point.

She wondered if the same could be said for Kassandra as far as Richard was concerned.

Hold on, girl, Janine thought wisely. *Let's not get too carried away with one afternoon of sex, thinking that it changed anything, really. Get real.* She didn't even pretend to imagine she could take Kassandra's place in Richard's life. Why would she? The circumstances that ended their relationship were totally different from those that had ended her marriage to John. Richard never asked to have his wife and daughter taken away so suddenly and without warning.

Janine wondered if he felt guilty about what had happened between them. Or, for that matter, if she did. Her answer was that the jury was still out as it related to her feelings. There were complications that first needed to be resolved.

In such a short time, it appeared she had fallen for—and slept with—a man to whom she still had not fully disclosed her purpose for being there. Although she felt the two were separate issues, Janine knew at the same time that they were inexorably connected. How would Richard react once he learned the truth? she wondered nervously.

Even if he brushed it aside as no big deal—after all, he stood to gain from honoring his contract with Callister-Reynolds; she was merely the go-between—there was still the reality that they were miles apart, figuratively and literally, in their lives. Expecting that anything could come out of this other than a bit of mutual comfort and companionship might prove to be a huge mistake.

One Janine couldn't afford to make.

"Tell me about your daughter, Lisa," Richard said at the table.

Janine put salad in her mouth while feeling the curiosity of his stare. "She's a wonderful little girl," she told him cheerfully. "Bright, charming, outspoken, eats like a horse and often seems to have far more energy than her mom."

"Sounds just like Sheena," he said sentimentally. "Kassandra used to say she had more spunk in her than anyone she knew—present company included."

Janine felt terrible and almost guilty that her own child was alive and well, whereas Richard's had been mercilessly taken away by a cruel twist of fate, along with her mother.

Janine looked across the table. "This might seem strange, but I wish I'd gotten to know your wife and daughter," she found herself saying. She meant it, as awkward as it sounded under the circumstances. Having gotten to know Richard somewhat, Janine couldn't help but feel she would have liked the woman he loved, and the creation of that love.

"I wish they'd gotten to know you, too," Richard voiced matter-of-factly, surprising Janine. "You and Kass...wow! You probably could have been best friends."

Janine hardly knew what to say to that, but thought of how bizarre life could be in the ways that people came together and were pulled apart. Not to mention those who had never met in the first place, yet were joined in spirit by a common thread. In this case that common thread was Richard Lowrey.

They ate in stilted silence for a moment or two, then he asked her, "What happened to your marriage?"

Janine stopped chewing, allowing food to digest and her stomach to stop churning. "It was never really much of a marriage to begin with," she admitted as much to herself as to him. "John, my ex, was really only interested in a trophy wife. And later, my being a mother to his child. He felt comfortable appeasing his carnal desires elsewhere."

Janine suddenly felt like crying. Perhaps it was because she had never put her marriage into its proper perspective before now. Certainly not to another living soul. *To a man she'd just made love to.* It made her realize just how much her life had been wasted to this point.

To her chagrin.

"Your ex husband was a damn fool," Richard said unequivocally. "With you, he had everything a man could want—and he threw it all away like garbage!"

Janine nearly wilted under the fire of Richard's gaze. She couldn't argue with his astute observation about John, something she had believed to be true but had often suppressed in favor of her perceived shortcomings as a wife.

"Thank you for saying that," she uttered, the fork shaking in her hand.

"I meant it." He pursed his lips. "You deserved better."

She eyed him thoughtfully. "So did you."

"Yeah. I guess we both deserved a hell of a lot more than we ended up with."

Janine tasted her wine—a zesty Merlot—while wondering if there was a double meaning to that as she considered the passion they'd shared. Maybe ending up with each other was not the best move for either of them. Or maybe it was the best possible thing that could have happened to both....

They each seemed to slip into thoughts of their own misfortunes and self-doubts for the rest of the meal, keeping the conversation, when there was any, strictly superficial.

Afterward, Janine volunteered to do the dishes while Richard took Kimble out for a walk. He appeared genuinely grateful for something that to her seemed the least she could do, all things considered. She used the time alone in his house to contemplate where this was headed, if anywhere.

Am I setting myself up for a great big fall? Janine opened the dishwasher. It was still too soon to tell, and she wasn't sure if it was even wise to think about a real relationship between them, given the scars they both carried.

Yet there was no denying that Richard had made her feel more alive and desired than she'd felt in many years. She couldn't help but hope the same was true for him—that after the way he'd given himself to her, maybe even a small piece of his heart now belonged to her.

But there was still the formidable task of convincing Richard that it was in his best interest to work with Callister-Reynolds rather than against them. Not to mention her own best interest.

As well as that of the buying public that, no doubt, would be eager to embrace the prizewinning African-American photographer's new works.

After loading up the dishes and turning on the dishwasher, Janine put away the leftover food and tidied up the kitchen. As Richard had not yet returned, she found herself wandering about the exquisite home that she had barely seen. Each room was neat, attractively furnished and spacious. She couldn't help but compare it to the considerably more cramped apartment she and Lisa lived in.

That Richard lived alone made the place seem even larger. A woman's touch, though, seemed evident throughout. But how was that possible? It was almost as if Kassandra had never left. Clearly, she realized, Richard had chosen to leave things pretty much the way they were when his wife and daughter were still alive—as though changing or getting rid of anything would somehow tarnish their memories.

Janine entered a bright and colorful room that was filled with dolls and toys. Obviously this was Sheena's room. The small picket-style bed had a patchwork spread of floral and solid colors, topped with fluffy pillows, as though waiting for Sheena to somehow return to it. The rather eerie thought sent chills up Janine's spine. She could only imagine the torture Richard had put himself through, spending the last three years worshipping the dead and ignoring the living.

Stopping at a closed door, Janine hesitated for a moment,

but decided, against her better judgment, to go into what she assumed was Richard's bedroom. He had never indicated any room was off-limits, she thought, convincing herself it would be all right.

The first thing Janine noticed was the portrait. It was a captivating painting of Richard's late wife, whom she'd recognized from the newspaper clipping. Kassandra Lowrey seemed to be gazing directly at her with soulful eyes that were an enchanting café au lait color. Vibrant, long groomed locks cascaded across her slender shoulders, surrounding a taut face of high cheeks and perfect proportions. She wore a strapless tea rose dress with a low-cut bodice, revealing a hint of cleavage. Her complexion was a perfect shade of golden brown, dotted with a few moles, adding spice to her facial features.

She was incredibly beautiful, Janine thought enviously. Almost hauntingly so. In that instant it seemed hard to imagine anyone, *especially her,* being able to ever take Kassandra's place in Richard's life. It was hard enough to compete with a ghost. Any ghost. But with one that had her looks and immortality in death, it would be virtually impossible.

Janine felt some of the old insecurities returning—the ones that began with the mother who once told her she would never be able to keep a man. Just as she had failed to do with Janine's father. This in spite of the fact that her mother had carried the torch for him till the day she'd died.

To Janine, her mother's chilling words had seemed painfully true after she'd divorced John, though she was the one who had sent him packing. *Maybe I'll never be good enough or pretty enough to keep a man,* she told herself. *Or at least to keep him from straying when the first thang in a short skirt with a big ass comes along.*

The thought disturbed Janine more than she cared to admit

and she tried to put it out of her mind. Along with John's painful betrayal.

Richard's room had a king-size bed and antique oak furniture. The curtains on the window were open to show a beautiful view of the spacious green yard with groves of cypress trees in the background.

Janine again met the penetrating eyes of Kassandra Lowrey before leaving the room, wondering if she could ever feel comfortable in there, where the "lady of the house" gave her the creeps. She found it hard to imagine making love in that room with Richard's late wife present, as if possessing what was still her domain—and man.

The entire prospect left Janine feeling weak and considering if Richard felt Kassandra's presence in the same unsettling way. Obviously not. Otherwise he would have gotten rid of the painting a long time ago.

It was clear that Kassandra still had some sort of strong hold on Richard and anyone who threatened to come between them, Janine could see for more reasons than one. The fact that they'd made love on the living-room couch and floor instead of his bedroom and *bed*, with Kassandra looming overhead, spoke for itself.

Don't even go there, girl, Janine thought, having no desire to intrude further into the man's business than was necessary. She closed the door and toured the rest of the house, discovering what appeared to be a darkroom behind another closed door. Or at least, that's what it had once been. From the looks of the dried-up developing trays and lack of anything resembling recent picture-taking, it was evident that the room had not been used for some time. This was indicative of Richard turning his back on his career and incredible talents, as well as the obligations he had to Callister-Reynolds and to himself as a professional.

Janine seriously wondered if she was capable of getting Richard to reverse his current feelings about putting his photography skills on indefinite hold. *Can I reach somewhere inside the man that hasn't been reached before?* In the back of her mind she feared that the wounds were too deep and hardened to ever get him back to where he had once been.

But she had to try, even if she recognized that getting personally involved with Richard could make things just a little bit stickier.

As her aunt Josephine once told her, "Girl, you put one foot in front of the other and you can get somewhere—no matter the obstacles."

In the study Janine found a wall-length pine bookshelf stacked with books and magazines, along with a forest-green recliner, gold contemporary sofa, TV and portable DVD and CD player. There was no camera equipment visible in any room, as if Richard had rid himself of the tools of his trade after the accident. She guessed that it was his plan to, in fact, take no more photographs or write about them for the rest of his life.

I have to do something about that. She felt determined, and prayed that it wasn't already too late.

Browsing the bookshelf, Janine's gaze settled on a shelf that was filled with books authored by Richard. She pulled out one titled *Black Beaches in America.* Opening it, she saw magnificent photographs of African-Americans occupying pristine beaches across the country, making use of the water for swimming and scuba diving. There were wonderful tidbits about each beach and the local community. His magnificent captions on each page seemed to be nearly as powerful as the pictures themselves.

"There you are…" The voice startled Janine so that she nearly dropped the book.

She turned and saw Richard standing there, favoring her with an uneasy gaze.

Chapter 17

Richard stared at her across the room. Janine was seemingly transfixed on one of his books, as if painstakingly enthralled by it. He might have thought this the fascination of a serious fan of his work. But in this case, he suspected that the interest might be more a reflection of her occupation. After all, Janine was an editor, lest he forget. It was only natural that a shelf full of books would pique her interest.

Right now his own interest lay with her—the beautiful and sexy lady he had come to know intimately in one dizzying afternoon. She had unleashed a passion and hunger in him like he hadn't felt since Kassandra had died. He had acted on that need that had been building up inside him like a volcano ready to erupt. Janine had reciprocated in kind, appearing to be equally desirous of him.

The whole thing left Richard with a confusing mixture of guilt and a renewed sense of purpose. There was a strong feeling of having somehow let Kass down by making love to another woman in their house. Yet another side of him was beginning to come to terms with the fact that it was time to get on with his life, and maybe find someone else to share it with, if only for a short time.

Richard fixed his eyes on Janine, regarding her from head to toe, and instantly felt himself wanting her again.

"Hi," he said apologetically, realizing he'd caught her off guard.

"Hello," Janine responded cheerfully. "I was, uh, just admiring your work."

Richard shrugged off the notion, no longer moved by admiration, which he'd he once sought like it was the most important thing on earth. For all the books' worth and the success he had enjoyed, it now seemed like an anvil around his neck, no longer worthy of his time and appreciation.

He sucked in a deep breath and stepped closer, honing in on the book in her hands. "Not much to admire. It wasn't my best work. That is, if I'm to believe some of the criticism." He could smell the sweet naturalness of her skin, enticing him. "Hope you didn't get too bored while I was giving Kimble some exercise."

"Not at all," she told him, seeming anything but bored. "I was just hanging out." Janine glanced back at the book. "And I wouldn't put much merit in critics' opinions. Everyone knows they're merely failed authors or wannabes looking to make a living by putting down successful writers."

Richard frowned. "Yeah. But the strange thing is that some of them become successful in their own right as a result of putting many of us through hell and back."

Janine batted her lashes skeptically. "That may be, but who's going to remember them at the end of the day? One success story could hardly compare with the other."

Janine studied the cover of the book in her hands curiously. "So what does the *E* stand for in your name? Hmm...let me guess...Edward?"

Richard chuckled, wrinkling his nose at the same time. "I don't think so."

"Evan?"

"Getting colder, I'm afraid."

"Eric?"

"Nope."

She mused for a long moment and favored him as though a light had gone on in her head. "Edgar?"

"Bingo!" Richard smiled.

"After Edgar Allan Poe, I take it?" Janine deduced.

He nodded, impressed. "My mother was big on Poe."

"So am I."

"Cool. I prefer Dickens myself," he admitted. "Along with a little bit of Shakespeare and Emerson, and a lot of Toni Morrison."

Janine flashed her teeth, which were sparkling white. "These days I think I'm partial to a new author I'm just now discovering."

"Is that right?" Richard teased her, feeling as if they were already an item, even when he knew that wasn't the case. Yet.

"I think it's *more* than right." She raised her eyes at him glowingly, then placed the book back on the shelf. "How many of these have you written and photographed, anyway?" she asked casually.

"They're all there," Richard muttered unenthusiastically. "At last count, there were nine of them."

A thoughtful look appeared on Janine's face. "When was your last one published?"

"Three years ago."

She favored him with an intrigued look. "And no plans to do any more?"

Richard pondered the notion. "Not at the moment. But who's to say what the future holds?" He wondered if she could possibly understand where he was coming from. No one could know how difficult, if not impossible, it was for him to pick up and return to that former life, even if he wanted to. Some things were better left alone.

"I really think you should reconsider," Janine said straightforwardly, taking him by surprise. "From what I've seen, you're very good. The public would embrace you and your work if given a chance again, I'm sure."

Though flattered and sure Janine meant well, Richard couldn't help but think she was speaking more like an editor, rather than the person he'd made love to this afternoon. This was not entirely welcome, but he knew she was merely trying to help him get over the hump.

And perhaps it was time he got off his ass and over the self-pity and went back to work. Could be that he needed someone like Janine to light a fire under him.

"Maybe you're right. I'll think about it," he promised, mindful that his publisher had been pressuring him to complete the two books remaining in his contract or return the advance, which he no longer had. His attorney had already advised him that there were no loopholes in the contract that would allow him to keep the money free and clear without delivering the books. At least, none that he could afford to try and exploit in a protracted and costly court battle. The bottom line was that he had a real responsibility here to do the right thing and finish what he'd started, even if his heart wasn't entirely in it.

Richard considered Janine and her powers of persuasion. Those who enjoyed his books and pictures would surely welcome him back with open arms, if he was willing to resume his career. They would understand the hell he had been put through and respect that he'd needed time away to get himself back together.

Yet lingering in Richard like a malignancy was the tragedy that had disrupted his career and his life. The hurt still went too deep. He just wasn't sure he could ever climb out of that misery and be whole again.

But maybe with Janine's encouragement and friendship, he could. He smiled at her and was very happy she was there. "Would you like a glass of wine?" he offered hopefully.

Janine smiled back at him contentedly. "Yes, I think I would."

They only made it through a few sips of wine before making love twice more on the couch and carpet, both able to sustain longer each time. Their bodies, like their minds, seemed to be perfectly synchronized, finely tuned, much like the pieces of an expensive watch. Each gave more than they took, yet took plenty and came back for more. Soon they were spent, sweaty and laughing like two children at play. Only, their actions were much more adult and pleasing.

Richard felt a lump in his throat as he looked at Janine, wrapped in his arms as though she was his very own pride and joy. She had closed her eyes for a moment of inner peace and relaxation and looked like an angel with just the right blend of brown sugar. He had wanted to take her to his bedroom to make love, but was held back by Kassandra's presence, both in the painting and in spirit. It was as if he would be disrespecting her by making love to another woman in *their* bed. Under Kassandra's watchful and resentful eyes, no less.

Yet even this could not prevent the powerful feelings Richard was admittedly starting to have for Janine Henderson. He wanted her—needed her—for as long as she was there and available for what they'd started. After that, he didn't dare think about tomorrow.

Or the next day.

Or beyond.

He only wondered, after this gorgeous New York woman had awakened passion long dormant in him, how he could possibly go back to the way things were before, once she returned to her own world. The thought of returning to a life void of affection and companionship scared Richard more than he cared to face up to. He had never been meant to be by himself in life, not like some men he knew who only wanted to play the field but always came home alone. That wasn't him. He'd always needed the companionship and support of a woman to make his existence worthwhile, and he had realized that even before he'd met Kassandra. Now he had to face the very real prospect of being thrown back into that abyss with possibly nothing to hold on to to keep him from going under completely this time.

Opening her eyes, Janine lifted her head and kissed Richard firmly on the mouth. He kissed her back, loving the sweet taste of her tongue, then kissed one of her breasts. It was honey brown, with a darkened nipple that rose and became taut with his kiss as if he were casting a magical spell upon her.

"As much as I would love to just stay right in this spot forever while you're doing that," Janine hummed, "I think I'd better go. I have some work I need to finish up." She pulled away from him, her breathing labored.

"I understand," Richard muttered, feeling a bit guilty in maybe taking up time she had obviously set aside for her work. He wasn't sure exactly what editorial duties would have her here in his neck of the woods. She'd been vague on that for some reason. But he would take all the time she could spare before going back to New York and the life she had there without him. He was hardly in a position to think otherwise.

Richard watched as Janine put on her clothes. Even this routine function had taken on an entirely new meaning in his pleasure and desire for her. He wondered if he'd felt this way when watching Kassandra. *Did that simple but sexual task turn me on with my wife?* It bothered the hell out of him that he couldn't remember. It was as though time had eroded some of his precious memories, causing them to be misplaced deep in the recesses of his mind, perhaps lost forever.

Another possibility occurred to him. Memories of the past were in all likelihood being interfered with—or upstaged— by current and more persuasive thoughts. Thoughts which he had little to no control over. Richard eyed the source of his uncertainties. This lady had managed to single-handedly turn his life upside down in a short time, causing him to have to reevaluate everything he thought he wanted.

And needed.

At the door Richard said nonchalantly to Janine, though his desires for her company were anything but indifferent, "If you have time tomorrow or Friday, I thought maybe we could go up to San Francisco for the day. I could show you around the famed City by the Bay." He realized he was being presumptuous in asking, putting her on the spot, but he did so anyway.

Janine seemed to have reservations but quickly turned this around, as if she, too, didn't want to pass up the opportunity to spend some quality time together for as long as they could. "Sounds wonderful," she told him. "Only, Friday would be better."

This actually worked better for him, too, thought Richard as he pasted a smile on his lips. "Friday it is. I suggest you bring your camera. You may need it."

Janine met his eyes daringly. "Only if you bring yours."

Richard suspected he had been caught in a trap of his own making. He looked away thoughtfully. In fact, he had locked away his camera equipment, uncertain if he would ever use it again. Having it lying around, he figured, would only remind him of the wonderful life he'd had with Kassandra and Sheena.

Now he was being challenged to use his photography skills again by a woman who was as clever as she was beautiful. Since he had suggested Janine bring a camera, it was only appropriate that she toss him a *quid pro quo*.

Maybe it was time to get behind the camera again, he thought with some optimism.

Especially with Janine Henderson as the subject of his lens. He could only imagine what stunning images he could take of the lady from New York.

Richard faced Janine, met her gaze and said, "You have yourself a deal."

Chapter 18

Richard knew he would be less than honest if he were to say that Kassandra had had absolutely no problems leaving her laid-back life behind in Jamaica while adjusting to the hustle and bustle of southern California. Not even his presence in her life early on was enough to prevent a few bumps and potholes on the road to happiness.

Fortunately those were of relatively short duration, as they were both determined to make their marriage work no matter what it took. Settling into Richard's cramped Los Angeles apartment, they'd had a clear understanding that it would only be until they could find something better.

They soon did—a rented house in the Valley that gave them a little breathing room and less smog to fill their lungs.

It didn't take Kassandra long to find work, as her international-tourism background and multilingual skills gave her a decided edge in the competitive marketplace. Richard's work—which had been limited to freelance photography for mostly small, obscure magazines and newspapers—took a turn for the better after he took a photograph of a deer. The poor creature had somehow found its way into the middle of freeway traffic during rush hour and lived to see another day.

Being in the right place at the right time had not come with the territory for Richard as a photographer. But the instincts for capturing great images were always there. He knew a good thing when he saw it. Driving down I-5 and seeing this magnificent deer as fascinated with the vehicles dancing around it as the occupants of those vehicles were with the deer was too much to pass on. He pulled off to the side, grabbed his camera and went through a roll of film, seemingly capturing the deer he dubbed "Sassy" at every conceivable angle of confusion, intrigue and fear.

One particular photograph, in which Sassy seemed to be looking directly at Richard, as though he was its savior, won him an International Picture of the Year award after appearing in *Urban Travel* magazine.

Suddenly, offers Richard could have only dreamed about began pouring in, for interviews, plum assignments and visual books. In spite of being a bit overwhelmed, he knew his fifteen and a half minutes of fame would be short-lived so he sought to take full advantage of them. He'd been given enough work to keep him going for a couple of years or more.

It was actually Kassandra who had talked Richard into authoring his first book of pictures.

"You can do it, darling," she'd said, her Jamaican accent as thick and wonderful as ever. "I'll even help you pick the perfect setting and perfect way to describe it. So long as there's no coauthoring here, thank you. I don't want to steal any of your thunder, mon."

For his part, Richard would have loved to have coauthored every book he'd ever done with Kassandra. Between his skills behind the camera and her astuteness with the travel industry and exotic locations, they would have made a dynamic pair. But she was happy and secure enough in herself to assist and support him in any way he asked while taking none of the credit. This selflessness in Kassandra's character was part of what made the fine-as-she-wanted-to-be woman so very special to Richard. Along with love like he had never known before or could imagine again.

On the day Richard had signed his first contract with Callister-Reynolds, he and Kassandra celebrated by vacationing in Maui, Hawaii. It turned out to be the perfect island to photograph and put in a book. The people of color there were as hospitable as could be and they had marvelous stories to tell about life on the island.

They stayed in a condo on Kaanapali Beach, journeyed by helicopter to photograph the Haleakala Crater and braved the perilous drive to Hana. There they explored the Black Sand Beach and witnessed the most beautiful rainbow either had ever seen.

In between work was ample time for play. They went swimming in the warm waters of the Pacific Ocean and danced the night away at hot ethnic clubs like it was their last night on earth. Kassandra had brought with her from Jamaica a zest for fun, sun, sand and sex—all of which Richard found agreeable in every conceivable way. They enjoyed each other tirelessly and their love grew deeper in the process.

One night, after making love, Kassandra said, "I think I'd like to have a baby now, Richard. It would be nice to have a beautiful little child of our own to chase around like a butterfly."

Richard felt his heart thumping wildly. He had dreamt of

having children someday, banking on the fact that they would inherit most of their physical traits from their mother. But they'd skirted the issue, with Kassandra wanting to enjoy her work and freedom from child-rearing responsibilities for a few years.

He had to be sure. "What about your job?"

"What about it?" She batted her long, curly lashes dramatically. "I do love my job and would work for as long as I had to. But I love the thought of being the mother of *your* child even more, Richard. I just hope you don't mind seeing me with my belly sticking out like I just swallowed a balloon."

Richard wrapped his arms around Kassandra and her still-flat stomach, barely able to contain his enthusiasm. "Are you kidding? Baby, you'll be the most beautiful pregnant woman the world has ever seen. I want to have a child with you more than anything in the world, Kass," he assured her. "Now that I already have my Jamaican princess."

His eyes connected lovingly with hers.

"Oh!" Kassandra cried openly. "Why are you so good to me, Richard Edgar Lowrey?"

She kissed him hard on the mouth, and he responded endearingly, "That's an easy one. Because I love you, Mrs. Lowrey, and always will."

"Is that a promise?" Kassandra asked with a teasing gleam in her eyes.

"It's more than a promise," Richard said. "That love is guaranteed to be there for as long as I live and beyond."

Richard could not imagine a time when he wouldn't love Kassandra. Life as he knew it for them was just beginning, with the better part of their lives to look forward to. Their love for each other would only grow over time, he had no doubt about that.

They kissed and cuddled again for a long while and Richard felt renewed arousal enveloping him like a shroud.

"What do you say we start working on creating that baby, sweetheart?" he asked anxiously.

Kassandra flashed him a brilliant smile as only she could, while letting her actions speak for her.

They were to have lots of practice on increasing their family over the next three years before their efforts paid off in style with the birth of a beautiful, healthy girl.

Chapter 19

"So, when do I get to meet this lady?" Henry Lowrey asked.

Richard blinked from across the table at the Bay Restaurant where he and his father had lunch once a week. "Not really sure about that, Pops," he muttered. "Maybe the next time she comes back to town. If there is a next time...."

Henry sipped coffee, staring at him unblinkingly. "Do you want there to be a next time?"

Richard was beginning to feel uncomfortable with the Twenty Questions, though they were not unexpected. After all, his old man was still sharp enough to be able to read him like a book and even between the lines. That didn't mean he had to always like it.

"Yeah, I guess I do," he spoke candidly. "But I can't control what happens in the future. Right now I'm just kind of playing it by ear, you know what I'm saying? If it's in the cards, we'll probably see each other again. If it isn't, then we won't. Simple as that."

"This isn't some damn card game, Richard," snapped Henry, his brows stitched. "If you really like this woman, then say so. Hell, son, you know I'm not gonna pass judgment on you for liking someone other than Kassandra. She's been gone for three years now, for heaven's sake."

"I know that, Dad." Richard raised his voice more than he intended to. His underarms dripped with perspiration and he could feel his heart racing as though ready to have a heart attack on the spot.

Henry's brow furrowed. "Then what's the problem?"

Richard sighed exhaustedly. "There's no problem." He thought about it for a moment or two. "This dating thing scares the hell out of me, Dad. I don't know if I'm up for it at this stage of my life. I mean, what am I supposed to say or do without feeling that it's all wrong?"

"It's only wrong if you make yourself believe it is, son." Henry lifted his fork, along with a stack of sliced garlic potatoes. "There's nothing wrong with trying to find someone who can make you happy, just like Kassandra did. And you say and do what feels right."

"It's always so simple with you." Richard both admired and disliked this in his father. The way he saw it, everything was not *always* black and white. Gray areas sometimes could not be avoided, like fog on a rainy day.

Henry begged to differ.

"That's because it *is* simple, Richard," he insisted. "The only thing hard here is you going on some sort of guilt trip, just because you find yourself interested in somebody else— like you're cheating on Kassandra or something. Well, it don't work that way, son. You're *not* being unfaithful to the memory of your late wife if, after three long years of living like a monk, you develop feelings for another woman."

Richard knew that in the strictest sense his old man was right. Problem was, rational thinking aside, he still felt that in enjoying Janine's intimate company he was somehow being untrue to Kassandra, as sure as if it was her who was sitting opposite him at the table.

But even if he overcame this feeling of compunction, there were still other complexities standing in the way of any type of real relationship between him and Janine. For one, they lived too far apart. If only she lived in Monterey. San Francisco. Oakland. Hell, even Denver would be a lot closer than New York.

Damn, he muttered to himself.

Of course, he'd been down this road before when Kassandra lived in Montego Bay. But the circumstances were different. Or so he wanted to believe. They were both young and adventurous with no serious obligations. Free to do essentially whatever they liked. Live wherever they wanted. Go where life took them.

The situation was not as flexible this time. Janine had a child, for one thing. He couldn't seriously expect the woman to uproot her daughter and herself to move across the country, abandoning her career in the process.

I would be hard pressed to do the same, if our positions were reversed.

Let's face it, bro, he mused, *why would any woman in her right mind want to make that sacrifice for you—of all men?* To shack up with a thirty-eight-year-old has-been photographer who was still grieving for his late wife…and probably always would, to the point of being a serious risk for anyone who expected his undivided attention.

"When is she leaving?" Henry asked, interrupting Richard's thoughts, while stuffing roast beef dipped in brown gravy into his mouth.

"This weekend, I think," mumbled Richard.

Henry frowned. "That don't leave you much time to plot some strategy."

Richard gripped his coffee mug so tightly he could feel pain in his knuckles. "There's no strategy to plot," he stressed. "We only met two days ago, for crying out loud." It somehow seemed as though they had known each other much longer. "What do you expect me to do—ask for her hand in marriage?"

"Son," Henry said hoarsely, shaking his head while ignoring the sarcasm, "I haven't seen you *this* unsettled…off balance…since…well…not since the accident. Something's obviously going on inside that head of yours. The way I see it, your lady friend has something to do with it."

Richard gritted his teeth. "Why don't we just change the subject," he strongly urged, tired of being psychoanalyzed.

"If you say so." Henry regarded him respectfully. "But when you feel ready to talk, I'm here."

"I know that." Richard tossed his food haphazardly about the plate, having suddenly lost his appetite. Inside he acknowledged that since meeting Janine he had become unglued. Hell, this woman was driving him crazy. He didn't know if he was coming or going, moving ahead or simply going around in circles. It made him uncomfortable, while at the same time, it had an intoxicating effect on him that he hadn't felt in years. There was something about Janine Henderson that truly caught his attention and imagination, independent of Kassandra. Janine was warm, gentle, smart, inquiring, sexy as hell and, most of all, *genuine*. He was sure he could trust her, beyond all else—something he never thought he'd be able to say about a woman after Kass's death.

Janine had even managed to talk him into getting his camera out of cold storage where he had more or less banished it, having had no desire to even look at it...much less use it again.

Yet there was still some mystery to the lady, he sensed perceptively. Like she was holding something back. Or perhaps keeping secrets she wasn't yet ready to share.

Not that he was any less guilty on that score.

He had managed to keep from Janine his hesitation on embarking on a new relationship. His unwillingness to make love to anyone in his bed—the one he'd shared with Kassandra. His reluctance to remove Kassandra's and Sheena's things from his home, as if to do so would be removing them from his life.

Including the painting of Kassandra in the bedroom that seemed almost like Richard's lifeline to his late wife.

Whatever Janine was holding back, it surely could not measure up to his own less-than forthrightness.

Richard pondered if the barriers that stood between him and Janine like a roadblock—mostly distance, along with his own weakened state of mind—allowed for anything other than a good time for a few days and some short-term memories.

He could only wonder.

Chapter 20

Thursday was a day of reflection and uncertainty for Janine. She stood on the shore watching the seagulls and cormorants nestled on rocks like they were afraid of the water. Farther out were dozens of sea lions and harbor and leopard seals seemingly just as intrigued by humans, who flocked there to watch them with fascination. She wondered if their world was fraught with the same type of emotional dictates that ruled the world of humans.

Janine felt as if she was making serious progress with Richard in spite of herself and the personal attachment she'd made to him. That he was willing to begin taking pictures again suggested he might be sliding out of the deep despair that had served as an impediment to his photography for three long years.

Yes, I am making some major headway, she thought positively of her assignment.

In that sense, it was only a matter of time before Richard

resumed his career and started photographing images for the books he still owed Callister-Reynolds.

But how long "a matter of time" would actually be was still up for debate.

She was hesitant to pressure the man any more than she already had—which was certainly less than her employer would have wanted—fearing that it might just backfire. She felt Richard's fragility as much as her own. Attempting to find some balance between what had been and what still could be was precarious at best.

And dangerous at worst.

In many ways Janine felt she was going through the same inner turmoil as Richard in putting circumstances behind her that she would just as soon forget, but couldn't any more than he could.

Janine was suddenly more aware and afraid of the future than at any time since her divorce. After being content to be on her own and raise her daughter alone, she now found herself wondering if that could possibly be enough. Richard had reached something deep down inside her that she believed was gone forever.

But she was not afforded the comfort of looking too far ahead as to where their relationship might go from here—not when there were so many potential land mines in the way, threatening to explode upon impact. She had been hurt too badly in the past to let down her guard, and Richard had obviously been, too.

Janine considered if this would mean a stalemate to the flames that passed between them like electrical currents.

She wasn't sure if, at the end of the day, the photographer extraordinaire was destined to be in her future.

Janine called Lisa that afternoon. She was her usual bubbly self.

"Mommy, Bernadette took me to the zoo!" Lisa cooed. "We saw lots of really cute animals."

Janine had not taken Lisa to the zoo this summer, but had planned to at some point. Now she wondered if she should have found the time earlier, before Bernadette had done the honors and it became a case of too little too late.

"I'm happy to hear that, sweet pea," Janine told her, forcing sincerity. Inside she was furious at herself. "Mommy will be home Sunday," came a promise. "Daddy will bring you home the same day. Is that all right?"

"For real?" Lisa said the way a child does when needing extra reassurance, or simply flat out disbelieving.

"Cross my heart."

Lisa made a giggling sound of approval. "I've missed you, Mommy," she sang. "Have you missed me?"

"More than I can say, sweet pea." Janine felt like crying for some reason. They had only been apart for less than a week, but it seemed so much longer. There was something about a mother–daughter bond that could not be adequately described, other than to say it hurt so deeply to be away from Lisa for even a few days that she could feel it in every fiber of her body.

Janine found herself wondering if this bond was similar in father–daughter relationships and separation. She supposed it depended upon the father and daughter. In spite of his love for Lisa, Janine doubted that John could relate to the gut-wrenching agony of being apart from her, even for a little while. But Richard was a different story. His bond to his daughter was apparent—made even stronger by death. Janine knew that Sheena's absence in his life was more powerful than she could relate to. She tried to imagine what it would be like to not see Lisa for three years or to know that she would never see her again till arriving at the Pearly Gates.

The mere thought made Janine quiver.

"Daddy says that he and Bernadette might get married," Lisa uttered with a strange excitement in her voice.

Janine wasn't sure what to make of Lisa's apparent approval of this possible marriage, never mind the shock Janine felt, other than that Bernadette had obviously made an impression on *her* child. Janine cringed at the prospect of Lisa already seeing Bernadette as a "second" mommy.

"Oh, really?" Janine muttered sourly.

"Are you mad at Daddy?"

Janine sucked in a deep breath while wondering if Lisa had read that in her inflection. Or if John had suggested as much. Or if his bride to be had suggested it.

Was I telegraphing to my little girl thoughts I hadn't meant to? Janine wondered with a sense of alarm, unsure exactly how she felt about this news, if anything.

"No, I am not angry with your father." She tried to assure Lisa as much as herself. "We are no longer together. But he will *always* be your daddy." She sighed. "I hope Bernadette makes him happy."

Even then Janine couldn't help but wonder how long John would be happy for. For all his talents as a lawyer, John had shown himself to be a man who was incapable of settling down with one woman for any length of time. She had serious reservations that it would be any different with Bernadette. Here today, gone tomorrow. Janine should know, having failed herself at keeping John faithful to her.

Other troubling thoughts cropped up in her mind, like what effect another divorce would have on Lisa. Janine feared for her daughter being put through another divorce, the breakup of her second family. In spite of Lisa's resiliency and ability to bounce back from heartbreak and disappointment, the emotional scars this time around might be too deep to overcome.

"I hope someone can make you happy, too, Mommy." Lisa broke her thoughts wistfully.

Janine smiled at the tender, genuine wish. She had never given Lisa any indication that she wanted or needed someone in her life in order to be *happy*—other than her. In fact, Janine had consciously tried hard to indicate that she was not devastated over the divorce or the man responsible for it. Whatever had gone wrong in their marriage, she did not want her daughter to suffer anything beyond the normal parent–child separation of a broken home.

But Lisa had evidently seen through her like a window, Janine thought sadly, and had sensed her loneliness. Even when she hadn't felt it herself.

That is, until very recently.

She suspected that Richard must have seen it as well, perhaps mirroring his own loneliness.

"I hope someone can, too, honey, someday," Janine said to her daughter, thinking that hope springs eternal, as the saying went.

In her mind, Janine knew someone had already made her happier than she had been in a long time.

What she didn't know was for how long the magic would last.

Janine wondered unnervingly about the inevitable sorrow that seemed destined to come as a result of her involvement with Richard Lowrey.

Chapter 21

The drive to San Francisco was smooth, the traffic light. It was a sunny day with not a cloud in sight, save for one or two that stubbornly managed to cling to the sky like lint on a shirt. Richard seemed preoccupied for the first part of the ride and Janine chose not to intrude on his thoughts, her own mind working overtime as if trying to decipher hieroglyphics. She wondered if it had been wise to accept his invitation to San Francisco, thereby prolonging what seemed like a dead-end street.

The other side of her knew it was an offer she couldn't very well refuse, for Janine wanted to enjoy Richard's company for as long as possible on a personal and very private level. There was still the fact that she needed him to get comfortable with the camera again…Callister-Reynolds was depending on it.

"You're awfully quiet over there," she said as a means to strike up a conversation, favoring Richard's pensive profile. "Hope it isn't the company."

Richard glanced her way, his mouth curving into a crooked smile. "Not at all," he assured her. "Actually, to tell you the truth, it's the company I've been thinking about…."

"Oh?" Janine felt her knees tremble. "And just what have you been thinking about, Richard? Or shouldn't I ask?" Some sexual thoughts came to mind, making her feel a slight tingle between the legs.

He gave a throaty, sensual laugh. "Well, that too. Most definitely. But what I've been thinking about even more is just how much I've grown to care for you, Janine, in such a short amount of time. It's as if we've known each other forever."

"I know," Janine had to admit, a warmth coursing through her veins. "I feel the same way."

"It was like that with Kassandra," Richard said. "I thought that type of comfort zone with another human being only came along once in a lifetime." He paused. "Guess I was wrong on that one."

Janine was truly flattered to be compared to his late and beloved wife in any respect. But she was also a little uncomfortable with it. She feared that favorable comparisons inexorably led to unfavorable ones. The last thing she wanted was for Richard to see things in her that fell far short of Kassandra in his eyes.

Stop it, Janine ordered her mind. *You have as much to offer Richard or any man as Kassandra.*

Janine just wasn't sure she truly believed her own words where it concerned Richard Lowrey.

"There is definitely some nice chemistry between us, Richard," she began with trepidation, "but it could hardly be compared with what you had with Kassandra over time…."

Richard sighed, bemused. "You may be right about that. It hasn't really been long enough for us to get that kindred spirit, soul mate thing going. All I know—" he looked at her in earnest "—is that I'm already starting to dread the thought of your leaving, baby."

"That's sweet," Janine was moved to say, wishing it didn't have to come to that, but knowing it was an inevitable consequence of the trip. "So am I," she responded sincerely.

Richard put his hand on Janine's and she wrapped her fingers around it. Neither of them said a word, though the mental connection and energy coming from their bodies was definitely there.

As was the great uncertainty Janine felt inside.

In San Francisco they went on a whirlwind sightseeing tour. It was clear to Janine that, not too surprisingly, Richard was no stranger to the City by the Bay, as he seemed to know it inside out almost with his eyes shut. They visited Golden Gate Park and then crossed over the Golden Gate Bridge to Marin County. Later they went to Nob Hill, Chinatown, Union Square and the Presidio.

Janine and Richard both took tons of pictures. At first Richard seemed tentative, as if to release the shutter would somehow cause it to explode. But gradually he began to use the camera like an artist would his paintbrush and canvas. Janine could see from the twinkle in his eyes that the magic Richard conjured up behind the camera was making its way back to the forefront of his existence. It seemed as if she had definitely turned the corner in a big way in her assignment for Callister-Reynolds.

Take things one step at a time, Janine reminded herself wisely, not wanting to put the cart ahead of the horse.

For lunch, they ate at a crowded seafood restaurant at Fisherman's Wharf. Richard had grilled swordfish and Janine went with the broiled salmon.

"I'm glad you came, Janine," Richard said, his voice genuine in expression.

"Thanks for inviting me," she said sheepishly. "The guided tour of the city has been wonderful. And the company even better."

"That works both ways." He stared appreciatively at her glowing face. "Maybe someday you can bring your daughter to visit," he suggested. "I'm sure she would love to ride the cable cars. Or take a boat out in the Bay."

Janine was shocked, though she tried not to show it. Was he inviting her *and* Lisa to visit him? She somehow doubted this, deciding it was more likely a general invitation any local might give to a visitor to come to San Francisco to ride the cable cars or take a boat ride in the Bay.

Maybe even with him serving as tour guide, Janine contemplated, *given his penchant for such.*

She also had to consider that the suggestion was possibly merely an offhand comment, just for effect, and not meant to be taken in the literal sense.

Certainly not as a personal invitation to intrude upon his solitary life, somehow causing the ghosts of his beloved Kassandra and Sheena to grow restless.

"That would be nice," Janine told Richard, smiling as best she could. He tossed her a smile in return, but seemed happy to leave it at that.

Janine, caught up in the fantasy of such a get-together, found herself trying to imagine what it might be like for Lisa and Richard to meet. She wondered if Richard would measure up to Bernadette in her daughter's eyes as someone she could relate to. Look up to. Play with. Share laughter with.

And would Richard be just as enchanted with Lisa? Janine

wondered hopefully, mindful that his wounds ran deep where they concerned a lovely little girl named Sheena.

As far as Lisa knew, there was no one even on the horizon in Janine's life, much less a serious connection.

Certainly not someone that she could easily envision, Janine thought, if given time and opportunity, falling in love with. But this was something she could not allow herself to feel even in passing. It would only make it that much more difficult when the time came for her and Richard to say goodbye.

Richard's eyes grew ravenous while focusing on Janine's plate. "That salmon looks *really* tasty. Mind if I sample a piece?"

Janine squared her shoulders. "Be my guest."

He stuck his fork into one of several chunks she had sliced up. Putting the piece in his mouth, Richard hummed jazzily, then licked his lips invitingly, causing Janine to experience a surge of desire within. She had not realized a man could have this type of effect on her simply by producing a sensual sound and rolling his tongue over his lips. But then, it was obvious to her in the time she'd spent with him that Richard Lowrey was not just another male that she could easily take or leave. He had seen to that.

Janine nervously forked a piece of her salmon. "Do you play golf, Richard?" she asked in an attempt to quell her libido. She knew that outside of Tiger Woods and a few others, African-Americans had not taken up the sport to the same degree as basketball or football. Still, the man did live right next to a championship golf course.

Richard gave a slow nod. "I'm definitely not in Tiger's league," he said matter-of-factly. "But I can hold my own on the links." He sighed. "Golf was really Kassandra's game. Her father was a pro and taught her everything she knew. It was one of the reasons we moved to Pebble Beach. Had all the comforts of Jamaica, right down to playing golf in her own backyard." Richard's face crinkled depressingly. "Damn...."

Janine swallowed regretfully. "I'm sorry."

"Don't be." He shrugged it off, jutting out his chin. "Everything I—we—had and lost...just hits me every now and then. I'll deal with it."

Janine tried to think of something—*anything*—meaningful to say, but nothing would come to the surface that she felt could ease his pain instead of possibly making things worse. No one deserved to be put through what he had, she thought dolefully. She hoped her presence in his life, albeit brief and with no clear direction, had succeeded in giving him something positive to hold on to.

Richard looked out the window musingly. "My dad and I try to come up here a couple of times a year just to get away from things. You know what I'm saying?"

Janine nodded and sipped her iced tea. "You're pretty close to your father, aren't you?"

"Yeah." Richard turned around. "He's my best friend. No matter what hell I've put him through over the years, he's always there for me."

It was a bond Janine envied, for she felt just the opposite about her father. He had never been there for her or her mother in the ways that counted most.

"Maybe I'll get to meet your father before I leave," she suggested, hoping she wasn't overstepping her bounds.

Richard gave an agreeable bob of his head. "I think he would like that. In fact, I know he would. But I have to warn you—my old man can be a trip sometimes. He likes to speak his mind, regardless of what anyone else thinks. And ever since my mother passed, he even has a roving eye for the ladies—especially the young, nice-looking ones."

Janine chuckled softly. "Thanks for the warning. I'll do my best to keep him in check."

What she wasn't nearly as certain about was checking her own inner strength and emotions as far as Richard Lowrey was concerned.

They rode a cable car to Lombard Street and back. At the pier, Richard turned the camera on Janine, insisting she was better to photograph than any natural scenery. Though charmed by his words, she felt slightly uncomfortable at the prospect. While most people considered her attractive, Janine had never believed she was particularly photogenic. Richard seemed determined to prove otherwise. And she was happy to be his subject—especially if it meant getting him comfortable with the camera again.

It wasn't till late that they arrived back at Pebble Beach and 17-Mile Drive. The Ghost Tree stood like a haunting apparition and the restless sea converged several conflicting ocean currents. Neither Richard nor Janine were quite ready to see the day end, so they went for a drink.

"Do you believe in fate?" Richard asked abruptly at the table, his eyes focused sharply on Janine's like gray marbles.

"I don't know," she replied tentatively, not sure where this was leading. "I suppose. Do you?"

He nursed his cocktail. "Yeah. I believe most things happen for a reason," he indicated soberly. "Sometimes beyond our comprehension."

His eyes dropped and Janine knew he was thinking about the fateful loss of his wife and daughter. This was his Achilles' heel, she thought. Just the type of thing that could send him back over the edge.

"I try not to put too much faith in why things happen as

they do," Janine told him. "Otherwise we might drive ourselves crazy. To me, it's best to simply go with the flow and let life take care of itself one way or the other." She wasn't sure she totally believed that, but it sounded right at the moment.

"Point well taken." Richard favored her. "Still, you have to admit, it was the strangest of coincidences that we were fortunate enough to meet at Pescadero Point when we did. I can't help but think that there must be an underlying reason to it somewhere in the scheme of things. It might be fun trying to figure out what bizarre forces of nature brought us together and gave us something so warm and special."

A surge of guilt spread through Janine like wildfire, threatening to engulf her. As much as she wished that their meeting had been strictly serendipitous—though in fact, the particular time and place was—she knew otherwise. Now the time seemed right to level with Richard on at least this much.

The man needs to know the truth once and for all, she thought.

Bracing herself, as if about to go down a water slide, Janine sipped her drink and uttered anxiously, "Actually, Richard, I have a *small* confession to make...."

In her mind, however, it seemed huge and possibly unforgivable.

Richard held up a hand, as if directing traffic, stopping her before she could utter another word. "I'm not a priest, Janine. Just a man. You don't have to confess your sins or secrets to me. As far as I'm concerned, whatever's happening here between us, we're both starting from scratch. Anything else doesn't really matter—"

"But, I think *this* does—" Janine tried to say, while her courage and conviction were still there.

Again Richard checked her. "No buts. Whatever your

reasons are for being in town, neither of us could have planned what would happen between us. No way! Am I right, or what?"

There was no denying that things had not gone exactly according to plan, conceded Janine. *Okay, they had gone completely awry.* She hadn't wanted to fall for Richard Lowrey or have him attracted to her. She certainly hadn't intended to sleep with him or feel that it was the most natural thing for them to be joined at the hip and somewhere in between.

Maybe there were strange forces at work, she considered. Well beyond her relatively small-scale mortal objectives. And those of Callister-Reynolds and Dennis DeMetris.

Janine looked at Richard now. "Yes." The word came out shakily. "You're right about that."

He grinned broadly, lifting his drink. "Amen. Here's to making the most of what we have, whatever it may be."

She raised her glass a little tentatively and the two clinked before they put the glasses to their mouths.

What exactly do we have? Janine honestly wasn't sure if it was each other, or if this was merely a mirage, like water in a hot desert.

She wondered how long either of them could realistically expect things to last, even under the best of circumstances, before the roof caved in....

What Janine feared even more was being caught under the rubble with no way to escape or make things right.

Favoring Richard and knowing she had made him feel good about himself again, Janine tuned out all negative thoughts. She enjoyed his company more than she had any right to, and didn't want it to end.

Not this moment.

Not this night.

They went back to her room and made love well into the wee hours of the morning. Janine relished the closeness she felt with Richard in their lovemaking. He was every bit as gentle a lover as he was demanding. Each tapped into the other's erogenous zones as though knowing perceptively every nook and cranny that needed satisfying, and going about it with skill and the utmost determination. Over and over again, as if to make certain it was everything they both wanted, and much more.

Temperatures rose to blistering heights while they tried different positions as if to explore their deepest fantasies and create new ones. The full moon gave way to the rising sun as darkness turned to a pale early-morning gray.

When it was all over, Janine had lost count of the number of times she'd climaxed, caught up more in making sure Richard experienced much of the same feverish and orgasmic ecstasy. She wished with all her heart that there were some way to bottle up their intimacy to use and reuse every time their bodies demanded it. But she knew this was not possible. There was no mystical formula for hanging on to something so wonderful, other than precious memories. And bodily reactions to thoughts that conjured up vivid, stimulating images that attached to the mind like magnets.

Janine wasn't prepared to look beyond that for anything else. She didn't dare, when looking at the big picture—one that may not leave room for a lasting relationship or even an occasional one.

She suspected Richard felt the same way.

There were too many hidden and visible obstacles for either of them to think otherwise.

Chapter 22

They were just entering their fourth year of marriage when Kassandra gave Richard the news he'd waited for over three years to hear. It was on a rainy, hot and muggy day in New Orleans where they were on a combined vacation and business trip. Richard was working on his third book, photographing the French Quarter, while Kassandra was doing an article on Mardi Gras for a travel magazine. They tried to schedule trips together, intent on spending as much time in each other's company as possible.

To Richard, it was a partnership made in heaven but nurtured on earth.

In the supper club of the Bourbon Street hotel they were staying in, the attractive couple dined on spicy red-hot Cajun food and warmed their ears to the mellow sound of jazz music. Sitting at a table by the wall, Kassandra leaned into her husband and whispered in his ear, "I think I could get used to this, mon."

"I wouldn't even want you to try," Richard told her, feeling less than enthusiastic at the prospect of calling New Orleans home, colorful as it was. "At least, not on a permanent basis."

Definitely a fun place to visit. But with mosquitoes as big as yellow jackets, cockroaches that looked like flying saucers and alligators that took no prisoners, at least not alive, he was in no hurry to give up the comparatively manageable earthquakes and smog of southern California.

"You're probably right about that," Kassandra told him. "After all, we wouldn't want to see our child baking alive in this damn awful heat...."

Richard's eyes latched on to her face, which was bright with anticipation.

"Are you...?" He could barely get the words out, his rapidly beating heart about to bolt from his chest.

"You're going to be a *father,* Richard Lowrey," Kassandra sang mirthfully.

His mother had once told Richard that giving birth to him was her proudest moment. He'd shrugged at the notion, believing she was giving him way too much credit for coming into this world. Now, looking at the mere prospect of having his own child to love and cherish was almost overwhelming.

"Well, say something, mon." Kassandra gave him a look of worry. "Please tell me this is what you wanted to hear—"

Richard found his voice again, and responded elatedly, "Yes! Yes! Yes!" He laughed like his funny bone had been tickled. "You've made me the happiest man in New Orleans, Kass. Make that the whole world!"

"Really?" she asked, as if feeling the slightest doubt.

He leaned over and kissed her firmly on the mouth, forcing

himself to pull away from the temptation of her sweet lips. "What could be more rewarding to a man than knowing that his beautiful woman was finally going to have *his* baby?"

Kassandra beamed. "We kept trying and trying and the Lord has finally answered our prayers. You should be holding a little Lowrey girl or boy by the end of the year."

Richard had already begun to count down the days and nights till the big event, like everything else in between paled by comparison.

"What do you say we go back to our room and celebrate?" he proposed, a suddenly overwhelming desire to have her building to a fevered pitch.

Kassandra took about a second to think about it. "I'm up for that. I could do with some serious celebrating behind closed doors."

"Oh, yeah?" He held her soft and supple hand. Even that turned him on.

"Must have something to do with the pregnancy—turning me into a wild woman," she teased him. "Impending motherhood. Or maybe I just want to be with my man right now in any way he wants me."

Fanciful thoughts crept into his head like sugarplums, and Richard could barely wait to put them into practice. He took Kassandra's hand and they headed upstairs, both in the mood for another kind of nourishment.

This woman of my dreams, thought Richard, *has become a reality in all the best ways.* Whatever he'd done to deserve her, he would gladly do a million times over, if the result were the same.

They stayed in a luxury suite, courtesy of Kassandra's travel agency, and made the most of it. Richard's book had taken a decided back seat to their love child.

* * *

In early November, Sheena Connie Lowrey was born. With her dark brown curly hair, big, bold chocolate-colored eyes and light complexion, she was every bit as captivating as her mother, Richard thought. He could only imagine how beautiful she would be someday as an adult.

It had never occurred to him that her life would be tragically cut short.

Chapter 23

Henry Lowrey cocked a brow intriguingly as he shook Janine's hand in the living room. Richard watched from the side, admittedly more nervous than he thought he would be in bringing her to meet his old man. He wasn't sure how things would go, but felt it was important, even if the future between him and Janine was still very much a question mark.

"Nice to meet you, Mr. Lowrey," Janine said politely.

"Nice meeting you, too, Janine," he said. "And why don't you call me Henry? I'm way too young to be a mister."

She gave an amused chuckle. "All right—" she smiled "—Henry."

He crinkled his eyes, his weathered face softening. "Can I get you anything to drink, Janine? Richard? I have coffee, tea, soy milk, beer, gin, Coke…"

"Coke sounds good," Janine said.

"I agree," Richard seconded, deciding against his first choice of beer.

"Two Cokes coming up." Henry nodded with a smile. "Why don't you both make yourselves at home. I'll only be a minute."

Richard waited until his father had walked away before favoring Janine. He tried not to let her see his unsteadiness. It was the first time since Kassandra died that he had introduced Henry to a woman.

"What are you thinking?" Janine asked as though reading his mind.

Richard managed a smile but did not speak right away, for fear of saying something he might regret. "It's nothing, really."

She frowned. "Are you sorry I came?"

"Not at all," he promised knowingly.

"You sure?" There was doubt in her face.

"Positive." Richard tried to reassure her and himself. "I wanted you to meet my father. Believe me, he's grateful for the company. He's pretty much kept to himself since my mother died."

"You mean like you since your wife and daughter died?" Janine asked straightforwardly. She furrowed her forehead. "I'm sorry—I shouldn't have said that."

"No big deal," Richard insisted evenly, feeling the sting as surely as if she had just slapped him across the face. The truth often hurt, especially when one was confronted with it head-on by a beautiful lady. "I guess my father and I both have a stubborn streak in us a mile long. Maybe two or three miles," he admitted.

"Maybe it's time for one of you to change that." She looked up into his eyes cautiously.

"Yeah, maybe," he owned up, and considered that she had single-handedly been responsible for him opening himself up to another for the first time since Kassandra had died. It was definitely something he hoped to build on, along with returning to photography.

Henry came in with a tray holding two glasses of Coke and ice, a bottle of beer and a plate of chocolate-chip cookies. He set them on the table. "Help yourself."

Janine took one of the glasses and a cookie, and sat on the couch. Richard sat beside her.

With the beer in hand, Henry flopped onto the recliner. He eyed Janine thoughtfully. "Richard tells me you have a daughter."

"Yes." She smiled. "Her name's Lisa."

He took a swallow of beer. "I'll bet Lisa is about as pretty as her mother."

Janine colored. "Thank you. But I'd say she's even prettier." She added, "Mothers tend to think that way."

Henry favored Richard with a glint in his eye. "Hear that, son? Her little girl is not only pretty, but, from the sound of things, she's very special—just like Sheena was."

Richard shifted uncomfortably. "Yeah, Dad, I'm sure she is."

He met Janine's eyes and knew instantly that she felt his sorrow over the loss of his beloved daughter. There was no doubt in his mind that Sheena and Kassandra were in a world somewhere where no more harm could ever come to them. He also believed that if they were still alive, there would have been a bond between them, Janine and her daughter—had they met under other circumstances.

"So, you're an editor from…New York, is it?" Henry looked at Janine, leaning back in his recliner.

"Yes," said Janine effortlessly, sipping her drink.

"What do you edit?"

"Books," she responded.

"Interestin'. Richard's publisher is in New York. Did he tell you he's got eight books published?"

Richard regarded Janine coolly. "Actually, it's nine, Dad," he volunteered.

Janine smiled. "Yes, he did mention it. I looked at some of them. Richard's a wonderful photographer."

"He is, ain't he?" Henry said proudly. "People from all over the world have said the same thing."

Suddenly Richard didn't like the tone of this conversation. His old man had been riding him all along to get back to taking pictures and completing his book deal with Callister-Reynolds before, as he put it, "They come with the cavalry and lock your ass up in a cell for breach of contract."

In spite of this dire warning, Richard had responded that he needed time. That time had turned into years, before he knew it, making the situation worse all the way around.

Henry understood his pain, but he couldn't make things right any more than Richard could in his head. There was nothing in the world of professional photography that accounted for dealing with the loss of loved ones.

But lately, Richard was trying, more than he had in some time, to turn his life around. To make his father proud again. He sensed that Henry had found an ally in Janine.

Had he also found an ally in her—beyond intimately? Richard wondered uneasily. Being an editor, he could only hope Janine wouldn't think less of him if he failed to revitalize his career and get more books published. He wasn't sure he could take that sort of rebuff, though he planned to do every damned thing he could to avoid it.

Somehow the thought of Henry and Janine ganging up on him rattled Richard. He was never one for being backed into a corner, even if he knew it was in his own best interests. If he was going to get back into photography full-fledged, he would have to make it happen himself.

"Richard took some great shots in San Francisco yesterday," Janine volunteered, reaching for another cookie.

Henry sat up and stared at his son, wide-eyed. "You didn't tell me you'd gone up to 'Frisco and taken pictures…."

"It was a last-minute decision," Richard said tonelessly.

He hadn't mentioned it precisely because he didn't want his old man to get the wrong impression.

Henry grinned. "Well, I'll be damned. I'm glad to hear that." His gaze slanted toward Janine. "Looks like you've had a real positive effect on Richard."

Janine blushed. "I'd say it works both ways, Henry."

Richard felt a flutter inside. There was no question that this woman had done something to him. Exactly what, he wasn't sure—other than that it was truly incredible and left him wanting for more. He didn't need to look any further than that for the time being.

That still didn't stop Richard from contemplating how this all might play out in the final analysis for him.

For her.

For them.

And mostly as it related to his feelings for Kassandra.

"Richard, if I were you, I wouldn't let this lady get away," Henry said. "If you do, I just might go after her myself." He gave a gravelly chuckle, though he appeared very serious.

Janine looked uncomfortable, while batting soulful eyes at Richard.

He laughed unevenly, aware his matchmaking father had put them both on the spot. "I think you're embarrassing Janine, Dad."

Henry turned a brow crookedly. "Seems to me, son, that *you're* the only one here on the hot seat."

Richard felt himself begin to perspire. "No one's on any hot seat here," he mumbled dismissively. "As for me and Janine, I think it's best that we just wait and see how things go. I'm sure she'd agree." He didn't think it was too smart to make any premature plans for a relationship with someone who, by all accounts, would be on the other side of the country by this time next week. Living a life that likely didn't have room for him.

"Fair enough," Henry said, knowing when to back off.

Janine, nibbling on a cookie, made eye contact with Richard, then tilted her head in the direction of the front door. He understood, standing.

"We'd better go now," he said, gazing Janine's way.

"So soon?" uttered Henry disappointedly.

"Janine has other things on her agenda besides entertaining us, Pops."

Henry nodded and stood, as did Janine.

At the door, Henry told her, "Hope I get to see you again, Janine."

"I hope so, too," she said sweetly.

Richard gave his father a warm pat on the shoulder and they left.

"I really like Henry," said Janine on the way back to the inn.

"And he obviously likes you," Richard hummed.

Out of his periphery, he saw Janine stare at his profile. "Does that bother you?" she asked.

"No." He met her gaze. "Why would it?"

"I don't know," she responded with a shrug. "Correct me if I'm wrong, but it just seems like you're not too comfortable having your father think you might actually be happy being with someone other than Kassandra."

Richard frowned, tightening his grip on the steering wheel. "Not true," he indicated. "Maybe I just didn't want to give him false hope that you were going to be around when we both know otherwise." Not to mention, he had his own mixed feelings at the prospect that she would soon be leaving—perhaps for good.

"Well, I'm sorry, but that can't really be helped," Janine said defensively. "I happen to live in New York. We both knew that going in."

"You're right," Richard muttered resignedly.

"That doesn't mean we can't visit each other sometimes," she offered. "If you like—"

"Yeah, sure—that's cool." His terse response was meant to discourage what seemed like an impossible situation to Richard. He had been in a long-distance relationship before and, though it was difficult, he'd made it work till they were living in the same place, sharing the same space. But that was then. In this case, it seemed like the best they could hope for was the occasional visit here or there.

And maybe that was the best thing all the way around.

For both of them.

In Janine's room they made love again as if they'd been doing so for years. It was intense and sustained, as if to make this last night one to remember.

For his part, Richard knew it was a night he would not soon forget. Janine's presence had been so giving and strong that for the first time he had begun to actually imagine a life with someone other than Kassandra.

One that for the longest time had seemed impossible to conceive. One that was capable of filling his heart with such joy and his body with cravings that had him longing for Janine's touch, scent, kisses and mere presence.

He didn't know if this was good or bad; if he was happy or sad; if feeling this way was completely sensible or utterly foolish.

Well past midnight, Richard found himself suspecting the cards were stacked too high against building a life with Janine.

But even those misgivings would not stop him from keeping hope alive—something Richard was just starting to appreciate again.

Chapter 24

The footprints in the sand marred what was otherwise a picturesque, golden beach. The deep blue hues of the ocean seemed to be asleep with only a hint of a ripple. Peeking from beneath a cottony cloud was the sun, its rays shining down on Janine and Richard like beams from an alien spaceship. A few seagulls danced along the shoreline as if unsure in which direction to go.

It was barely 8:00 a.m. on Sunday—Janine's last day at Pebble Beach before returning to New York. She and Richard had made love again that morning after going at it for much of the night, deciding to say goodbye with a walk on the beach. It had proven to be much harder than Janine could have imagined. Neither of them seemed to want to say much of anything, as if nothing could adequately express the deep sadness both felt at this moment.

Janine favored Richard. He was wearing a Sacramento Kings jersey, brown sweats and a pair of black athletic shoes, that contrasted with her pink sleeveless T-shirt, green sport shorts and white running shoes. She watched his rigid profile and could see the melancholy in his face. He was looking straight ahead, as if unable to meet her eyes or touch her spirit, for fear of breaking down. She wondered if he was thinking about Kassandra and Sheena at that moment.

Or maybe I'm the one occupying his thoughts, Janine said to herself, admittedly preferring such for at least as long as she was there.

She hoped Richard was thinking about their lovemaking and intimacy—something that had engaged Janine's own thoughts; she was still caught up in the afterglow and dreading the prospect of having to leave him. Or perhaps he was more absorbed with the uncanny comfort level they had developed between them, as if they'd been a part of one another's lives far longer than five days or even five years.

These were things that spun around in Janine's mind like a top and made her weak in the knees. It had never been her intention to become attracted to this man and want to be with him. Not even John had affected her so powerfully when things were good between them.

The one thing Janine was sadly forced to come to grips with was that whatever magic they had created could not last, even if they wanted it to. Richard had his life and she had hers. Each had been disrupted momentarily by the presence of the other. All that was really left was to carry on as if what they had together had never existed except in their minds.

It would be a monumental task, if not damn near impossible. *I can still feel him inside me,* Janine thought desirously, *and his powerful arms around me.* Even if she wanted to, she could never forget Richard Lowrey and what he'd meant to her.

But she had to push it to the back of her mind. Or go mad.

Things looked much better as far as Janine's professional objectives were concerned. Though unsure just how much progress she had actually made in convincing Richard to return to photography, she had a sense that she'd succeeded in cutting through his reluctance and resistance to the degree that he was on the way back. She hoped that his inner strength and convictions would propel him into doing the books for Callister-Reynolds.

It somehow seemed inappropriate to request any more of Richard at this point, if ever. She'd set the chain of events in motion and the rest would be up to him.

Janine again gazed at the contours of Richard's face. There were tiny dark hairs shadowing his strong jawline from not shaving the night before. They were holding hands as if they were high-school sweethearts. Or an old married couple.

"Richard…?" Janine heard her voice say.

He turned to face her but said nothing.

"You seem miles away."

Richard sighed. "I'm right here…just thinking," he said, as if pausing for more thoughts. "I don't really want *this* to end."

Janine involuntarily cocked an eyebrow as his earnest words rang in her head like a bell. "I don't, either, Richard," she freely admitted, with her heart and not her head. "But it's unrealistic to think that this could work."

His eyes trained down on her. "I think it could if we really wanted it to."

She averted the intensity of his stare, which seemed to penetrate her very being. "Oh, Richard…" she gasped. "If only it could. But we live too far away from each other, baby—"

Richard stiffened. "Kassandra lived in Jamaica when we met," he pointed out. "It, too, seemed hopeless. But somehow we found a way to make it work."

Janine now felt a bit uncomfortable being compared to his late wife. *Just because Kassandra gave up her life to be with a man doesn't mean it's right for me,* she thought, slightly miffed. *I'm not her.*

Janine feared that it would be the standard that Kassandra had set that she would always be measured against in any serious relationship with Richard. Whether it was fair or not. Good or bad. Right or wrong.

"I'm *not* Kassandra, Richard," Janine felt compelled to say, staring him straight in the face. "And I never will be."

Richard looked taken aback. "You don't have to be, baby," he said categorically. "This isn't a contest between the two of you. I like you for who you are, Janine. Nothing more or less."

"But you don't really know who I am," she stated sharply. "I'm a single mother, Richard, with a young daughter and a scarred past. The few days we've spent together, though incredible, should not be confused with reality. Mine or yours."

"Why not?" he challenged her. "What we had was as real as anything I've ever experienced." Richard's voice broke and he averted his gaze, then back again. "I think I know something about scarred pasts. Maybe it's time, Janine, for both of us to start thinking about the future."

Janine looked out over the ocean, unprepared for this discussion. The thought of being in a real relationship again both thrilled and terrified her. She had little doubt that Richard was a truly wonderful man and could potentially be a wonderful friend to Lisa. Maybe even be a father figure. Yet there was still that gaping wound in her heart inflicted by John that meant her heart was not easily yielding to another.

She fixed her eyes on Richard's handsome face, his eyes warm with hope and sincerity. A part of Janine wished she'd met him before hooking up with John and before Richard had found love with Kassandra. Things might have turned out differently all around. But there was no going back…no room for second-guessing….

Now was now.

Janine took a deep breath. "I'm not sure I'm ready to make any future plans, Richard," she told him honestly, "with you or anyone else. To be perfectly frank, I'm still trying to come to terms with a husband that caused me so much pain and regret that it left me empty and bitter. I don't know if I could ever put myself in such a vulnerable, trusting position again."

Richard stopped in his tracks, prompting Janine to do so. She faced him.

"Look, I would never hurt you, Janine," he insisted, placing his hands on her shoulders.

Janine believed he meant it in his heart, causing her own to skip a beat.

"I'm sure you wouldn't," she agreed. "Not intentionally, anyway. But you don't know that for sure, do you? Sometimes people are hurt even when others try hard not to hurt them."

Richard gave her a weary look and breathed out of his nose. "All I'm asking you, Janine, is to give us a chance. Give me a chance. We both deserve something better than what we have. Even if there are no guarantees…."

Was there ever a guarantee for happiness? Janine contemplated, as if it came with a warranty and could be easily replaced if defective. Was having "no guarantees" therefore a recipe for disaster? she mused, while thinking logically that it was more a candid assessment of real life and the acceptable risks that accompanied any worthwhile relationship.

It was as tempting an offer as Janine could ever remember receiving. The notion of trying to have a long-distance relationship with this man was far from unappealing. Quite the opposite, in fact. She knew a lot about Richard—at least as much as he had allowed her to—and on a personal level, felt very comfortable with him intellectually and sexually. But Janine wasn't living in a fantasy world, either. Trying to make this work was fraught with many obstacles that seemed invariably ready to stand in the way of progress, like a steel door, her reasons for being in Pebble Beach notwithstanding.

Even if he was a man who any woman in her right mind would be crazy not to want if given the opportunity.

She wet her lips and said hesitantly, "Let me think about it, Richard, okay? I'm just not sure we're right for each other as far as a future. Your wounds run too deep. So do mine." Her eyes met his. "You can't or won't let go of the past."

Richard flashed her a befuddled look. "What are you talking about?" he asked, as if he had not a clue.

"I think we both know what I'm talking about," Janine stated.

"If you mean Kassandra—"

"Think about it." Janine's voice cracked, but she remained determined to speak the truth. "You've turned your house into a living shrine to your late wife and daughter, Richard. We couldn't even make love in your bedroom, for heaven's sake. And, frankly, I'm not even sure I'd want to, with Kassandra glaring down at me from that painting like a beautiful goddess, or like a she-devil standing guard over her man—"

"You were in my room?" Richard's eyes bulged and his nostrils flared in disbelief, taking a step back as if slapped.

"I wasn't snooping," Janine insisted defensively, though it must have seemed like the contrary. "It was when you were out walking Kimble that day. I only wanted to see what the house looked like. I didn't think you'd mind."

Richard's hard features softened apologetically and he

sighed. "When Kass and Sheena died, I felt as if I'd died with them. My whole damn world came crumbling down like a sand castle. I wasn't sure I could make it without them. Keeping the bedrooms the same as when they were alive seemed to be the only way to cope with their loss. It made me feel as if somehow Kassandra and Sheena were still close by." He paused, taking Janine's hands. "I never thought anyone else would come along to dominate my thoughts and give me a new reason to be enchanted and enthusiastic about life again. But you have, Janine."

Her hands shook inside his in that moment and Janine was speechless. She had not planned to try to take the place of Richard's beloved wife and daughter, not that she ever could or would want to. But suddenly she didn't want to shy away from being a part of this man's life and allowing him to become a part of hers.

Maybe there was such a thing as a second chance. And maybe they owed it to themselves to see if it was meant to be for them. Whatever else came with the territory, they would just have to deal with it.

In its own time.

Janine hugged Richard and felt his arms wrap around her like tentacles. "I'm sorry," she uttered, "about everything...except us."

"No need to apologize about anything, baby," Richard stressed, pulling her closer. "Everything is good—and it'll get better...."

They remained holding one another for some time as the waves crashed into the shore and the sun came out full force. Janine almost wished they could have remained that way forever. Caught up in their own little world where anything was possible.

But sooner or later, the time would come when they

would have to put this extended, long-distance camaraderie into practice.

And to the test.

She wasn't wearing blinders. It would not be an easy relationship to make work, even under the best of circumstances. They lived on opposite coasts, and there was no talk of either moving. Both had been through some difficult times, though Janine couldn't help but feel that Richard's tragedy far exceeded her own in terms of impact.

She pulled away from Richard and kissed him a little desperately on the mouth. He returned this kiss in kind and they enjoyed each other for a long moment before resuming their walk down the beach, hand in hand.

Alone in her room a few hours before her flight to New York, Janine took a moment to reflect. She and Richard had agreed that there would be no teary goodbyes. But no timetable had been set for the next time they'd say hello.

Could I ever be enough for him? Janine mused with some misgivings, while fearing that Kassandra's long and beautiful shadow would always loom over them like a dark cloud.

Equally of concern to Janine was whether or not Richard could learn to care for her daughter the way she would want any man in her life to. Or would the soul of his lost daughter forever stand in the way? she wondered.

Janine looked out the window at the picturesque view of Pebble Beach and couldn't help but envision it being uniquely depicted someday by Richard. She wondered if when all was said and done he would ever return to his photography and books or if he would somehow end up wasting his considerable talent by continuing to look backward rather than ahead.

Think positive. Like the man said, *Everything is good—and it'll get better....*

"And what about your career, girl?" Janine asked herself out loud, as if in doubt. She wanted to believe it was solidly on the right track. Yet she knew that it could just as easily be about to be derailed like a train gone awry.

Only time would provide the answers.

For now Janine felt the real pangs of having to leave Richard, just when it seemed as though they had found themselves.

And each other.

Chapter 25

Sheena was barely a year old when Richard and Kassandra went house hunting. Richard's books had proven to be an enormous success, surprising him and his publisher. A seven-figure advance to do several more books had suddenly provided him and Kassandra with the financial security they had previously only dreamt of.

Richard was afforded the opportunity of picking and choosing his settings for photographing, while Kassandra was able to quit her job and become a full-time mom and part-time travel writer.

The search for the perfect place to raise their daughter took them up and down the state of California, where Richard had lived most of his life, having little desire to live anywhere else. Kassandra stood by her man, feeling right at home in her adopted state.

The Monterey Peninsula beckoned them from the moment they set their sights on Pebble Beach, which had always been famous for its golf tournaments and scenic beauty. Situated between Monterey and Carmel, Pebble Beach's Del Monte Forest was breathtaking with its endless cypress and pine trees, peaks and valleys, sandy white beach along a rugged coastline and proximity to the Pacific Ocean. Wildlife freely roamed the forest, as much a part of it as the trees and huckleberry bushes. Elegant homes there were among the most sought after in all of California, if not the entire country.

The Lowreys found the ideal house in the middle of Pebble Beach's renowned 17-Mile Drive. It impressed them with its architectural elegance, size, style, structure and amenities, which seemed endless.

"It's our *dream* of dream homes," declared Kassandra exultantly.

Richard was in total agreement. He'd waited all his life to have something like this. The place would tie up much of their money. But what the hell? It was worth every penny and then some, for the sparkle he saw dancing in Kassandra's eyes.

They would live in paradise. And grow old together loving every moment of life and each other.

Richard pulled Kassandra close to him and declared, "A house is not a home, baby, till it's filled with love. Our love."

"It will be filled with such love, darling, and so much more." Kassandra lifted her chin and planted a long succulent kiss on his lips. "What did I ever do to deserve you, mon?"

"You came into my life," he said smoothly, and knew it was that simple.

She kissed him again. "I don't think I've ever been happier, Richard. With you, Sheena and now this—" she marveled at their new home "—I have everything I could possibly want and need."

Richard kissed his wife this time. He, too, felt he had everything he could ever want in life, both personally and professionally.

It seemed as if they had their whole lives ahead of them....

Chapter 26

"I might've made a big mistake," Richard said thoughtfully at his father's kitchen table.

"How's that?" Henry lit a cigarette.

Richard stared into his walnut-brown coffee as if the answer would suddenly appear. He'd been reflective ever since leaving Janine's room late that morning. There were so many things unresolved as to how they would make this bi-coastal relationship work. He sometimes wondered how he'd managed it with Kassandra. Before her, he had never even thought of going after a lady who wasn't practically within shouting distance from his house.

But, he knew, things happened. And usually for a very good reason.

What he didn't know was whether that line of reasoning was applicable this time around.

As it now stood, Richard felt that he had absolutely no

interest in moving to New York, with all the big-city headaches that went along with it.

The question was, if their relationship progressed, would Janine be willing to uproot her life and that of her child to move across the country to Pebble Beach and 17-Mile Drive to live with him? He had plenty of room for both of them and was tired of living in a big, empty house alone.

But he was thinking of things from his perspective. Janine may have other ideas, Richard considered. If she came, maybe she would want her own place. And space, where she could do her own thing, without feeling some sense of obligation under his roof.

That wasn't the only thing weighing heavily on Richard's mind. He felt guilty about giving himself to someone other than Kassandra. He had promised her—or his late wife's memory—that there would never be another to take her place.

Am I backing away from that promise? Richard asked himself, getting a whiff of the cigarette smoke filtering from Henry's nostrils.

He thought about the prospect of removing those things that belonged to Kassandra and Sheena to make room for Janine and Lisa. It seemed like an impossible task. He hoped it didn't come down to that, which he saw as somehow another assault on Kass and Sheena's memory, as if committing a mortal sin.

Richard looked up at his father, who was waiting patiently for him to speak. Stammering, he said, "M-maybe it wasn't such a good idea to try to keep this thing going with Janine—"

Henry peered across the table. "Why the hell not?"

Richard shrugged, not fully able to explain what he was feeling. "It's too soon."

Henry narrowed an eye. "Too soon for what—to get a life for yourself?"

"You know what I mean," he said curtly.

"No, I sure as hell don't!" A vein in Henry's temple threatened to pop out. "Listen to me, Richard. From everything I've seen and heard about her, Janine seems like a fine, decent woman. She likes you. You like her. So what's the problem?"

Richard ran a hand across the top of his hair, feeling hot under the collar. When he finally did speak, he said in a controlled tone, "It's *only* been three years since Kass died. I'm just not sure I'm ready to share *her* bed with someone else."

"You're as ready as you'll ever be," Henry insisted with an edge to his tone. "Three years is too long to mourn, son, even for you. If you don't want to share her bed with someone else, then dammit, son, get a new bed! Wherever Kassandra is now, do you really think she'd want you to give up the rest of your life moping around like a stray puppy, feeling sorry for yourself?"

Richard knew the answer to that was a definite "no." In fact, he recalled one conversation they'd had. It was while making love in the bathtub. Kassandra, slightly intoxicated, had said to him, "Doesn't get much better than this, darling. Sex, orgasms, more sex, more orgasms, sweet wine and an even sweeter, loving man."

He'd responded, almost foreshadowing the future, "No, baby, it doesn't get much better—not in this lifetime."

She'd looked him straight in the eye and said, "Just promise me one thing, Richard. If anything ever happens to me, I want you to find someone else who can make you just as happy as you've made me."

As much as he'd wanted to please her in every way, Richard had never made that promise. It was as though to do so would amount to some sort of self-fulfilling prophecy. Besides that, he could never have imagined anyone other than her quite fitting the bill.

Until now.

But even now he was filled with doubts, fears and second thoughts.

"I just don't want to get my hopes up again, Dad," he said tonelessly. "You know what I'm saying? Only to come crashing back down to earth like a damn rocket out of control."

"There's nothing wrong with getting your hopes up, son," Henry told him, inhaling deeply on the cigarette and blowing out plumes of smoke. "That's what life is all about. We all have to take chances. If you fall down, you get back up and try again till you get what you're after."

Richard took his still-steaming coffee with him to the living room as Henry followed, as if not wanting to let this end. He couldn't help but think that his old man always seemed to have an answer for everything, whether he wanted to hear it or not. Maybe that was a good thing. No one else knew him well enough to offer such sound and critical advice.

"What if this thing were to get serious?" Richard asked with some consternation, turning around. "Maybe Janine wouldn't want to move out here."

Henry hit him with jutting eyes. "Maybe she wouldn't," he agreed. "If so, then it would be up to you to move to where she is."

"To New York?" Richard's mouth hung open in horror, as if the notion was utterly outrageous.

Henry frowned, the cigarette dangling precariously from his mouth. "If that's what it took, why not? Could be that this time it's you who has to uproot yourself and leave everything else behind. Don't knock it until you've tried it."

Richard did try to imagine it, aware that his father had successfully relocated to Monterey from San Diego. Not to mention the many times they had moved when he was a boy.

But he was a man now, and relocating didn't figure into his plans. Going cross-country to the Northeast where winters could be brutal and sunshine was in short supply was something that would take some long and hard thought. At the moment he was not inclined to take such a drastic step in his life.

But he wouldn't rule it out altogether, either, Richard told himself. His career travels had told him that he could live almost anywhere if he had to. He could make the necessary adjustments. It was living somewhere where he didn't *have* to that bothered him.

As yet, it seemed he and Janine were still a long way from making solid plans to be together, much less live together.

He just wasn't absolutely sure he was ready to share his space again with someone other than Kass and Sheena. Or, for that matter, share Janine's space with her daughter. Maybe this wasn't a road Janine was ready to travel down, either.

Richard thought about his old man being alone all these years and seemingly able to cope with no problem. He'd often wondered if Henry had ever felt loneliness. Frustration.

The desire to be with another woman.

He fixed on his father's face. "Dad, why haven't you tried to find someone else since Mom died?" He thought it time to ask. "And don't tell me it's because you're too old and set in your ways." Not that this didn't have some merit in and of itself.

Henry's face looked weary as he contemplated the question. He took a final drag of the cigarette and squashed it in an ashtray like a bug before saying, "I was married to your mother for near thirty-eight years, son. That's nearly four times as long as you were married to Kassandra. I never wanted anyone but her. Never needed anyone but her. When your mother died, I felt that we had been married long enough to last her lifetime and mine. I still feel that way."

Richard nodded understandingly. "Yeah, I know exactly what you mean. That's just how I feel about my marriage to Kassandra. How the hell can I ever expect anyone to take her place?"

"Listen to me, son," said Henry, putting a firm arm around him. "Don't compare your situation to mine. You still have your *whole* life ahead of you. I don't. Your mother died after living a full life, and her body gave way to disease. Kassandra was taken away by an accident while still a young woman with plenty of life left. There's nothing you can do to bring her back. You can't throw away your life because of that, Richard—especially when there's someone out there who just may be able to make it meaningful again."

Richard stared at the words as though on paper. Once again, his father had overridden his protestations, reluctance and fears with some wisdom and sound observations. It was his time to make a new start, he realized. Janine was someone that he had really grown to care for in a short time, maybe far more than he was willing or wanted to admit. He owed it to her and himself to give this every chance to work, even if it meant a few sacrifices along the way and dealing with some unexpected obstacles.

Even now, Richard thought lustfully, he missed Janine's touch, smell, voice and chuckle. Most of all, he missed her companionship.

It made him wonder if he'd felt this way when he'd first

met Kassandra. After they had made love. After he had declared his love to her.

He tried to recall if the feelings were exactly the same this time around. Or entirely different....

Damn, he cursed inside, frustrated at these conflicting and confusing thoughts. *Have I changed my tune or what?*

It bothered Richard to think that he could not remember precisely the swirl of his emotions going through his head and body when courting Kassandra. He wondered if this was what happened when a person died—the memories slowly began to fade away, like seasons. Or like dusk turning to dawn. Till there was nothing left.

Richard sadly realized that the face filling his mind like photographs these days was not his beloved Kassandra's.

It was Janine's.

Chapter 27

The first six months after her divorce were the hardest of Janine's life. Much of it was spent wondering what she had done wrong. Or what she could have done right. She had followed her mother's footsteps to divorce court like a clone, though Janine had sworn to herself that she would make her marriage work at all costs.

But then, she hadn't expected that she would end up marrying a man whose overactive libido and wandering eye was usually directed at someone other than herself.

The most difficult part of it all for Janine was telling her daughter that her mommy and daddy would no longer be husband and wife. Trying to explain that to a five-year-old proved to be a challenge. Especially when Janine was still trying to come to grips with it herself, and feeling like she was a failure at life.

But Lisa was more perceptive and wise beyond her years than most kids her age. She took it hard, but understood that

Mommy and Daddy no longer liked each other the way people should who live together. Therefore, they had to live apart. But she would get to spend time with both of them so that her connection to her parents would not suffer irreparably from their decision to separate.

Lisa seemed to adapt easily enough to the custody arrangement and visitation schedule with no obvious signs of stress or maladjustment. Janine sometimes wondered if her daughter was hiding her emotions, or if they simply lived in a time when divorce and separation were so common that children tended to take it in stride. *Much more than the estranged parents.*

Either way, Janine was determined to bring her daughter up as best she could, even if it meant doing so as a single parent with only part-time help from Lisa's father.

Janine's biggest fear was that she would not be able to do enough to help Lisa realize that a healthy and loving marriage was not a fantasy, but something many people enjoyed, even if her own parents didn't. She wanted her daughter to have every advantage of kids with united parents, and had every confidence that someday Lisa would be able to find a man who would love her and treat her with the respect she deserved. That included a committed relationship built on trust, communication, give-and-take and understanding.

Janine's social life following the divorce was put on indefinite hold. She had dated in high school and college before she met John. But those seemed like distant and forgettable memories. John had poisoned her against men—at least for the time being. She was in too much pain and self-blame to want to go through another relationship where she could end up hurt and humiliated again.

Instead, she turned to work to sustain herself and to keep her mind on a track where emotional attachment was not an issue. But soon even that was not enough to compensate for the lack of a physical and spiritual relationship with an adult.

Perhaps that was why she'd relocated to New York, even if she hadn't realized it at the time. She was subconsciously trying to find Mr. Right *and* Mr. Wonderful.

Or hoping that he would find her.

But somehow the move only reinforced Janine's desire to remain single and unattached. She rationalized that it would only give her more quality time to spend with Lisa, without the complications and emotional roller coaster of dividing such time with another.

Then came Janine's trip to California.

And Richard Edgar Lowrey.

He had, in short order, made her reassess *everything* she had tried to avoid like the plague. He had made Janine question her very soul and what she wanted out of life besides Lisa.

Janine was not sure when she knew she was in love with Richard. Perhaps it was the first time they kissed—the feelings lingering well beyond the moment. Or the first time they made love. Or the last time….

Maybe it was when they went out on his father's boat. Or the trip to San Francisco. Or the walk on the beach, where Janine noticed no one but him and felt as if Richard saw no one but her.

It could have been the thought of having to leave Richard while wanting to stay with all her heart and body.

It might have even been the very day they'd met at Pescadero Point—love at first sight, which Janine wouldn't have believed was possible before. But now….

What she did know was that the feelings were as real as anything Janine had ever known or experienced. This devilishly good-looking man had made her feel wanted, needed and appreciated in the most wonderful way, which she had never felt before. Richard seemed to be telling her through his eyes, touch—his very essence—that she didn't have to be alone anymore.

And neither did he, Janine told herself positively.

What hadn't been answered early on was whether or not they could survive heartbreak and broken dreams and make a future for themselves.

Chapter 28

John F. Kennedy Airport was typically jam-packed that Monday as Janine waited for her daughter, feeling a little anxious. Her eyes finally latched on to Lisa through the throngs of people. Janine began waving wildly, as if trying to flag down a cab.

Lisa burst into a bright smile when she saw her, shouting, "Mommy! Mommy!"

Wearing a pink dress Janine hadn't seen before and matching ribbons in thick pigtails, Lisa carried her small orange-brown duffel bag. She literally jumped into Janine's arms as they embraced and kissed, openly displaying the affection between mother and daughter. Neither cared that they seemed to have attracted the attention of practically everyone else coming and going.

"Did you have a good flight, sweet pea?" Janine asked, eyeing Lisa's dress and noting a hexagon-shaped brownish stain on the front of it.

"Yeah. It was neat. They gave me chocolate ice cream."

Janine glanced again at the brown stain. "Yes, I can see that. Well, I'm glad to have you back, honey."

Lisa giggled. "I'm glad to have *you* back, Mommy!"

Janine smiled at her lovingly. "Come on, let's go get Murphy."

They went to the baggage-claim area and waited for the cat to emerge in his carrier before heading to the parking lot.

In the cab Murphy snuggled in a corner of the back seat. Lisa, beside him, had a glint in her eye as she asked, "Did you bring me a gift from California like you promised?"

"I brought you *gifts,*" Janine told her matter-of-factly, knowing the joy her daughter received whenever she bought her anything. This, in turn, gave Janine a warm feeling of satisfaction. Being a single parent without unlimited means, she strove to do everything she could to provide Lisa with a normal life. That included buying her things that were both practical and exciting to a young girl.

"Where are they?" Lisa voiced impatiently.

"At home."

Lisa crossed her arms and pouted.

"You'll see them soon enough," Janine promised her, seeing her displeasure. "They're not going to go anywhere." Favoring Lisa's dress, she commented, "Besides, looks as if someone already bought you a very pretty and very pink gift—aside from a little brown coloring."

Lisa looked at herself as if for the first time and smiled broadly. "Bernadette took me shopping at a big mall. She used Daddy's silver-colored credit card to buy me this."

John must *really* care for Bernadette, Janine thought with just a trickle of envy. He had once guarded his precious credit cards like Fort Knox, even though she had never been a free spender when they were married. John, on the other hand, had always had trouble appreciating the value of a dollar, spending money freely and often only thinking of himself.

Janine felt a little jealous for some reason at the thought of her ex-husband's girlfriend buying Lisa clothes—as if Lisa was *her* daughter.

I haven't even met the woman, Janine whined to herself, feeling at a huge disadvantage. She could only wonder what John had told Bernadette about her, as well as what he'd conveniently left out.

Has he suggested that I'm not a good mother? Janine winced at the thought, further imagining John implying that she was incapable of buying her own daughter clothes, or was too preoccupied to do so.

Now you're being ridiculous, Janine chastised herself. For all the hell that John had put her through, she knew he had never believed her to be anything but a totally devoted mother to Lisa. Even when his own interests were often elsewhere.

"It's a very pretty dress," Janine found herself repeating lamely to Lisa. "It'll be even prettier once I wash that stain out."

Janine looked out the passenger window for a bit, then turned back to her daughter. She smiled when she saw that Lisa had fallen fast asleep with Murphy.

She thought about Richard, wondering how he and Lisa would get along. The obvious concern was whether her daughter would like the man she'd fallen for and, in turn, if Richard would like Lisa....

Janine pondered just how much his daughter's tragic death would affect how he felt about Lisa. The hope was that Lisa would be judged on her own merits as a wonderful little girl that he could dote on.

Since arriving home late yesterday, Janine had spoken to Richard on the phone. They had made tentative plans to visit one another. Her reluctance to embark on a coast-to-coast relationship had given way to her overpowering attraction and connection to this talented man. They had tapped into something that neither could deny or resist.

Richard was nothing like John, Janine knew definitively. In fact, Richard had a way about him unlike any man she had ever known. He was sensitive, charming, laid-back, introspective and vulnerable all in one. He'd experienced love and success, pain and loss, high highs and low lows, yet still managed to have his head together at the end of the day and night.

He seemed to be changing courses in life, almost midway, thereby averting a disaster. Janine wanted to be a part of Richard Lowrey's life when he turned it around completely and found inner strength, contentment and hope again for tomorrow.

How big a part she played was unclear in Janine's mind. Right now there seemed to be more questions than answers about the future of their relationship. She still didn't know if it was fated to be long-term, or just a temporary fix to their mutual needs.

She hadn't dared look too far ahead for fear of being disappointed or too optimistic. But even this did not stop Janine from speculating on the various possibilities. For instance, if she and Richard became an item, maybe he would be willing to move to New York, giving up his precious Pebble Beach.

Janine reversed this to the possibility of her moving to California. Was relocating Lisa across the country even a realistic option? She peeked at her daughter and could see Lisa beginning to stir, wondering if John would be opposed to her taking their daughter to the West Coast. She imagined that he might be too wrapped up in his own romance with Bernadette or someone else to even care. But Janine couldn't rule out that he might try to fight her where it concerned Lisa.

An even greater sense of anxiety entered Janine's head, sending a shiver through her bones. All other potential obstacles to relocating aside, she had serious reservations as to whether or not she could successfully coexist with the spirit of Kassandra Lowrey in Richard's heart and home.

Serious, indeed, but a bridge Janine was willing to try and cross, no matter the difficulty. The man was that special.

Experience had taught Janine that nothing came easily in life. At least not hers. She would follow her dreams and pray that they would not lead her astray, but rather right into the arms of Richard Edgar Lowrey.

Chapter 29

On Tuesday morning Janine returned to work, not sure how she would handle explaining to Dennis her progress—or lack thereof—in getting Richard Lowrey to fulfill his commitment to Callister-Reynolds. She couldn't even begin to discuss the personal relationship she'd developed with Richard during her trip out West, much less its implications for the future.

But she did love and indeed need her job and was not looking forward to seeing it put in jeopardy. Janine tensed in the fear that she'd already reached the point of no return in that respect.

No sooner had she sat down at her desk in an office that was too small than Dennis came barging in, huffing and puffing like the Big, Bad Wolf.

"I see you made it back safe and sound," he said guardedly.

"All in one piece, thankfully." She batted her lashes and wrinkled her nose innocently.

Dennis hovered over her, one hand on his glasses as if to hold them up. "So how did our little trip go?"

Janine drew a silent breath. "I made some progress," she informed him.

He peered down at her. "Some progress, huh? Not sure I like the sound of that."

She swallowed, choosing her next words carefully. "I wasn't able to get a firm commitment out of Richard, Dennis—but I do believe that he will soon be working on a book for you."

A strained smile rested on Dennis's lips, and he said, with skepticism, "Well, did he tell you that, or what...? Speak up, girl!"

Janine clasped her hands together, feeling the heat of expectations burning inside. "Not in so many words," she stammered. "But he did pick up a camera before my very eyes and use it for the first time in years. I'd say resuming his career is the next logical step for Richard."

An irregular line deepened on Dennis's forehead. "The only logic I see here is that we have a contract that calls for *two* more books from Lowrey, with an option for two more after that. Frankly, I was hoping you would be able to get a more firm commitment out of the man than that."

Janine felt her face flush with the discomfort of clearly disappointing her boss, though it couldn't be helped. She was only human and couldn't force Richard to do anything he wasn't ready to do—but she had definitely made inroads to that effect. Still, Janine knew that she was basically being forced to choose sides in this battle between publisher and photographer.

"Richard's been through an ordeal, Dennis," Janine tried to explain, while feeling like she was walking on eggshells. "It's taken its toll on the man, both physically and emotionally. But he's starting to come out of it now…I could see that. You just need to give him a little more time—"

Dennis drew his brows together sharply. "We all feel for Richard and his loss," he said colorlessly. "But we can't run a business on sympathy. He either has to produce in a timely manner or we'll see his ass in court to collect the money he was advanced that other authors would jump at the chance to pocket!"

Janine was uncertain where to go from here. She feared that if Dennis put added pressure on Richard it might have the opposite effect of its intended purpose. But she also knew that Dennis and the publisher had every right to want the books Richard had signed a contract to do for them. Or return the advance money, which she suspected he had already spent a good deal of, if not all of, on his expensive digs on 17-Mile Drive.

"Let me work with Richard a bit longer, Dennis," Janine found herself beseeching. She quickly added, "I won't need to go back to California. We developed somewhat of a rapport when I was there." *If you only knew,* she mused dreamily, warmed by the very thoughts. "I believe I can get him to own up to his commitment without having to resort to a lawsuit or incurring more travel expenses."

Dennis scratched his goatee as if in search of fleas. "Fine," he said tersely. "You have till the fifteenth of August. That's one month from today. I hope for *your* sake, Janine—and *his*—that we have in writing a firm timetable for the delivery of his next book!"

Janine didn't bother to ask him what *her sake* meant. It was as crystal clear as the scowl on his face that she either delivered Richard's head on a silver platter, so to speak, or she started looking for a new job.

Suddenly the stakes had risen for Janine and Richard. Not only were they embarking on a new personal journey with unknown pitfalls along the way, but also their professional lives had become intertwined with serious consequences for them both, should either fail to produce.

Janine wondered with trepidation if they could survive the potential fallout. For the moment, she thought, unnerved, it was important that she first concentrate on her own survival in an increasing minefield.

That afternoon Janine had lunch with Flora at a deli on Madison Avenue. It was packed, but they managed to find a table in the rear near the kitchen.

"Girl, maybe you should go away more often," Flora said, a smile putting dimples in her cheeks. "Since you hopped cross-country, things have improved a hundred percent between me and Butch—especially in the sack—you know what I'm saying?"

Janine had met Flora's boyfriend only once and couldn't help but think that they were totally mismatched, aside from the age difference. But she wasn't about to tell Flora that, not when her own experience with mismatched partners was still fresh in her mind. Who was she to say what could and couldn't work, under the circumstances?

"I'm glad to hear that, Flora," she told her sincerely, and lifted a corned beef sandwich.

"You are?" Flora rolled her eyes theatrically. "Honey, let me tell you, there ought to be a law against the things this man can do under the sheets. And outside them, too. Ooh, I get all hot and bothered just thinking about it." Flora began dramatically fanning herself.

Janine chuckled and found herself blushing, her mind immediately turning to Richard and the times they had made love. Make that all-out *lust!* She felt a twinge between her legs and could almost feel him in her. And taste his mouth upon hers and all over her body.

Only now did Janine realize just how much she missed being intimate with Richard. Being able to please and be pleased by him.

Turn your mind off, Janine ordered herself, before realizing it wasn't her mind that was the problem at the moment.

"I heard that you didn't exactly twist Richard Lowrey's arm to get his books done." Flora looked across the table at Janine, causing her to come back to the real world. "Question is, did you get the man to *bend* just a little?"

"Yes," Janine told her truthfully. "As a matter of fact, I think I did."

Flora's eyes grew wide with curiosity. "Care to elaborate?"

Janine sighed thoughtfully. *Not about everything.* "Richard's begun taking pictures again," she said. "I'd say that's a good first step, considering what he's been through."

Flora dug her long, polished and perfectly manicured nails into a roast beef sandwich. "I agree. So how'd you manage to get him to do that?"

Janine wasn't quite sure how to answer. "Well, you could say I bribed him."

Flora studied her intently. "Hmm. Very interesting. So what *aren't* you telling me, girlfriend?"

Janine played with her sandwich. She was hesitant to share too much with the older woman, not knowing if she could trust Flora to keep anything said to her between them. It wasn't like they were the best of friends outside the office. But they were friends, nevertheless, and she needed someone to confide in.

Facing her, Janine said nervously, "Richard and I kind of hit it off...."

Flora's head snapped back in surprise. "You mean, hit it off as in the sack?"

Janine colored, wondering if it was wise to say any more. She decided to go with her instincts. "Yes," came a soft reply. "Richard's really a wonderful man, once you get to know him."

"Well, you go, girl." Flora beamed like a proud mom. "Obviously the brother's been lying dormant waiting for a terrific lady like you to come along."

"I don't think he was looking for anyone," Janine said defensively. "Richard truly loved his wife, Kassandra, and seemed content with that love—even though she's gone."

"But you can't live just on memories forever, honey," observed Flora, patting her hand. "He deserves better. And heaven knows you certainly do after practically living the life of a nun since I've known you. Maybe it was some sort of divine intervention that Dennis sent you to see Richard, though I don't know if Dennis is quite ready to put it in those terms yet."

Janine considered just that, in relation to her own feelings. "I do like being with Richard," she admitted, and that was understating her feelings, "but there are certain complications that may keep us from ever having any type of serious relationship."

Flora stuck a fork into some fries splattered with ketchup. "You mean, like the fact that he lives in California and you live in New York?"

"That certainly doesn't help matters any," Janine grumbled, knowing there was more.

Remembering that Kassandra had lived in Jamaica when she and Richard first met made Janine almost feel that their distance was a petty grievance by comparison, relatively speaking. Of course, she also knew that she and Richard hadn't yet reached the stage in their relationship, geographically or otherwise, that she believed he and Kassandra had achieved and managed to maintain till the very end. Maybe they never would, she feared.

"If you two were meant to be," expressed Flora hopefully, "you'll find a way to work it out—whatever the obstacles."

"That may be a tall task," Janine voiced with concern. "You see, Dennis has given me a month to get a solid commitment from Richard to fulfill his contractual obligations with Callister-Reynolds. If I fail, I could end up losing both the man and the job." Neither of which she was prepared to deal with right now.

Flora favored her over a mug of root beer. "Hmm… What does one have to do with the other? Or shouldn't I ask?"

Janine felt her underarms perspiring. After a moment or two, she acknowledged shamefully and with regret, "I haven't gotten around to telling Richard that I work for Callister-Reynolds. Yet."

Flora swallowed in disbelief. "I see," she uttered wryly. "Well, maybe you should. Don't you think?"

"Yes," Janine muttered weakly, knowing full well she really didn't have much of a choice. "The time just never seemed quite right. And then, you know, things sort of just got out of control—"

"I understand." Flora gave her a comprehending smile and patted Janine's hand again. "If you need my help, Janine," she offered, "I would be happy to run interference for you with Richard. You may have softened him enough that it wouldn't take as much to get him to come around on the contract issue—without jeopardizing anything between you two."

"Thanks for the support, Flora." Janine spoke gratefully. "But I have to sort this out all on my own. It's the only way I'll know I made the right decisions. Or even the wrong ones. And be able to deal with it, for better or worse...."

As tempting as it was to pass the torch to Flora or anyone else, Janine knew in her heart that this was something she had to do for herself. Even if it meant that she ended up coming out on the short end of the stick with Richard and Dennis. She didn't want to lose Richard or cause the company to lose their investment in him.

Could she possibly have her cake and eat it, too? Janine wondered nervously. Then she thought, *To hell with the cake—I'd settle for the man and his books.*

Chapter 30

For Sheena's fifth birthday, Richard and Kassandra had bought her a cocker spaniel. It was Sheena—thrilled to have her own little pet with a silky golden-brown coat—who'd named him Kimble.

"Kimble and me are never going to be apart," she'd declared emphatically.

Richard took her at her word, happy just to see that his baby girl was rapidly growing into a beautiful little lady. Her soft, nut-brown hair grazed small shoulders in curls. Wondrous, big brown eyes were luminous with life. A generous smile with a tooth or two absent lit up her entire face like a candle.

Richard couldn't help but smile himself as he focused the camera on his subject. With each passing day Sheena was looking more and more like her mother. He took the picture, knowing it would mean more to him than any of the thousands of photographs he'd taken around the world. It was his plan to capture Sheena in the best light for every birthday that came along.

He never considered that there wouldn't be many more birthdays to celebrate for his little shining star. There was no reason to think that.

Kassandra, who had become a very good photographer in her own right over the years, snatched the camera from Richard.

"Get over there with your daughter and Kimble," she commanded.

"Yes, ma'am," he chuckled.

Richard sat Sheena down on his lap while she held Kimble in front of the large living-room window.

"Ready when you are, baby," he told Kassandra, then produced a brilliant smile.

She snapped the picture. "Perfect. Just one more."

Richard put Sheena on his other knee. She took Kimble with her.

"This is fun, Daddy," Sheena giggled.

"Yes, it is," Richard seconded. He couldn't think of a time when he'd felt so content and at peace in his life. He had his family to thank for that.

"Say cheese…." Kassandra said.

"Cheese," they said in unison. At the last possible moment Richard kissed Sheena on the cheek just as the picture was taken.

Kassandra set the timer to take one final picture of the entire family. This one was taken in front of the fireplace, which had seen plenty of use lately and had a nice fire going.

Richard held Sheena to his chest with one arm and placed the other snugly around Kassandra. She cuddled Kimble, who seemed quite at home with all the pictures, never uttering a bark of protest.

Before the picture was taken, Richard put his mouth to

Kassandra's luscious micro braids and whispered into her ear, "Thank you for giving me a beautiful daughter to go with a beautiful wife."

Kassandra, never entirely comfortable with her beauty, replied, "It's you, Richard, who make us beautiful, baby. Never forget that."

It was all Richard could do to keep from shedding a few tears as they looked at the camera, smiled together and watched the flash momentarily blind them.

Richard didn't know it at the time, but it was to be one of the last pictures ever taken of them together as a family.

Chapter 31

The photographs came to life one by one. Each was of Janine. Richard was starstruck by her ravishing beauty as revealed in the prints. She reminded him so much of Kassandra—there was no mistaking the similarities in the texture and fullness of the hair that surrounded the face like a halo, finely chiseled bone structure, beautiful light brown complexion and pure enchantment in the eyes. But somehow Janine's look was still distinctly her own.

Richard stared at the images of the gorgeous lady he was rapidly falling for in ways he would not have thought possible. Janine had been gone for just two days, yet he missed her as if they'd spent months—even years—apart.

He wasn't sure what to make of these feelings for a woman he had known less than a week.

Have I fallen in love with Janine Henderson? Richard had to ask himself as if the thought had never occurred to him. He wondered if that was what gnawed at him like a puppy with an old shoe.

Love.

Is it Janine that I'm finally ready to give my heart and soul to?

Richard looked at her tantalizing image in the enlarged prints—reminiscent of Kassandra in many ways—prompting him to question if, in fact, his interest in Janine was merely as a reflection of the woman he believed could never be replaced.

Richard left the darkroom with one print and joined his father in the study, where Henry was stretched across the couch like he owned the place, his old eyes glued to the Mariners playing the Tigers on TV.

"What's the score?" Richard asked disinterestedly.

Henry yawned. "Tigers are up 1–0 on a suicide squeeze play."

Richard lost his train of thought for a moment before he glanced at the screen. Suddenly all the conflicting emotions building up like hot steam left him feeling confused and uncertain. He had no idea what the hell he should or should not be feeling or wanting.

Henry looked up as Richard sat beside him, sensing that something was wrong. "Everything all right, son?"

"I'm not sure," Richard moaned with a sigh.

Henry furrowed his brow, noting he was holding something. "What's that you got there?"

Richard glanced at the enlarged photograph of Janine, then handed it to his father.

Henry peered at it approvingly. "Nice. You still got the magic with the photography, Richard. That's good—real good." He paused, raising a brow hesitantly. "So what's your problem?"

"Nothing." Richard swallowed. "I don't know... Maybe everything."

Henry studied his son, then the picture. "Janine's beautiful in a sophisticated way—just like Kassandra was." He favored Richard. "That's what this is all about, isn't it? She reminds you of Kassandra and what you once had?"

Richard gave a slow, uneasy nod.

"Now you're feeling it again," said Henry knowingly, "something deep in your heart for this woman. Am I right?"

He had always been able to read him so clearly, Richard thought. Better than anyone else. It must be a father-son thing.

"Yeah, Dad," he admitted, "you are. I'm just not sure I should have these feelings for Janine the way I do. You know what I'm saying?"

"Why not?" Henry said. "There's no law anywhere that I'm aware of that says you can't fall in love twice in your lifetime."

Richard licked his lips. "Didn't say anything about love."

"Didn't have to, son. I'm your old man. I've been around long enough to be able to see it in a person's eyes. Especially yours, where I've only seen the love bug once before."

"This is crazy," Richard said, feeling as if he was becoming discombobulated.

"No, it's not," Henry insisted, leaning forward. "You're human, Richard. You should know as well as anyone that there's no supernatural formula to falling in love. It happens when it does. You can either go with it or ignore what you know is true."

Richard set his jaw. He knew he could no more ignore what Janine was doing to him than what Kassandra had done fifteen years earlier. But even that couldn't wipe away the guilt that still tore through him like an internal enemy.

He regarded his father. "I feel as if I've disappointed Kassandra in a major way," he said. "As if I somehow need to try and explain *this*—"

Henry shifted his body and leveled a hard gaze at Richard. "Son, there's nothing to explain. Especially not to a woman's spirit. Kassandra's dead and gone to heaven or wherever people go when they leave this earth. She never expected you to carry on your life as if she was still here or that you somehow owed your allegiance to her even in death. It's time to put her to rest and regain control over your life."

That was easier said than done, yet he knew he must try and rebuild his life.

And find love.

He fervently hoped that both would include Janine. But he couldn't presume that she had similar feelings for him. Or that she would be willing to make any major sacrifices to that effect. Love should not be confused with lust or liking a whole lot. *Can I settle for anything less in a woman than total, all-encompassing love?* Richard asked himself doubtfully, while feeling instinctively that Janine would not settle for anything less in a man.

Richard decided that he had to keep his own emotions in check until he found out if they could really bridge the gap that separated them geographically, physically, mentally and maybe even spiritually.

"I suppose you're right," he told his father slowly.

"I know I am." Henry nodded with satisfaction. "You'll see."

Richard thought about regaining control over his life. It had to begin where he had lost it. He looked Henry in the eye. "I think I'm ready to go back to work now, Pops," he remarked, glancing at the photograph of Janine. It was she who had inspired and encouraged him to pick up the camera again. He couldn't thank her enough. But he would try to.

"That's great, son." Henry patted him on the knee encouragingly. "You'll pick it back up in no time flat."

"I've made some inquiries with some local magazines for

freelance work," noted Richard. "I also hope to start soon on another book of pictures—assuming Callister-Reynolds still wants my stuff."

He had little doubt they wanted something from him—if not the remaining books he was contracted for, then the advance money owed them if he reneged on his part of the bargain. He was betting on the books, since Callister-Reynolds hadn't taken legal action against him yet, knock on wood.

Richard knew he could not live forever off the interest, dividends and growth potential from the small investments he'd made in stocks, bonds and a savings account. There seemed little other choice than to return to the only means of financial support he had ever been any good at. *I'm doing this for me, first and foremost,* he told himself determinedly.

Henry drew a breath and broke into a grin. "How could they not want you back? Everyone knows you're the best in the business at what you do. I'm proud of you, Richard. Sitting on your ass feeling sorry for yourself was getting you nowhere fast. You've got too much talent to let it go to waste forever. Kassandra never wanted that. And I know Janine, being an editor and all, will also be delighted to know that you intend to get your brilliantly photographed books back on the market where they belong."

Richard looked forward to sharing the news with her. But first, he wanted to focus on *them.* The present. The future. And what might or might not be in store for them when the sea smoothed itself of ripples.

Richard sighed and gave Henry the benefit of a warm gaze. "Dad, I appreciate your being there for me, man," he said with feeling. "I know I haven't always been the easiest son to put up with."

Henry placed an arm around his shoulder, bringing them close together. "We're there for each other, Richard. That's what being a father and son is all about. I try not to overstep my bounds, and so do you. But when one of us needs a little shove, we know we can count on the other to do the right thing."

The two men embraced, expressing the genuine love, warmth and friendship they shared.

Chapter 32

The next two weeks were like a whirlwind as Janine and Richard carried on their long-distance relationship by phone, the Internet and through vivid imaginations. Much of the communication revolved around missing each other, wanting each other and having each other, albeit from afar. Neither spoke much about the future and they spoke less about the past, as if to do so would somehow threaten the present.

Several times Janine attempted to broach the subject of the books Richard was under contract to do with Callister-Reynolds. But to do so would mean having to tell him that she worked for the publisher and had been assigned the task of bringing him back into compliance with his obligations. This was something she thought would be better to tell him in person, though she'd failed to do so before.

Janine felt guilty about being less than upfront with Richard from the beginning, but there had been mitigating circumstances. Such as becoming deeply attracted to the man himself over and above the business implications involving the photographer/author. Her one hope was that she and Richard would still be able to hold on to what they had, no matter the outcome of his dispute with Callister-Reynolds. Or even her own rather precarious future with the publisher.

Janine did discuss Richard's photography with him and was pleased when he gave her every indication that it was something he was ready to pursue again on a full-time basis. She could only assume that meant he intended to start work on a book for Callister-Reynolds. But this was an assumption she could not bank on and with only two weeks before Dennis's deadline, Janine invited Richard to visit her, hoping to resolve the impasse once and for all.

She wanted desperately to see him again, as well as introduce him to her daughter, not to mention get him and Dennis to come to terms with one another. It would be a delicate balance, to say the least, she thought uneasily.

But worth the trip on all counts.

It was two days before Richard was due to arrive when Janine received the package in the mail from him. She opened it with all the enthusiasm of a child on Christmas morning. In the box was a letter, a large padded manila envelope and two small gift-wrapped packages.

She opened the letter and read it first.

Dearest Janine,

I cannot tell you how much I've missed your company these past weeks, sweet lady. I think I've already made this clear to you by phone, e-mail and online chats, but it seemed necessary to say it again, anyhow.

To be honest, I never thought I'd ever look twice at

another woman again after Kassandra died. But then you came along like an angel from the heavens and turned my life upside down. Actually, I think it was more right side up. Either way, it seems like something akin to a miracle.

I've asked myself a thousand times if what we shared when you were here was real or an illusion borne out of loneliness, heartbreak and being where we were, when we were. I suppose that's why I was thrilled when you invited me to New York to spend some quality time together. Now we can see if what I think I feel, and perhaps what you feel, is something lasting and substantive. We both deserve the happiness that has eluded us in recent memory and not the pain that has followed us like a dark cloud.

I've sent along pictures I took of you in San Francisco that I thought you'd like to have. They came out great—an obvious reflection of the subject. See for yourself….

There's a little something extra for you in the package that I wanted you to have. It's my way of bringing what moves me in so many ways right to your doorstep.

I also bought Lisa a cute gift I saw in a shop. Hope she likes it.

Looking very much forward to meeting your daughter and seeing you soon.

Fondly,
Richard

Janine felt deeply touched by the letter and her heart melted for the man who wrote it. She knew that, regardless of everything else, there was something between them that neither could walk away from—at least not yet.

Maybe never, as they sorted out the depth of feelings tested against the realities of their lives, histories and circumstances that went well beyond their control.

Janine lifted the small package addressed to her and opened it. Inside a box was a CD. It was *Sarah Vaughan's Greatest Hits*. Janine smiled, thinking of when she had heard this remarkable woman's voice at Richard's house. She held the CD up to her chest, knowing her mother was somewhere up above, approving.

Janine grabbed the other small packet addressed to Lisa. She shook it, trying to guess what was inside, quickly realizing she didn't have a clue. *Now, what would he be getting my sweet pea?* she wondered keenly.

Lisa was in her room. A coloring book and crayons were spread over her bed with Lisa and Murphy in the center of it all.

"I have something for you, sweet pea." Janine got her daughter's attention.

When Lisa looked at the wrapped box, her eyes shone like headlights. "What is it?" she asked, practically springing from the bed.

"I don't know, honey. It's from my friend in California."

"You mean the man who's coming to visit us?"

Janine nodded. "Yes."

She was not sure how Lisa would take it when she first approached the subject of Richard. Since her divorce, Janine had never gone out on a date with anyone so much as twice, much less been intimate with a man. For the most part it had been just her and Lisa. On the other hand, John had kept a steady string of women like a revolving door for his daughter to meet.

Remarkably, Lisa had seemed to take it in stride, as though it was what she'd come to expect of men.

Or at least her father.

Will she hold me to a higher standard than John? Janine asked herself with some disquiet. She pictured Lisa viewing Richard as somehow intruding on their lives, thereby never truly giving him a real chance as Lisa apparently had John's girlfriend, Bernadette.

Moreover, Janine thought about the effect her becoming involved with someone other than Lisa's father might have on the relationship with her daughter. The last thing she ever wanted was to sacrifice the quality of their mother-daughter connection—not even for Richard, something Janine was sure he could relate to with the memories of his own father-daughter bond.

At least in the short term Janine was certain that her fears were exaggerated. Lisa had been quite curious about Richard, asking all kinds of questions. All the while she had shown no resentment or rejection of having Richard in Janine's life. In fact, Lisa had even embraced the possibility that what they had could turn into love, marriage and a second daddy for her.

While such notions were premature at this point, Janine felt relieved nevertheless that Lisa seemed to give her tacit approval of the special friendship before ever meeting Richard. It also bode well for the future should such a friendship give way to anything lasting between them.

Lisa ripped the paper off the box, showing little patience for maintaining the suspense. It reminded Janine of her exuberant anticipation and joy when opening the gifts she had brought Lisa from California.

There was a seashell inside the box. It was painted in three different shades of blue.

"It's from the ocean," Janine said, pleased. "If you put it up to your ear, you'll be able to hear the sounds of waves crashing against the shore."

Lisa put the shell to hear ear and listened. She quickly broke into a big grin. "I can hear it, Mommy!"

"Let me see if I can."

Janine enjoyed these shared special moments with her daughter. She knew how quickly children became adults and were no longer there for such innocent fun and frolic. That is—she thought sadly of Sheena and many others like her hit by fatal tragedy—if they were fortunate enough to reach adulthood at all.

Putting the shell to her ear, Janine heard the hollow sound, as if in a deep cavern. It reminded her of when she and Richard were walking along the beach and the sweet sounds of the gentle, swaying ocean sang in the background, as if to forever remind them of their time spent together.

Lisa quickly reclaimed her prized possession and Janine went back to the living room, content to see her daughter happy and grateful that Richard had been so thoughtful to buy her something.

Janine opened the manila envelope and pulled out a framed 11 x 14-inch picture of herself. The first thought entering her mind was that she could hardly believe the stunning image was *her face*. It was almost surreal with its vivid colors, pronounced yet muted features, and larger-than-life appeal. It said as much about the photographer and his talents, she thought, as the subject.

Janine removed several 5 x 7-inch prints of herself, laughing while viewing them, as she remembered the joy that had possessed her from top to bottom being in Richard's company when they were taken.

Suddenly she longed to be with Richard again in every way and Janine found herself counting down the hours till his arrival.

She phoned him that night, desperately needing to hear his voice as the next best thing to being in his protective arms.

"Thank you for the pictures," she told him. "Especially the framed one. Lisa thought I looked like a model."

Richard laughed sensuously. "She's not alone, there. Only, you look better than any damn model I've ever seen."

"Flattery will get you everywhere, baby," Janine said teasingly, enjoying being thought of as attractive, maybe even beautiful, in Richard's eyes. Especially when she had often felt just the opposite during her marriage.

Still, Janine couldn't help but feel that she could never quite measure up to the *unreal* beauty of Kassandra. She wondered how often Richard had compared them in his mind and if the comparison could ever be a fair one to her.

I'd rather not have to compete with Kassandra in the looks department or otherwise, Janine told herself insecurely, though a part of her wanted to believe she was as attractive as any woman when at her best.

"I'm counting on it," she heard Richard say, feeling the strong desire for her in his inflection.

I feel it, too, darling, the voice in Janine's head told him, and it was reinforced by a renewed surge of adrenaline. Forcing her mind in another direction, she uttered, "Lisa loved the seashell."

"I thought she might," he said. "When I was a kid I collected them. I thought I could use the shells to help me to locate some hidden treasure." He paused. "Maybe in a strange but wonderful way, I have."

The soft patter of Janine's heart skipped a beat or two—she was happy to be thought of as someone's discovered *hidden treasure.*

"I've missed you, Richard," she cooed unabashedly.

"I've missed you, too, baby."

The words settled in for a while between them, as if they spoke for themselves and nothing else was needed.

Janine thought about the dilemma she'd created with Richard and Callister-Reynolds. It made her think about how odd life could be when circumstances arose that could change one's entire perspective and reshape lives and events forever.

She wondered how such serendipitous events would shape their lives when the final pages were written. When the last photographs were taken....

"You know, I'm afraid that when I see you, Janine," voiced Richard, his tone as smooth as could be, "I won't want to let you out of my sight ever again."

"Hmm. That works both ways," Janine said with a catch of her breath, and thought warmly, *A man of my dreams.* Suddenly she imagined herself being cuddled by Richard while kissing him passionately. Then she thought of them making love, causing goose bumps to form on her skin. Showing unrestrained yearning, she murmured into the phone, "I wish you were here right now, baby...."

"Oh, yeah?" Richard cadenced lasciviously into the phone.

"Yes," Janine reiterated, "instead of thousands of miles away."

"Now, be careful what you wish for," he warned deliberately. "You just might get it for longer than you possibly know what to do with."

It was a warning that Janine took to heart. She wondered if Richard was challenging her, himself—or both of them—to a serious, long-term commitment.

Might they both get everything they bargained for in each other—and then some?

Maybe that's what all this was leading to, Janine mused wistfully. Finding untold joy at the end of the rainbow. Dreams that *really* came true, like Dorothy's in *The Wizard of Oz.*

Right now, Janine couldn't imagine wishing for anything

or anyone more than one incredibly handsome, intelligent and talented man named Richard Lowrey to get along with her wonderful daughter.

She wanted only for them to coexist harmoniously in the complex scheme of things in her life.

Inside, Janine knew that the rough waves that lay ahead were such that they might never get the chance to put the plan into action.

Chapter 33

On their tenth anniversary, Kassandra had presented Richard with an oil portrait of herself. It had completely floored him, as the painting was stunning in its portrayal of her almost classical beauty and refined features. The blend of deep brown and tender russet colors of her painted eyes was enchanting, much as Kassandra's real eyes were, only magnified in their exaggerated intensity. Her intricately woven braids hung beautifully across bare shoulders, framing the perfect tautness of her high-cheeked face with its light golden-brown complexion. The fullness of Kassandra's breasts was outlined in a red silk dress that contoured every curve of her body.

There was a gothic feel to the painting, as if it had been rendered in the nineteenth century, thought Richard. A gold-painted wooden frame, its architecture superb, enhanced the image. He could almost imagine the portrait on display at an

African-American art museum, so captivating was the image before him.

"Do you like it?" Kassandra asked anxiously.

Richard was virtually speechless, totally intoxicated by the painting, but more so with the woman herself.

"I love it!" he avowed jubilantly.

She raised her cheeks into a delightful smile. "The painting was done from a photograph you took of me last year during our trip to Jamaica. Do you remember?"

Richard reacted gleefully. "Like it was yesterday," he told her, thinking back.

It was but one of many photographs he had taken of Kassandra in her homeland, dating back to the day they had first met. She had proven to be a natural before the lens, with beauty and grace, which made her all the more photogenic, and his job easy.

Yet even pictures of Kassandra had to take a back seat to the painting Richard admired now, with its larger-than-life image, wonderful mixture of oil colors and three-dimensional, vibrant presentation.

"Somehow the painting seemed like a fitting way to capture that wonderful occasion," Kassandra said, "and ten wonderful years of marriage."

Richard knew it was something that he would always treasure. Like the woman herself—the love of his life. It was an anniversary he would remember forever.

Richard gave Kassandra a grateful look. "Thank you, darling," he said to her, emotion nearly overwhelming him. "What can I say? Everything about the painting, its subject, is stunning."

Kassandra fluttered her lashes lovingly. "And everything about you, my man, has been *equally* stunning these past ten years," she declared. "I could not have asked for a better man to share my life with and father my child."

"And I couldn't have asked for a better woman to be my wife and the mother of my daughter than you, Kass." Richard felt warm tears slide down his cheeks as he reached out to his wife. "I love you so much, baby."

"I know," she told him softly. "About as much as I love you."

Kassandra moved into Richard's waiting arms and they kissed with the urgency of the moment and held one another as if both somehow sensed that each and every precious moment together must be cherished and explored to the fullest.

Chapter 34

Kassandra's mesmerizing eyes shone down on Richard with the radiance she had in life. Richard stared at the oil portrait sentimentally, distraught with emotion and a renewed sense of guilt.

"Why the hell did you have to die, Kass?" he asked out loud, as if she could hear the words and feel his tremendous pain. "I loved you so damn much. I never wanted to be with anyone else. I didn't think there ever could be anyone else...."

Richard paused and dabbed at his eyes where tears had formed with nowhere to go but out.

"I've been so lonely, baby," he told her. "So disillusioned about everything. Nothing seemed important to me once you went away." He sniffled, moving closer to the painting that hung on the bedroom wall like a permanent fixture. "Someone else has come into my life, Kass—much the same way you did—without warning or expectation. Her name is Janine Henderson. I think you would approve of her. She's like you in the best ways, even if she could never take your place. She would never try to. Janine is very much her own woman. As you were."

Richard found it hard, indeed damn near impossible, to tell Kassandra about another woman—something he never thought he'd do. Yet he knew there was no other choice if he were to continue to make a new life for himself while reconciling with his previous life—the life he'd had with his beloved Kassandra and their wonderful daughter, Sheena. Deep down he was sure Kass would understand, wanting him to be happy and to live a life that stood for something other than grief, regret and self-pity. But another part of Richard somehow felt the need to explain what he was feeling, to convince Kassandra that he was doing the right thing by getting on with his life.

"I care for Janine a lot," he said, peering at Kassandra's painted soulful eyes. "I may even love her. She may love me. We have to see how that plays out. Janine has a daughter named Lisa, the same age Sheena was when—" Richard sighed sentimentally. "I guess what I'm trying to say is that Janine and I may have a future together and I wanted to let you know that I'll never abandon you, Kass, or what we had with each other. It's been three long years since you and Sheena left and I think it's time for me to move on as best I can. To make something of the life you helped create in me."

Richard took in the beautiful face of the woman who had once been everything to him, knowing it could no longer suffice in fulfilling the needs and desires he had as a human being and a man. It was Janine who now filled his thoughts with longing, togetherness, excitement, possibilities and, yes, very possibly, love.

Richard met Kassandra's steady gaze head-on and realized he felt no shame or regret in admitting his feelings for another woman. It was as if he had suddenly come to terms with the past—and his past love—and could now move forward without compunction or hesitation.

Even if he didn't know exactly what the future held, or where such a future might carry him.

Near or far.

Here or there.

With Janine or on his own.

He would take one day at a time and let it happen as it was meant to.

It was nearly nine in the morning when Richard rang Henry's doorbell. Kimble was at his side, resisting the urge to run from the porch and chase a squirrel that was doing a sprint toward a maple tree.

Henry opened the door, yawning. "What time is it?"

"Time to get up, Pops," Richard said lightly. Since retiring, his father had, deservedly so, gotten rid of his clocks, no longer bound by the rules of time and schedules.

Kimble barked and slipped past Henry inside. Richard followed.

"Behave yourself, boy," Richard yelled at the dog, who had scooted into the kitchen as if hot on the trail of a cat.

"He'll be all right," Henry said, unworried.

Richard favored his father. "I need to leave Kimble with you for a few days."

Henry's left brow lifted crookedly. "Oh? What's up?"

"Going to New York," he said calmly.

"Hell, it's about damn time." Henry grinned excitedly. "I'm glad, son."

"And I'm nervous as hell," admitted Richard, butterflies filling his stomach like hotcakes. He was not sure how this trip would fare, even with the best of intentions. He didn't know if he was cut out for this type of long-distance romance thing anymore. What if the bright lights and big-city atmosphere didn't work for him? He was not particularly comfortable visiting New York City, associating writing success with personal failure. He knew he had to get past this. If not, there was no telling how it might impact his relationship with Janine.

"I know everything will work out just fine with you and Janine." Henry said, trying to encourage him. "And don't worry about Kimble. I'll take good care of him."

"I know," Richard said confidently. He was less confident about going to New York—to Janine's world—where he was no longer in his comfort zone. He was worried that the magic that had existed between them in idyllic Pebble Beach might no longer be there in the Big Apple. More than two weeks apart seemed almost like a lifetime, making them practically strangers again, forcing them to essentially start from scratch—along with all the second-guessing and uncertainties that accompanied it.

Richard turned his thoughts toward Janine's daughter. He wondered if he could relate to her as he had his own daughter and how Lisa would relate to him. There was a fear that she would see him as trying to encroach upon her father's territory.

Richard conceded that perhaps in some ways he might be stepping on the other man's shoes in entering Janine and Lisa's lives. But that simply came with the territory, just like his own past, which they would have to deal with. For his part, Richard believed that he could come to accept both Janine and Lisa for who they were, independent of Kass and Sheena, and more importantly, what Janine and her daughter represented for the future and his life.

Richard's mind moved on to the other matter weighing on him: Callister-Reynolds. It was time to square things up with them, he knew. Honor his commitment, about which they had not always been patient, though they had stuck with him in spite of his inability to finish the books in a timely fashion.

"Can I get you something to eat?" asked Henry, almost as an afterthought. "Drink?"

Richard waved him off. "I'm cool. My flight leaves in a little over an hour. I'll have something on the plane."

"Where are you staying?"

Richard knew the question was not one of a prying nature, but was rather fatherly concern in case of an emergency.

"I made reservations at the Hyatt in Manhattan."

He had volunteered to stay at a hotel, figuring it would be best all around, especially for Janine's daughter. It was enough that she would be meeting him for the first time as a man her mother was romantically involved with. There was no reason to further complicate matters by staying with them. Janine had not argued against it.

"Just give me a quick buzz to say you made it safely," requested Henry. "I don't want to jinx you or anything, but I'm not too happy with the problems they seem to be having with planes these days—sometimes before they ever get off the ground."

Richard smiled from one side of his lips. "I'll be fine, Pops," he assured him, promising, "I'll call you when I get there."

Henry's face wrinkled. "You better get going then. Be sure and tell Janine and her little girl I said hello."

"I will."

The two men held each other's gaze affectionately for a time of thoughtful regard, and then hugged tightly.

A short while later Richard was aboard the airplane, anticipating his journey across the country. He had not been to New York in five years. He didn't expect much had changed.

Upon further reflection, he realized much had indeed changed since then, in more ways than one. In his personal life, Kassandra and Sheena were gone, while Janine and her daughter, Lisa, were very much alive.

Richard found himself pondering if he would be able to successfully have a relationship with the latter while he was still heartbroken about the former.

Chapter 35

Janine could hear the erratic beat of her heart as Richard made his way past other passengers and approached them. Minutes earlier she and Lisa had watched planes land at La Guardia and tried to pick out which one Richard might be on. Janine felt then relieved that he had made it safely, excited to see him again and nervous as to what to expect of him as well as of herself.

Richard, looking fit in a short-sleeved, blue-and-red polo shirt and black gabardine trousers, beamed as he approached them. An ink-black tote bag was strapped over his shoulder. "Hey, Janine," he said coolly. "What's up, baby?"

"Hi, Richard," Janine responded, feeling as though she was about to burst with joy through the yellow knit dress she wore.

He wrapped his arms around her unabashedly and then planted a short but sensual kiss on her mouth. His spicy cologne penetrated her nostrils pleasingly.

Richard then hugged Janine again and whispered, "I've

been thinking about you practically every minute since the day you left California." He made a humming sound. "All right, even before then."

Janine gave him a cheery smile. "I've been thinking about you, too," she happily admitted. More than he knew, and for different reasons.

Richard pulled away from her, as if remembering that they had company. He looked down at Lisa, in a pink sweater and blue denim jeans, who looked up with just as much fascination and curiosity. Her hair was in a ponytail, unlike Janine's, which was down.

"And you must be Lisa," Richard said sweetly.

"Yeah." She giggled.

"This is Richard." Janine said. "He's come to visit us all the way from California."

"Hi," Lisa said, blushing.

"Hi, back, pretty young lady." Richard gave Janine a wink, then turned back to Lisa smilingly.

"How's Henry?" Janine asked, feeling as though she had become connected to him as well.

Lisa crinkled her nose. "Who's Henry?"

"He's my father," Richard told her proudly. "And he's doing well. Pops wanted me to tell you both hello and that he wished he'd been able to come along for the ride."

"Have you ever been to Disneyland?" Lisa asked, batting curly lashes at Richard.

"As a matter of fact, I have," he said animatedly. "Several times. I'll tell you all about it."

By the warm, eager smile on Lisa's face, Janine knew then that her daughter had found a friend in Richard.

"Let's get out of this place," Janine said to all, noting the throngs of people and wanting to spend some private time with Richard.

* * *

They took a cab to Richard's hotel in midtown Manhattan, so he could check in and freshen up, then headed for Janine's apartment. It was hard having Richard stay in a hotel when it would have been much more convenient all the way around for him to stay at her place. But they both agreed that it might be too much, too soon for Lisa if he were to spend the night. At least at the beginning.

This, in spite of the fact that Janine would have liked nothing better than for Richard to share her bed every night he was in town.

"We're here," she announced colorfully, climbing from the cab that had pulled to the curb in front of her building.

Janine felt a bit self-conscious about her unimpressive, un-inspiring residence in the heart of the overcrowded city of New York, compared to Richard's lovely, spacious, expensive home surrounded by pine trees and shrubbery, with the beach and a sea of beautiful blue water in his backyard. But she knew deep down her concern was unwarranted. Richard was not the type of man to pass judgment or consider one person better or worse than another based on material items or lack thereof. His unas-suming nature was one of the things she loved most about him.

"This is great," Richard said sincerely, once inside. "It speaks of New York City and its unique charms and heritage."

"Maybe," Janine said, amused and relieved at the same time. "But to us, it's just home sweet home."

Murphy came bounding down the stairs like her tail was on fire, and jumped up on the couch.

"That's my cat," Lisa said merrily. "Her name's Murphy."

Richard smiled and waved awkwardly at her. "Hey, Murphy."

The cat, her brown-green eyes alight, seemed intrigued by the first-time visitor.

"Mommy, can I show Richard my room?" Lisa shouted, not shy about commanding attention. Or stealing it.

Before Janine could respond, Richard indicated, "I'd love to see your room…if it's all right with your mother."

"Fine," Janine said, pretending to feel left out. "If that's the way it's going to be." In reality, she couldn't have been more pleased that Lisa had taken a liking to Richard, and vice versa.

Lisa ended up giving Richard a tour of the entire place, short though it was. Afterward they had dinner, which Janine had made beforehand, counting on Richard being hungry following his long flight. It was nothing extravagant—baked chicken, greens, rice, gravy and biscuits. He seemed to enjoy the meal, for which Janine felt thankful, remembering his own tasty cooking and determined to try and keep up.

Seeking to impress their guest, Lisa was on her best behavior at the table. *Thank goodness for miracles,* Janine thought wryly.

At one point, Lisa asked Richard, "Do you have any kids?"

He gazed at Janine and she read his thoughts, painful as they were. She had not told Lisa about his family's tragedy, fearing it was neither the time nor her place to do so.

"I had a daughter once," Richard said, a quiver to his voice. "About your age. She died."

"How?" came the curious question of a child.

"Lisa—" Janine tried to admonish her for prying into dangerous and sorrowful territory.

"It's all right," Richard said, as if he felt this was something he should say to her. "My daughter and wife were killed in a car accident. Sometimes people are taken away just like that, even when they shouldn't be."

The gravity of this seemed to weigh on Lisa and she found

herself unable to respond, as if there were no words that seemed quite right. She just stared at him.

"They're in heaven now," he said with certainty.

"That's good," Lisa said, spirited again, knowing it was a good place to be when no longer of this earth. Just as quickly and perhaps seeking a more comfortable topic, she asked, "Do you want to see my shell?"

Richard grinned. "Sure."

Janine admired the ease with which he was able to shift his emotions in communicating with Lisa, and could only imagine how loving and tolerant Richard had been with his own daughter.

After Lisa was put to bed, Janine and Richard had their first time alone since he'd arrived in New York.

"Come here, baby," Richard prompted Janine in the living room.

She followed his command, moving into his waiting, strong and comforting arms.

He wasted little time in kissing her. It was a long and hard kiss, nearly making Janine melt on her feet. Or float on air. She wasn't sure which, only that it felt great.

"I've been waiting to do that all day," Richard murmured guiltlessly.

"Hope it was worth the wait," Janine teased him, licking her lips and tingling like crazy inside.

He pressed his mouth against hers again, this time more softly, sweetly. "More than worth it," he promised, looking into her eyes. "Just like seeing you again, Janine."

She felt her temperature definitely start to rise, murmuring, "I see you're as charming as ever, Richard."

"I can be a lot more charming than that," he declared desirously.

Richard moved to kiss Janine again, only she had beaten

him to the punch this time, grabbing his shirt and lunging toward him. They kissed each other for what seemed like forever, as if making up for the time apart. Janine could feel Richard's hardness pressed against her body, aching to get out. When he put his hand to one of her breasts and began caressing the nipple, Janine felt an electrical charge surge throughout her body, filling her with a wanton craving to give herself to him—and take as much in return.

But a cooler head prevailed for the moment, and Janine, biting her lip, nervously removed Richard's hand, afraid that Lisa might catch them. Though her daughter was usually a sound sleeper, Janine feared that this would probably be the one time Lisa wanted Mommy to come tuck her in. Or, Janine could imagine, Richard to read her a bedtime story.

"We'd better chill things till we go back to your hotel," she told him, as anxious to be with Richard as she sensed he was to be with her.

"All right," he agreed patiently. "So, when will that be?" Richard favored her greedily.

She sighed, feeling his yearning, which surely matched her own. "As soon as I can get someone over here to look after Lisa."

Janine called the sitter, who lived two blocks away.

The retired schoolteacher and widow arrived ten minutes later. Phyllis Fisher was a bit on the plump side, with fine walnut-colored skin and short, curly, snowy white hair. She had raised five children of her own and had eight grandchildren and two great-grandchildren.

If Phyllis was a bit surprised to see that Janine had male company, she didn't say so. She had never known Janine to have a date since she'd begun caring for Lisa. While Phyllis may have thought it odd that a young, healthy, attractive woman seemed satisfied with no romance in her life, she never offered her opinion.

For that, Janine was grateful. She was also happy that she had waited until someone truly worthwhile entered her life, no matter how long it had taken.

Richard treated Phyllis as though she were his own grand-mother—with respect and admiration. Phyllis responded in kind, as if an old and wise relative or close family friend.

"You be sure to take good care of Janine, young man," she told him firmly. "She's far too special for anything less."

Richard showed his teeth and was deferential. "Yes, ma'am," he said. "And I agree, Janine's definitely one special lady."

Phyllis nodded approvingly, smiling at Janine and saying, "I think I like him."

Janine responded matter-of-factly, "I know I do."

She was amazed and excited that Richard had fit so effort-lessly within her world, more so than she feared she had within his. It was almost like Richard had become a new man, with renewed confidence and purpose in life.

Maybe this would make it easier when talking to him about Callister-Reynolds.

But right now it was their time to reacquaint themselves emotionally and intimately with each other.

And nothing, Janine prayed, would stand in their way.

Chapter 36

They barely made it inside the room before devouring each other like hungry lions. It had been more than two weeks since Janine and Richard had last made love, but it might as well have been two years for the raw sense of urgency and delirium that had them actually ripping off the other's clothes as they moved unavoidably toward the king-size bed. Janine had never known such a fervent appetite for another human being in her life, one she found to be beguiling. Nor, frankly, had she ever experienced the thrill of being wanted so much by another.

These sensations left her light-headed and in need of a quick fix. A fix that only one man was capable of providing.

Richard, sensing her overpowering need mirroring his own, brought his face to Janine's in an almost smothering kiss as they sank to the bed. Their nude, taut bodies were perfectly aligned and in harmony. He left Janine breathless as his torrid kisses trailed down her flesh methodically yet deliberately.

Within moments of Richard putting his face between her thighs, Janine climaxed violently, shuddering from head to toe. She would surely have done so again had she not wanted to return the favor. She took him in her mouth and felt Richard shiver with delight, his breathing labored, before he, too, soon exploded in a body-jerking orgasm.

"I want to make love to you now," Richard said with a grunt. "*Real* love."

"I want you, too," Janine said breathlessly, her heartbeat echoing in her ears.

They made love to each other, neither holding anything back. It was as if both had been reborn and they were experiencing the exhilarating fulfillment of intimacy for the first time.

Only, it turned into a second and third time, until they lost count of the times each had pleasured the other and had been pleasured.

When they were totally spent, Janine suddenly felt as though anything was possible. Richard Edgar Lowrey was not only a superb lover but a superb giver as well. He understood what it meant to totally appease and be fully appeased.

Janine felt a little envious at the thought that it had been another woman who had first benefited from Richard's gentle affections and unselfish devotion. His thorough lovemaking and sensual love. His tender touch and manly smell.

Janine wondered about the strangeness of these feelings under the circumstances. She questioned if she even had the right to envy Kassandra.

Or did she simply wish to fill her shoes?

Shouldn't she just be satisfied that Richard was ten times the man and lover John ever was?

Janine knew even then that it might not last. She tried to turn her mind off and simply enjoy the moment.

And the man.

"Stay the night?" Richard spoke softly, his eyes registering a desperate quality.

"I can't," Janine said regretfully, ignoring the cravings of her body and mind. "I didn't make arrangements for Phyllis to stay and watch Lisa overnight." She snuggled against him. "Besides, I don't think it would look too good if I showed up in the morning to greet my daughter all sleepy-eyed and in a state of perpetual bliss."

He kissed her shoulder begrudgingly. "Yeah, I know."

She kissed his nose, hating that they had to spend even one minute apart while he was in New York. "How long will you be able to stay in New York?"

Richard thought about it. "Long enough, I suppose." He smiled awkwardly. "You trying to get rid of me already, baby?"

Janine colored. "Of course not, silly. I just want us to spend as much time as we can together. I want you to get to know Lisa...." She hoped that didn't scare him off.

Then there was the issue of the books he owed Callister-Reynolds, Janine thought uneasily—and the high stakes for them both.

Richard kissed the tender spot above Janine's breasts, drawing a sigh from her lips. The he licked one of her nipples, watched it rise, and licked it again, the sweet pleasure making it hard for Janine to concentrate on anything else but the moment at hand.

"I want nothing better than to get to know *both* of you," he told her through clenched teeth.

Janine bit her tongue and forced herself to move away from his exquisite attention. "I think you already know quite a bit about me, Mr. Lowrey," she told him carnally.

Richard grinned sinfully. "And I like every inch of what I know about you, baby." He kissed her right breast, then her left.

Janine basked under the heat of Richard's wandering eyes and lips. Holding her breath, she forced herself to roll away from him. Standing before this sexy, beautiful man, Janine felt amazingly comfortable in her nakedness, as though they had been together for years and knew each other inside out. Over and beyond. In every nook and cranny, and more.

She regarded Richard's sinewy body and inviting posture and immediately felt a twinge of fresh desire. Janine somehow resisted, knowing it was best to go now or risk staying well into the night.

"It's really good to see you again, Richard," Janine told him in what was probably the understatement of the year. Or decade. If not the century. She leaned over and kissed him, brushing against his hard body. "*All* of you, baby."

He flashed her a wide, confident grin that told Janine he knew she was all his. And suggested that he was all hers.

Janine had conveniently arranged to take work off for the next few days, wanting to give herself and Richard every opportunity to blend both in and out of bed. Richard gave no indication he was planning to go to Callister-Reynolds and she didn't volunteer her role with the publisher as yet, holding back for as long as possible while they made the most of their personal time together. Any thoughts of this coming back to haunt her gave way to the feeling that what she and Richard had developed was stronger and more resilient than anything that might stand in their way.

Including their professional obligations.

With Lisa, they took in New York City like tourists, visiting the Rockefeller Center, the American Museum of Natural History and the Statue of Liberty, among other things. Conspicuously absent were the twin towers of the World Trade Center.

They rode the Staten Island Ferry for a spectacular view of the city's skyline. Everywhere they went, Richard brought along his camera, snapping pictures left and right like a man who knew what he was doing and did it well.

Janine wondered if he might actually do a photographic book on New York City's attractions. It seemed like a good idea, she mused, as it was one of the most dynamic cities in the world—especially from the point of view of a person of color and one whose talents were proven in capturing the heart and soul of a place.

At Lisa's request, they spent one day upstate at the county fair. Richard showed no hesitation in spoiling her as if she was his own daughter. At one point he won a big teddy bear at a basketball-shooting booth, demonstrating his skills with the ball and hoop, and presented it to an overjoyed Lisa. Janine couldn't remember a time when her daughter seemed to have such fun with someone other than her mother.

She somehow couldn't imagine Lisa being as receptive to John's girlfriend, Bernadette—though Janine knew her daughter was comfortable with the woman.

Shifting her thoughts to Richard, Janine wondered whether in his kindness toward Lisa, he was, in fact, giving her the attention and affection he was no longer able to give to his own daughter, but longed to. Lisa, Janine suspected, was soaking it all up like a sponge, due to the absence of such consideration from her own father.

Janine took none of it for granted, happy that these two important people in her life seemed to like each other just as much, and praying that nothing would change this.

Each hour of each day is a blessing to be cherished, she thought. Tomorrow would take care of itself.

In between their outings, whenever they could, Richard and Janine slipped into his room to make love and enjoy exploring each other's bodies. Their familiarity with one another had become so natural that to Janine they seemed to be able to act and react without cues or instruction. With John it had been quite the opposite. There was often no intimacy to speak of. When they had sex at all she was usually the one who initiated it and was often left unfulfilled.

Janine could never imagine such emptiness with Richard, who seemed to go out of his way in insightfulness and selflessness, as much as demonstrating unbridled desire and passion. The notion that they were only at the beginning of their journey thrilled her.

At the same time, Janine was very much enjoying each and every precious moment with this man who had opened up to her like a flower in full bloom. Richard had looked his tragedy squarely in the face and decided not to let it defeat him, because of all that he still had to offer.

In the process he had given her things that had long been missing in Janine's life: warmth, compassion and attentive affection. Maybe even love.

The fact that Richard's stay would only be temporary left Janine shaken. She honestly didn't know if their relationship could survive nearly three thousand miles of separation, even with the best of intentions.

And the baggage each carried like a thousand pounds on their shoulders.

She could only hope that at the end of the day, tragedy would turn into triumph. Sadness into happiness. Despair into delight.

Janine wanted to believe that somehow, in some way, there

would be a light at the end of the tunnel bright enough to withstand even the darkest hours of the past or future—including
the terms of Richard's contract with Callister-Reynolds.

And her role in affecting that.

Chapter 37

Richard made dinner, mastering Janine's kitchen like it was his own. The truth was that he felt as though it was home, insofar as the company he was keeping was concerned, and the fact that he was made to feel so comfortable. Janine had been everything that had attracted him to her in California, and then a whole lot more. Lisa, sweet and pretty, had eerily reminded him of Sheena.

Richard wasn't sure if his fondness for Janine and her daughter was a way of trying to recreate his family.

Or if, in fact, he had found a new family.

What was plain to him was that there was real chemistry here with Janine and Lisa and he wanted nothing more than to build upon it...and see what happened.

Following dinner, Lisa was put to bed, falling asleep immediately like a little angel. Afterward, Janine took Richard by the hand, leading him to her bedroom. A white oak dresser and chest sat on opposite walls beneath framed rustic landscapes. In the corner was an old-fashioned rocking chair. The centerpiece of the room was a queen-size water bed.

Speaking softly, Janine uttered, "If we're quiet, we can fool around a little without waking Lisa."

Richard, his libido raised to dizzying heights whenever he was near Janine, promised, "I'll be as quiet as a mouse."

He brought her body to meet his, looked into the chocolate fudge of Janine's eyes and they kissed. Richard felt her arousal as much as his own. They disrobed and sank onto the bed, each kissing different parts of the other. He caressed her firm, rounded breasts. They were perfect, he thought. Just like the lady herself. Perfect in every way.

Richard put his face between Janine's legs, seeking out that which gave her the most pleasure. Finding her clitoris, he kissed it, enjoying the feel of her in his mouth. He heard a soft gasp escape from Janine's mouth while he fulfilled her. It pleased him to please her. Within moments, her body began to shudder and he knew she was climaxing. He gripped Janine's hips firmly while continuing to ride the wave with her.

Feeling an urgent need to be deep inside her, Richard lifted up and sandwiched himself within Janine's splayed legs. He moved into her easily and they began to make love with the wonderful symmetry and passion they had become accustomed to. They met each other time and time again until reaching the ultimate height of gratification.

Their pleasure was hushed, separate and simultaneous, as an internal eruption rocked the foundation existing between them like an implosion.

Afterward they held each other for a time, their bodies slowly recovering and their labored breathing returning to normal. Neither spoke a word, for there was nothing to say that hadn't already been said in their lovemaking.

Richard ended up staying the night, though he got up early and pretended to come over after Lisa had awakened. The three of them had breakfast together.

Looking into Janine's beautiful face at the table, seeing the gleam in her eyes, Richard knew in his heart what he had believed before arriving in New York. He had fallen in love with Janine Henderson. It had only been reaffirmed these past few days.

He hadn't wanted to feel this way. Not with Kassandra still occupying the better part of his heart and soul. But Janine had done something to him, something remarkable and unimaginable—she had given Richard a new and glorious reason to feel as he did toward her.

What he didn't know for sure was where she stood regarding her feelings for him.

He had to find out, and he knew the perfect place to do so.

Chapter 38

When Richard suggested they go to the Empire State Building, Janine had no idea what he had in mind. She'd seen *Sleepless In Seattle.* But she had also seen *King Kong.* Visiting the world-famous landmark was anything but predictable.

Janine had been there only once before when she and Lisa had first moved to New York City. They'd gone to the observatory on the eighty-sixth floor, not daring to go any higher.

Richard and Janine took the elevator all the way to the top. The day was sunny and warm, with just a few clouds dotting the blue sky, as if purely for show. The panoramic view of the city was spectacular, if not a little dizzying to Janine from that height. She had to admit it was also very romantic, especially in the company of someone so special.

Richard had simply asked her to wear something nice. Janine settled on a purple silk Fuji blouse with a black choker and matching earrings, and a black skirt, along with low-heeled pumps. She wore her hair down, just as she knew he preferred it. She marveled at Richard, resplendent in a beige blazer, an ash-blue shirt, caramel-colored pleat-front twill trousers and brown loafers. His handsome face shone brightly.

As Janine stilled her nerves and turned to New York's skyline, Richard reentered her line of vision. He took Janine's hands and gazed down at the uncertain face before him.

Janine could feel a slight trembling in his fingers as Richard said evenly, "I love you, Janine. At least, I think that's what I'm feeling. I thought I'd never feel this way again. It can only be love...."

Janine's heart skipped a beat and she tried to get used to the word *love* again, as if she was hearing it for the first time. With John, the word had meant nothing other than a way to try and manipulate her into turning her back on his lies and infidelity. But she knew it meant something entirely different to Richard. He was not the type of person to ever take the word or his feelings lightly.

And neither was she.

Janine held his gaze. "I think I love you, too, Richard," she understated, knowing in her heart it was the real thing and not some sort of schoolgirl infatuation. *A girl has to hold back just a little*, she thought craftily.

Till now, Janine hadn't been willing to confront this realization for fear that she would only end up being hurt. Or hurting him. Or having her daughter hurt. She couldn't live with any of those hurts.

She wondered if he could.

Richard smiled warily, with an upward curve of his generous mouth. "Oh, you *think* so, huh?"

"How about I *know* so," Janine told him straight out, unwilling to deny the complete truth any longer.

"Even better for this gentleman to hear!" He grinned more easily now, leaned forward and kissed her lips heartily. "Tasty, too."

She smiled, kissing him again, and then used her pinkie to wipe lipstick from his mouth. "So are you, baby."

He loves me, Janine thought dreamily, her heart still racing nonstop. She didn't want to waste thoughts thinking beyond that for now. She just wanted to savor the moment for all it was worth.

"How much does Lisa know about us?" Richard asked, a serious look in his eyes. "About me?"

"She knows that we're seeing each other," Janine responded hesitantly. "Like girlfriend and boyfriend, minus the explicit details. She also knows that you live on the other side of the country. And that you're a professional photographer. And a damned good basketball player who likes seashells."

Richard gave a brief smile at Janine's words. He took one of her hands again and, after a moment or two, said evenly, "I'd like you and Lisa to move to California."

California? Janine's eyes grew wide with surprise…and questions entered her mind. She wondered what capacity he was referring to in asking them to move to California. When and where? Even *why* seemed an inescapable thing to ponder, under the circumstances.

"Not sure we could afford that," Janine tried to say lightly, though she felt the seriousness of the request from the rigidity of Richard's posture. "Not on an editor's salary."

Unlike writers, who could live anywhere.

Janine felt the dampness of her palm in Richard's large hand. *Is he asking me to quit my job?* What could she and Lisa possibly live on in another state?

Surely not his earnings, Janine thought. Which were on

hold at the moment until he got back on the Callister-Reynolds bandwagon.

Richard favored her in earnest, loosening his grip on Janine's hand. "I think you misunderstood me, baby. I wasn't referring to your simply relocating across the country and looking for a place to live."

Janine elevated a brow. "Are you asking me to move in with you, Richard...?"

He nodded firmly. "Yes. There's plenty of room for you, Lisa and me." He added assuredly, "We can be happy together, Janine. I know it."

"I'm sure we could—" she stated flatly and sucked in a deep breath.

Richard read the hesitancy in her voice. "But...?"

Janine licked her lips, weighing her words carefully. "But we haven't even known each other for a month, Richard," she uttered realistically. "Don't you think that's a little soon to start thinking about living together?" She assumed that was the gist of the request, as opposed to marriage—which couldn't be taken lightly in and of itself.

"Not really," came Richard's reply, as though he'd given this plenty of coherent thought. "Some people know each other for years before they decide to live together—only to find out they didn't really know each other at all, turning their so-called relationship into a disaster. It's what you feel in your heart that counts, baby girl. It doesn't matter how long it takes to feel it. Or how short a time it takes."

Janine found it hard to argue against this logic. She had waited much longer before she'd started living with John. Yet she had failed to see that they were never meant to be together.

Until they no longer were.

With Richard, it seemed as if they really had climbed

mountains in just over three weeks, she thought. But she still wasn't quite certain whether that meant they were truly ready to live in the same house.

His house.

Kassandra's house.

Another fear Janine had was that maybe living together in Pebble Beach would actually change the way they felt about one another for the worse rather than for the better. Being in such close proximity and on the other side of the country…

Instead of on *this* side.

Am I prepared to drop everything for this brother? Janine asked herself, peering into his wondrous eyes and keen stare.

She found herself fumbling with her words. "I live in New York, Richard. My job's here. Lisa's school…"

"You can find another job," he countered, as if it was the simplest thing to do. "Lisa can enter another school."

"It's not that easy, honey," Janine told him as much as herself.

"Why not?" Richard frowned. "If we really *love* each other we should be together—don't you think?"

Janine batted her eyelashes. "You mean together in California." Her brow wrinkled. "Why not New York?"

Richard gazed out at the endless sky. "This is a great city, don't get me wrong," he said in a wavering voice, "but I don't belong here. At least, not on a full-time basis." He turned to Janine. "And I'm not sure I can deal with a long-distance relationship where we see each other once a month and on holidays, if we're lucky."

Somehow Janine had known they would end up at this crossroads. It had only been a matter of time. It was a moment where distance threatened to drive a wedge between them like a wall separating two rooms. Yet she, too, believed that sustaining any type of serious relationship while living on opposite coasts would be difficult, if not next to impossible. Many people had tried it. Most had failed, no matter their good intentions.

Janine had to wonder if they were doomed from the start in this relationship. Much like two ill-fated strangers finding love aboard the *Titanic*—only to have it sink in deep waters.

Did they have to live together on his terms—in his California—or not at all? It was a position she hated being in.

In the back of Janine's mind was the fact that Kassandra had succumbed to Richard's wishes and given up Jamaica to be with her man. She had sacrificed everything for him, but at a heavy price, dying a horrible and premature death.

Do I really want to follow in her footsteps? Janine wondered, unnerved.

She felt uncomfortable at the pressure of somehow trying to live up to Kassandra's legacy.

It was something Janine feared was doomed to failure, thereby making her wonder if she should even try.

"Can I think about this, Richard?" Janine looked up at him, trying to stay steady. "What you're asking is pretty big in my book. There are lots of things to consider. Aside from my job, Lisa and I just moved to New York this year. I'm not sure either of us is up to starting over again so soon. And even though I have full custody of Lisa, my ex could still try to fight my taking his daughter across the country to live."

She wasn't sure how much of a legitimate concern that truly was, or even if John would have any legal ground to stand on should he try to interfere with her choice of where to live with Lisa.

What Janine did know was that she would not make a decision like this on top of the Empire State Building, where the air was thin and the atmosphere not particularly conducive to making a rational decision.

Richard put his arms around Janine, nestling her against his body. "I'm sorry, baby," he said in almost a whisper of sincerity. "I didn't mean to pressure you into a quick decision. I understand that this is something we both need more time to think about." He sighed. "The only thing I know for sure is that I love you and want us to find a way to be together. I never thought I would want or need anyone again. But I do. I need you, darling…."

Janine's eyes watered as she looked up at him. "I want and need you, too," she assured him. Perhaps more than she had ever wanted or needed anyone.

Janine pondered if that would be enough for either of them.

There were other considerations to factor in. She had a child who had to always come first—at least so long as Lisa was still a minor—even over Janine's own overpowering needs and desires. And over her love for this man, who had stolen her heart.

Then there was the noticeable fact that Richard hadn't mentioned marriage, as if the subject was totally off limits in his way of thinking. *As though he were still married to Kassandra.* Not that this was something Janine was anywhere near ready to dive back into, herself. Her disastrous marriage to John was still too fresh in her mind. Still, she wondered what Richard's thinking was on the subject. Perhaps he had only asked her to move in with him, as opposed to tying the knot, out of respect for her own misgivings about getting remarried after a failed marriage the first time around.

Yet Janine kept coming back to the notion that in his heart of hearts Richard might consider himself forever wed to his late wife—and therefore unavailable to any other woman in that regard.

Including me, she thought, feeling cold in spite of the warmth of Richard's protective embrace.

Not lost on Janine was also the very reason she had first laid eyes on Richard Lowrey. He owed Callister-Reynolds something. Unless he was prepared to pay up, the future seemed tenuous at best for both of them.

Chapter 39

Richard wondered if he had overstepped his bounds in practically insisting that Janine move to California to live with him. What the hell had he been thinking—that she would pack her bags right then and there and actually come back to California with him on the spot?

Dream on, man, he thought, angry with himself as he sat in the hotel bar.

Asking Janine to disrupt in a major way the life she had successfully made on her own without giving it much, if any, forethought, was just plain dumb.

He seriously doubted he would have reacted any differently had it been her who'd asked him to move across the country.

But I'm the one who asked her, Richard ruminated, *and I probably shouldn't have—not so soon, anyway.*

Comparing Janine's situation with Kassandra's was like comparing apples and oranges, Richard thought knowingly while nursing a drink. Yes, Kassandra had come to America to be with him, leaving behind her beloved Jamaica. But they were much younger and without serious obligations, aside from each other. Janine had her daughter to consider. And her job, which he had no damn business dismissing like it was not as important to Janine as his used to be to him. And maybe could be again someday.

The truth was, he knew practically nothing about Janine's professional life. Yes, she was an editor, but she didn't exactly go out of her way to talk about the job. How attached she was to it, if it was something she planned to build a career out of…possibly with this publisher, in particular. She obviously hadn't worked there very long. He wondered, though, if it was just long enough to keep her in New York and away from California.

If that was the case, Richard mused, feeling the bittersweet liquid drain down his throat, he hadn't left himself or her much wiggle room to keep what they had alive. Richard could no more expect Janine to walk away from her life than he was prepared to at the moment. He had no desire to leave behind the dream house he and Kassandra had carefully claimed as their own and had hoped to remain in for a lifetime.

Maybe Janine felt the same about planting roots in New York City, with neither of them willing to budge.

Troubled by this, Richard found himself wondering if it had been a mistake to come to the Big Apple in search of love and commitment from a woman he hardly knew. Richard could only hope he hadn't bitten off more than he could possibly chew.

"Would the gentleman care for some company?" the familiar voice asked dulcetly.

Richard looked up and saw Janine standing above him like an angel, a wide smile spreading from cheek to cheek. They had agreed to meet there this evening and then maybe go elsewhere for a bite to eat. As usual, she was a sight for sore eyes with that long, thick raven hair riding her shoulders like a shawl, her gorgeous and shapely body in a snug-fitting, spaghetti-strap red dress, and her deeply personal brown eyes all but making him forget about his second thoughts.

"The gentleman would *love* your company," he responded with a tender smile, standing.

They held hands and found a table, where Janine ordered a drink.

Feeling things were a bit awkward between them after their earlier encounter, Richard tried to put Janine at ease. And maybe himself, as well.

"Look, Janine…about this afternoon—"

"It's all right, Richard," she uttered understandingly. "You didn't do anything wrong. I'm sure we'll find a way to work things out." She paused, meeting his eyes tentatively. "I don't want to lose you, baby…."

He smiled at her, feeling a sense of relief and hope. "Neither do I."

Her drink came, and Richard thought about not only their future but also his future as a photographer and author. He had come to some decisions about jump-starting his career and wanted to share them with the woman who had in such a short time come to mean so much to him in so many ways. He credited Janine with getting him to pick up a camera again, in the process giving him the confidence he had sorely lacked. And along with it, the motivation and inspiration that the time was right to return to what he did best.

"I have some good news," he told her. "Well, sort of…."

"What?" Janine waited with openmouthed anticipation, as if she could read his mind. "Tell me."

Richard tasted his drink thoughtfully. "I've signed on to do some freelance photography with a couple of Bay Area magazines. May also be able to sell some stuff to the Associated Press. I've worked with them in the past."

Janine beamed. "Wonderful," she said enthusiastically. "I'm delighted to hear that, Richard."

"But that's not all," he hummed, a catch to his voice. "I'm going to see my book publisher in the morning to talk about doing two books of photographs that are way overdue...."

Richard watched anxiety fill Janine's face like a bad omen. He had expected just the opposite. Had he said something wrong? If so, he hoped she would enlighten him.

"What is it, baby?" he asked warily.

When Janine did not respond, as if a bone was caught in her throat, Richard said, perplexed, "I thought you'd be pleased. After all, you were the one to encourage me to get off my ass and get back to work. So now I'm doing just that."

Janine moistened her lips, her face still seriously strained, as if she knew something he didn't. "I am pleased," she stated raggedly. "More than you know. It's just—"

"Just *what?*" Richard leaned forward, his eyes narrowed.

Janine tasted her wine and seemed unable to look at him. Stammering, she said, "Do you think we can talk about this in your room, Richard?"

He raised his brow. "All right."

For the life of him Richard couldn't imagine what was so unsettling to her that Janine couldn't tell him there. He wondered if it could possibly have anything to do with his photography...or books.

He decided it was more likely personal in nature.

He had never known Janine to mince words since they'd met. Yet here she was, trying to arrange in her head, apparently, how best to say what was on her mind. He wondered what he was missing here.

Suddenly Richard felt an uneasiness take hold of him like a scolding parent. She's wasn't getting cold feet about *them,* was she?

Or maybe Janine was beginning to have doubts about him and his ability to regain his photography skills and career, he considered. Whatever, leaving him hanging was nerve-racking.

Richard sat on the bed, watching and waiting, trying to remain calm. Janine was standing, as if her knees had suddenly become inflexible. Their eyes locked.

"On the day we met at Pescadero Point," Janine began, her voice trembling, "it wasn't *exactly* coincidental, Richard."

"I know, I found you there, baby, remember?" he tried to say, even while wondering if maybe it hadn't been the other way around.

"Let me finish," she insisted, and gave a long sigh. "You see, I work for Callister-Reynolds."

This got Richard's attention in the least expected way.

Janine watched his reaction, pursed her lips and continued with some effort. "Dennis DeMetris asked me to go to California to try and persuade you to complete the books you still owed them, before the publisher took more drastic measures."

This can't be, thought Richard, disbelieving what he was hearing. But the words he heard told him otherwise. He found himself virtually speechless with shock and disappointment. It was as if he had suddenly entered the *Twilight Zone.* Only, there was nothing supernatural about this.

When Richard's voice finally surfaced, he said emphatically, "You mean this whole thing between us was just a damn charade to *trick* me into abiding by the terms of my contract?"

"No, baby! It's not like that at all!" Janine cried, fidgeting.

"I had every intention of telling you why I was there. But…things began happening so fast between us, I couldn't think straight. Things that I hadn't counted on. I became attracted to you… It made it harder to want to put a damper on what had been so beautiful…."

Richard digested these last words, but found that they meant nothing to him at the moment other than empty, hollow sounds. He felt nothing other than betrayal and anger over his own failure to see through her ruse.

"You let me fall in love with you," he spat, "and led me to think you actually felt the same for me, when all you really wanted was to use my family's tragedy and my personal grief for your own damn self-serving purposes?"

"It wasn't like that, Richard," Janine insisted, desperation in her tone. "I didn't want to make matters worse by telling you some story that you probably wouldn't have believed. I tried to coax you into resuming your photography and working on another book, hoping that would be enough without tarnishing what we had experienced in those few wonderful days. Then, when I knew I had to come clean, I tried, and you wouldn't allow me to."

Richard vaguely remembered that, but as far as he was concerned it was inadequate as it related to the bigger picture. Everything he'd thought they had was a pathetic lie. He blamed himself for not seeing this coming before it boiled over into this sorry-assed attempt at covering her tracks. If only he'd been sharp enough to avoid being blindsided like a deer caught in headlights.

But I was too busy feeling sorry for myself and letting my emotions get in the way of common sense.

This wasn't even about him and her. But it sure as hell felt like it. It wasn't even about him and Kassandra, per se.

It was all about Callister-Reynolds and the bottom line.

They didn't give a damn about him losing the loves of his life. Or needing a satisfactory period—his own time and pace—to mourn their loss. It was all about *money,* either making more or getting back what they felt they were owed. When they couldn't get him to cooperate with their pressure tactics, a more subtle approach was used. They'd decided to send a pretty woman with a nice body and deceptive charm to seduce him into compliance.

There were words for women like that, Richard thought, looking at Janine angrily. Women who were paid for sexual favors, even if he wasn't the one to hand her the cash. She had used him and his emotions, all the same, for her own deceitful agenda—so the shoe fit, as far as he was concerned.

In spite of the strong animosity that raced through Richard like a fever, there was something deep inside him that found it hard to believe Janine had somehow engineered this romance under false pretenses, and without sincerity in her words and actions. He wondered if he could possibly have been so vulnerable and shortsighted that he had mistaken genuine affection and possibly love for pity and profit.

He gave her the weight of his narrowed eyes now. "Were you ever planning to tell me the truth, Janine? Or were you getting some sort of perverse thrill through this sham, watching me make a complete ass of myself?"

Janine sat beside him tentatively, shuddering from the force of Richard's glare following her. "You were never making an ass of yourself," she uttered remorsefully. "I wasn't playing you for a fool. Everything that went on between us was real, I swear to you. *Certainly on my part.* The situation with Callister-Reynolds was a totally separate matter. We were never supposed to happen. I wanted to tell you *everything*—"

"When, Janine?" he demanded, brow furrowed. "After I gave my heart, soul and *love* to you? Or when you got tired of putting out?"

The instant the words came out of his mouth, Richard knew that had been a low blow, even under the circumstances, and he felt bad about it.

But at the moment he didn't really give a damn if he'd insulted her. Why should he be the only one hurting here? Payback could be a bitch.

He regarded Janine sharply, vacillating between regret and resentment.

She wobbled before him. "I deserved that—even if it's not true." Sucking in a ragged breath, Janine indicated, "I was going to tell you I worked for Callister-Reynolds before you left for New York. I know I should have from the start. I just got caught up in everything that was going on between us. The last thing I wanted was to risk losing it in any way. I had somehow hoped that we had reached a point in our relationship where we could withstand a fork in the road." She gazed at his face tearfully. "I guess I was mistaken."

Richard's head snapped back. "You call keeping me in the dark about your little scheme while I was falling in love with you a *fork in the road?*" His nostrils ballooned. "How about a damn crater! Don't try and put this off on me, as if I'm the bad guy here!"

Janine sniffled, dabbing at tears staining her cheeks. "I'm not saying that, Richard," she said steadfastly. "It's all my fault and I'm paying the price for it now. When I came back to New York, I told Dennis that he had to give you more time to deal with your loss. But he felt three years was long enough and he was under pressure himself. He was giving you till the fifteenth of August to either commit to doing the books you owed or he would sue you for breach of contract." She paused. "My job was on the line—"

Richard shot to his feet like he'd sat on a pin. "So your damn job means more to you than your integrity?" he asked pointedly. "Not to mention your self-respect?"

"No," Janine responded curtly, "it doesn't. I never planned for things to turn out as they did. You have to believe that, Richard."

Frankly, he didn't really know what to believe anymore, he told himself, looking down at the woman who he now saw as having betrayed his trust in the worst way. Just when he thought he had found something and someone to believe in, the rug had been pulled from beneath his feet, bringing him down hard. He wasn't going to give her the chance to ever hurt him again.

Even with that conviction, Richard still felt his anger reach the boiling point. He wanted to vent his frustration at someone, though he was unsure whom. A likely choice would seem to be Callister-Reynolds, for pulling an underhanded stunt like this. But he wasn't prepared to let Janine off the hook, either, for being a willing and obviously masterful accomplice to the deceitful plan of action.

What Richard knew for certain was that he hadn't really known the woman he thought he had fallen in love with. At least, not her smooth and convincing ability to sit on something he had the right to know. And all without him suspecting in the slightest her underlying motives and questionable character.

Richard lowered his brows over an implacable gaze at Janine, his thoughts and feelings jumbled into a mass of confusion, disillusionment and self-pity. "Well, it looks like your job will be spared," he snorted unfeelingly. "I plan to earn my advance for the books I'm under contract to do and I'll make that clear to Callister-Reynolds." He sighed. "Now, do me a favor, will you, and get the hell out of here. I need some time by myself."

Janine stood in shock, meeting his eyes wanly. "I really am sorry, Richard. You have every right to be pissed. I'll understand if you never want to see me again." She sniffled. "I just want you to know that I never meant for it to turn out this way. I didn't want to hurt you any more than you've already been hurt. I didn't want to hurt *us*—"

"I *trusted* you, dammit!" Richard said stridently, her words meaningless to him. "I actually thought we could have a life together. I was willing to put the past to rest and start over. But I was wrong. Dead wrong."

"No, you weren't," Janine said adamantly. "We can still have that life together, baby, if you want. Nothing has to change with us—"

Richard's face contorted in fury. "But don't you see, *everything* has changed—and we can't put it back the way it was. Everything I thought existed between us was all under false pretenses." He rolled his eyes disgustedly. "If you really cared at all about what we had, you should have told me up front what you wanted from me. Instead, you played on my emotions and vulnerabilities, my guilt and regrets and my love for Kassandra—someone you'll *never* measure up to!"

Richard caught a glimpse of the deep hurt in Janine's eyes before quickly turning his head as if to avoid his own pain. And hers. "I think you should go now," he repeated, even if part of him wanted anything but that. He wished he could stuff the genie back into the bottle and everything would be as it was. And could be. But it was too late for that.

And too late for them.

Richard felt Janine's fierce stare, as if it was burning into him. Into his very soul. He suspected she wanted to say something—perhaps a last halfhearted attempt at defending the indefensible—but the words did not come out of her mouth. He wasn't surprised. They had reached the stage where both were running on empty, with really nothing more to say.

She backed away from him slowly but surely, then turned around and left the room without another word spoken between them.

Only then did Richard turn around and look at the spot where Janine had last stood, the sound of the door slamming shut reverberating in his ears. It had, for all intents and purposes, marked the ending of any future they might have had.

Richard put his hands to his face, suddenly wanting to be anywhere but there. He questioned why the hell he had allowed himself to so easily fall in love with Janine. What on earth had possessed him to lower his defenses to the point of bringing his deep-seated affections to the surface, where Janine was readily available to manipulate them? He had been content to keep his love for Kassandra stored away in his memories of her. He had never so much as eyed another woman, knowing no one could ever fill her shoes.

Now Richard felt ashamed that he had broken his vow to his beloved Kassandra and turned his heart elsewhere.

It was a mistake he would never make again. Not in this lifetime. Or any other.

Whatever feelings he had developed for Janine were badly misplaced. It would be hard, but he would get over her. There was really no other choice.

What wasn't clear to Richard was how he would go about the task of falling out of love with Janine Henderson.

Chapter 40

Janine felt she had reached the lowest point of her life. Things had gone horribly awry with Richard. He had reacted according to the worst-case scenario in her mind, disregarding everything that had developed between them as though it had not. She accepted full blame, though she knew in her heart that things had happened as they had because of the circumstances that had rapidly intertwined their lives like braids, rather than because of any attempt to deceive him. She wasn't trying to somehow capitalize on Richard's tragedy for her own personal gain. Or even professional gain, she told herself, given that it was *his* breach of contract that had brought them together in the first place. Her employment with Callister-Reynolds was strictly incidental.

These thoughts now seemed pointless as Janine played and replayed everything in her head from the beginning, wondering what she could have or should have done differently. Had Richard not shown up at Pescadero Point that day, it might well have dramatically altered everything that had happened thereafter. Looking back, Janine realized she should have insisted on telling him the full story, even when he didn't want to know.

Maybe I should have foreseen the potential complications when Dennis first asked me to go see Richard, Janine thought, staring blankly out the window in her living room.

Then I could have backed out while I had the chance—before exposing myself to this deep hurt and regret.

Janine wiped tears from her eyes, while pondering why she'd let her guard down and allowed professional objectives to give way to personal neediness.

Was it worth the havoc I've brought upon Richard's life and my own? she mused, knowing the answer was "no."

Sniffling, Janine realized that no matter her retrospection, there was little to be gained by beating herself on the head. She could no more change the past than the future. Both now seemed to be working against her.

Against them.

Just as the present was.

Janine knew only that she didn't want to see the ties that brought her and Richard together, woven inexplicably like a blanket, tear apart at the seams. They had come too far in a short time just to lose everything.

Again.

But there seemed little she could do to stop what seemed to be the writing on the wall. Richard had made his feelings perfectly clear and she was in no position to change them. She wasn't sure she should even try, no matter how much she still cared for the man.

Janine continued to gaze pensively out the window. The house was deathly silent, like a morgue. Lisa had gone to spend the weekend with her father and his girlfriend in Boston. There was still talk that they planned to marry, though Janine would believe it when she saw it.

But her thoughts were elsewhere. Janine felt her own life unraveling once more, as though she was somehow destined to fall short of happiness, or of a chance at a relationship of substance, fulfillment and love. Just like her mother.

It was as if she had been cursed from the very start. Genetically predisposed to choosing the wrong men to share her life with.

Janine feared that this would forever be her fate.

Something she could no more change than her height or race or the century she was born in.

She thought of Richard's parting shot at her.

Someone you'll never measure up to.

The words had jolted Janine like a bolt of lightning, hitting her where it was bound to inflict some heavy damage. It had, hurting her in the worst way possible. She was being told in no uncertain terms that no matter what she did or tried to do, she could *never* fill Kassandra's shoes in Richard's heart. Never measure up to the many wonderful attributes of his late wife, the mother of his child.

Had he expected her to reach these lofty standards?

Something in Janine suspected Richard had decided it would likely be an impossible task from the very beginning, but he was apparently willing to settle for something less—her.

Another side of Janine didn't want to believe this, preferring to think that the bitter words coming from Richard's mouth had been meant solely to respond to the pain he felt out of anger at her deception. Not that this made her feel any better. Or the message less stinging.

Someone you'll never measure up to.

The words seemed to keep coming back to Janine as if inescapable in their insinuation.

I never tried to measure up to Richard's precious wife, she told herself realistically. The task would have been impossible in one month's time, or even a year's. Kassandra's tragic death had ensured her a sort of idolatry or enshrinement in Richard's mind that Janine honestly believed she could never live up to. Except possibly with her own death, and thereby the immortality of her soul. But even that, she felt, would most likely fall short of the powerful specter of Kassandra left indelibly in Richard's mind.

Was it that important to Janine that *she* be accepted as Kassandra's equal to Richard, had they been able to make it work? Janine contemplated. *No, not really,* she thought succinctly. *All I ever wanted from the man was to be judged on my own merits, strengths and weaknesses—nothing more, nothing less.* Just as she knew Kassandra had been.

Was it even possible at this point, when the situation seemed so *impossible*, to make things right with Richard? Janine wondered with a sense of hopelessness.

Janine's pessimistic side feared she might never be given another chance at a relationship where so much seemed perfect.

A future with the right man.

The love of her life.

With Richard Edgar Lowrey.

Janine walked almost mechanically into the kitchen and lifted the cordless phone from the counter. The silence, and not knowing if it was over or not, was killing her. She dialed the Hyatt and asked to be connected to Richard Lowrey's room.

After a moment or two, the desk clerk came back on line and said, "I'm sorry, but Mr. Lowrey checked out this morning."

Chapter 41

Moving from Boston to New York had been traumatic for Janine and Lisa, much like being separated from parents with whom you had been intricately and unavoidably linked since birth and being sent to a boarding school two hundred–plus miles away. Even though she was no longer married to John, Janine felt the ties that bound them together through Lisa. Weakening those by distancing themselves was like throwing away a person's crutches and forcing them to continue the treacherous journey on the strength of faith and raw determination. Janine fully accepted the challenge, knowing there was no longer a place for her or Lisa in Boston.

In many respects, Janine had felt like a prisoner there, unable to break free from a bad marriage and a cheating husband, in spite of the divorce decree. Even her work as an editor had suffered. She couldn't help but feel that no matter what she achieved professionally, John's high achievements and status would hang over her like a storm cloud, always reminding Janine who the primary breadwinner was and, thus, the more superior person. John had been only too happy to perpetuate this perception and the greater importance of his job whenever it suited him, to lower her a peg or two.

Making a clean break from his psychological torment and overachievement was the only way Janine felt she could reclaim her life and self-esteem. It was the only way to save her daughter from the emotional baggage that came from a dysfunctional relationship in which the parents were in close enough proximity to keep the flames of discord burning.

New York was a natural and appropriate place to relocate. It was close enough to Boston to allow Lisa to visit her father and maintain their bond, yet far enough away for Janine to start her life over without the dependencies of the past.

The job at Callister-Reynolds had come through the networking she'd done with other editors and people in the publishing business, along with a superior recommendation from her previous employer. Dennis DeMetris had hired Janine due to her proven skills as an editor, rather than merely filling a position for which there was an opening. Janine took her job and responsibilities seriously, knowing it was important for both her and her daughter to be able to support themselves and demonstrate an ability to make it on their own without a man.

For three months Janine had enjoyed her independence on the job and her independence from John and the life they'd had. Lisa had shown a remarkable ability to adjust and see the world brightly through a little girl's eyes. All seemed right with the world, or not quite wrong with their world within.

Then, quite inadvertently, Richard Lowrey had entered Janine's life, and Lisa's as a consequence.

Suddenly everything that once seemed orderly and accept-

able for Janine had become blurred with uncertainty and disappointment. What had been contentment, if not complete satisfaction, had turned into something far less. The freedom
Janine had once sought and successfully achieved from John
had come back to haunt her like a nightmare. She had
stumbled into something and someone wonderful that made
her reassess what it meant to live in the absence of a healthy,
loving, stable relationship.

In bed, trying to cry herself to a sleep that never came,
Janine wondered if things could possibly go back to the way
they were before she'd ever heard of Richard Lowrey.

A voice inside her head told Janine that his entry into her
life made it all but *impossible* to turn back the clock. She
couldn't pretend as if what had occurred between them—like
being on a magical, romantic journey where anything was possible—was nothing more than a figment of her imagination.

But that didn't change the facts any, she knew. Richard
Lowrey was out of her life.

Chapter 42

Richard spent hours walking around the city aimlessly, trying to get his head together and heal his pierced heart. New York had so much to offer, he thought bleakly. Yet the one thing he'd wanted most had turned out to be just another illusion.

A fraud.

A manipulator.

A con artist.

Janine didn't really want him. She wanted his photography and writing skills. She was only a pawn in his publisher's plan to tap into his vulnerabilities in order to get something from him. Those damn books. They would even stoop so low as to trounce on the graves of Kassandra and Sheena simply to try and make a buck. Or get a few back.

Damn them all to hell! cursed Richard to himself. And damn Janine for going along with it, he thought bitterly. She'd played her part to perfection like an Oscar-winning actress—

lulling him into believing she truly cared about the same things he did: honesty, togetherness, family and love.

Indeed, as far as Richard was concerned, Janine had only been interested in what she could get from him to further her career aspirations, with maybe some hanky-panky on the side as a fringe benefit.

He wanted more than anything to get the hell out of this damn city. There was nothing more for him here, Richard thought glumly. Certainly not real love, affection and dreams to build on.

It was all a charade, he told himself dejectedly.

And he had fallen for it like a lovesick schoolboy.

He had to get past this somehow and look reality squarely in the face. Janine Henderson was history! Whatever went on between them had come to an abrupt, regrettable and frustrating end—and nothing either of them did from this point on would change that.

There was no going back to the way things were before meeting Janine, Richard thought, returning to the hotel and feeling like a stranger in a strange city. He could no longer drown himself in regrets and sorrow, ignoring his obligations. He would give Callister-Reynolds their damn books and be done with it. Afterward they would go their separate ways for good. He wouldn't further associate himself with a publisher that disrespected him and what he was going through with deception, backhanded moves and cheap tricks. Let them find some other person to put the screws in.

He needed a clean break from everything and everyone that had hurt him—including Janine.

But not before completing some unfinished business.

Richard checked out of the hotel and took a cab to Harlem. He had the driver take him everywhere he wanted to go. He took pictures of Harlem's Apollo Theatre, the opera, Studio

Museum and other attractions, such as its elevated subway, Malcolm X Boulevard and some of the architecturally beautiful brownstones and row houses that dotted the area. He wanted to capture the true essence of black New York as part of his overall pictorial of the city and its many influences as the racial- and ethnic-minority melting pot of people of color in America.

Afterward Richard went to a building on West Fiftieth Street in Manhattan, where the Callister-Reynolds offices were located.

Richard took the elevator up to the ninth floor, hundreds of thoughts circling his head along the way like vultures. He wondered just how civilized he was supposed to act after the stunt they'd pulled. A good part of him wanted to rant and rave like a man who had lost all control and felt there was nothing more that could be done to ruin his life than what had already happened. But he thought better, as that would accomplish nothing meaningful.

What if he ran into Janine there? The thought entered Richard's head with mixed emotions. *I don't know what the hell there is to say that hasn't already been said.* She'd got what she wanted out of him and now he wanted nothing more to do with her.

Or so he tried to convince himself, thinking of the good times, before it had blown up in his face.

Richard grimaced. There was simply no other choice, he thought, but to leave well enough alone.

And to leave Janine Henderson alone.

Richard entered the lobby of Callister-Reynolds, with its fine contemporary furnishings, array of African violets on display and marble flooring. It almost seemed like old times. But not quite. This time, he was in no mood to rejoice over his achievements and partnership with the prominent publisher.

He ignored the young receptionist with pixie braids—chewing gum like her teeth needed the workout—and began to walk down the corridor that would take him to Dennis DeMetris's office.

"Well, look what the canary brought in," Richard heard the familiar voice say from behind.

He turned and caught sight of Flora McDougal sashaying toward him in a pink pantsuit and three-inch heels. She flashed him a bright, glossy smile. "If it isn't Richard E. Lowrey in the flesh! I was beginning to think we'd never see you again—not here, anyway...."

That very thought had admittedly crossed Richard's own mind on more than one occasion, he conceded.

"How are you, Flora?" he said tonelessly, glancing at the tight ginger-blond curls flat against her head.

"I'm just fine. How are *you?*"

Not very good, he thought, but said as if he believed it, "I'm okay."

"Well, good." She eyed him with a curious slant of the face, and moved closer. "The fact that you're in this building I guess says something."

Not exactly what you might think, Richard told himself. "Yeah," he muttered concisely, "guess it does."

Flora studied him. "So I hear that you and Janine have become *good* friends?"

Richard frowned at the thought, while not surprised that word traveled fast amongst all the coconspirators of what amounted to a setup. "Don't believe everything you hear, Flora," he said sharply. "It may be nothing more than hogwash."

She raised a brow. "Hmm..." she hummed. "Janine seemed to think otherwise. What's up between you two? Or shouldn't I ask?"

Richard wondered just how far this game of seduction and publisher scheming went up the chain of command. Had the whole office been in on the conspiracy—making him the laughingstock of Callister-Reynolds, if not the whole damn city of New York?

"Why don't you ask *her,* Flora?" he said curtly. "I'm sure Janine will tell you whatever you need to know. Right now, I need to see Dennis. See you later."

Richard walked away as politely as he could and hoped she would leave it at that. She did, though he could feel Flora's eyes on him like a hawk, trying to read his mind.

Only he knew what he was feeling inside, and the complex, inner workings of his brain. He wasn't prepared to share that—certainly not with her.

But he did want to give Dennis DeMetris a piece of his mind.

Dennis opened his office door just as Richard arrived at it. The two men eyed each other directly before Dennis fashioned a crooked grin on his lips and said, "Long time no see, brother."

Richard sucked in a deep breath. "Don't *brother* me, man," he responded unaffectedly. "Let's just get this over with."

He walked past Dennis into the office and became an author again.

Chapter 43

Janine wasn't sure what to expect when she went to work that afternoon. She wondered if when all was said and done Richard, feeling Callister-Reynolds had unjustly invaded his privacy, had reneged on his promise to honor his contract—costing them both dearly. Janine knew sadly that she'd lost any leverage she had in convincing Richard it was the right thing to do. This left her feeling useless and frustrated at the same time.

Is my job in jeopardy over the way I've handled this? she wondered with trepidation. She'd put personal over professional objectives. Issues of the heart above those of the workplace.

Now I'm paying the price, in more ways than one.

Janine felt as if she had lost her best friend. Best lover. And best love, by far. Perhaps Richard Lowrey was gone forever from her life. Her job seemed to take second place by comparison. Yet it was still there as far as she knew.

And Richard wasn't.

She assumed he had returned to California, having checked out of the hotel hours earlier. It also occurred painfully to Janine that Richard might have moved to another hotel to be as far away from her as he could.

It hurt her to think that the rift between them had been so wide, the bitterness so tart, that he hadn't even bothered to say goodbye. Not even to Lisa, who had grown to adore Richard in such a short time.

Is there anything I could say or do to repair the damage I've caused and allow us to start over? Janine asked herself, with hope fading fast.

Not that she could blame Richard for treating her like a pariah, Janine thought. For she felt like one. Someone no longer worthy of his affection, love and trust. She wasn't even sure she could trust herself any longer.

Janine went directly into her office, which she had neglected of late, deliberately bypassing the formalities and chitchat that accompanied every work setting, whether you liked it or not. Slumping into the low-backed, brown leather chair that occupied her walnut-colored desk, Janine glanced at her calendar. On it were notes she had made pertaining to Richard, his visit, his photography and his books. Their future and all the promise it held.

Suddenly Janine felt like crying, but she held back. She wasn't sure if it was pride, professional etiquette or a rejection of the misguided sense of bitterness that Richard had that put her in this position of weakness and regret. She had to take full blame for her decisions and choice of men to fall for—even if she regretted now giving her heart to Richard and having it thrown back at her.

She had to be strong under adversity and disappointment. If not for herself, then for Lisa.

Janine hadn't even noticed that Dennis had come in until

he said in a flat tone of voice, "Good afternoon, Janine. Glad you could make it in today."

She took that as sarcasm, given the fact that it was nearly 1:00 p.m. As it was, she had been so befuddled this morning over the way things were left between her and Richard that the last place Janine wanted to be was at work. After all, that was where her heartache and attachment to this man had begun. Then she'd decided maybe this was where she should be, confronting the source of her misery head-on, as the way to get past it.

Janine looked up at her boss expressionlessly. "I was feeling a bit under the weather this morning," she lied, and shuffled some papers on her desk for effect. "I'm feeling better now." Inside, she knew that she was feeling anything but good.

"Happy to hear that," he said indistinctly, touching his glasses almost on cue. "Thought you might like to know that Richard Lowrey came to see me this morning."

Janine tensed up even more. She noted a sort of twisted smile playing on Dennis's lips and suspected that it was the calm before the storm. She felt her knees quiver while wondering if this was where she would be given her two weeks' notice, after being told that she had failed in a big way to deliver on Richard and thus would be unceremoniously let go.

Not sure I can deal with losing Richard and my job in less than twenty-four hours, Janine thought, scared to death at the notion.

She fought back the fears and braced herself as best she could, but heard the unsteadiness of her voice in responding, "Oh, really?"

"Yeah, took me by surprise, too," remarked Dennis coolly. "The man still has a *definite* chip on his shoulder, but it looks as if your hard work paid off...." He adjusted his glasses.

Janine met his eyes with surprise but said nothing—afraid of what might come out.

"Lowrey handed me a tentative proposal for his next two books." Dennis hung on to that last word, as if still coming to terms with it himself. "Indeed, he's chosen the Big Apple as the setting for the first book of photographs. A brilliant idea, I thought. The city could use some positive attention these days, if you know what I mean…."

Janine did know and she could not have agreed more. She felt her pulse quicken with mixed emotions. Richard had decided to honor his contract, in spite of his feeling of betrayal.

But, she wondered, at what price to their personal relationship? She supposed that went without saying, and tried hard to move past what they had and could have had, to what was.

Janine shifted her thoughts to Richard's new book on New York City. She realized that, in fact, he had in all likelihood already gotten started on his photographic book tour.

When we were together and the whole city seemed like our private island, she thought. Instead of a place that would now be filled with sad memories and an ending of the road—their road.

Dennis tilted his head. "I have to be honest with you, Janine. For a while there I thought we—actually, you—might have struck out with Richard. But I guess I underestimated your strong influence in getting the man to snap out of the doldrums. Richard gave full credit to you!"

Again Janine found herself speechless. She was certain that any credit Richard gave her was purely cynical, even if she had been the one to bring him back into the fold. Such a victory seemed hollow, for it had come at the expense of their relationship and all it had come to mean to her. She considered her own loss immeasurable.

"I only did what you asked me to," Janine told Dennis, her voice lacking any real fulfillment and triumph. "I honestly wasn't sure if Richard would come around."

Dennis put his hand to his chin. "Well, he did, and you deserve a pat on the back for a job damn well done. I, for one, will sleep a lot better tonight knowing we're back on track with one of our most bankable authors."

Janine had a feeling it would be just the opposite for her. Sleep would not come easily this night. Or the next. Or the one after that.

Maybe never again.

"I'm sure you will," she said tartly.

Dennis, so caught up in his own self-satisfaction, never noticed the sarcasm. "By the way, your three—actually, four—month review has been completed," he said, smiling broadly. "Nothing but high marks across the board. I'd say your future with Callister-Reynolds is quite secure, Janine."

She colored, conflicting thoughts going through her head. "I'm not sure what to say."

"Don't say anything. You've earned it—as well as a raise…." Dennis watched Janine react with further astonishment, touched his glasses while looking amused and said, "Well, I'd better let you get back into the flow of things here." He started to walk away, then turned around at the last minute, as if by design, ripping off his glasses. "Oh, and one other thing, Janine. You'll be the editor overseeing Richard's next book. It only seemed appropriate under the circumstances. I'm sure you two will continue to work well together."

Dennis favored her with a dazzling smile and left the office with almost a hop to his step.

When she should have been jumping for joy at all this un-anticipated news, Janine felt like crawling under the desk and hiding. She had achieved the job security and pay raise she sought for her and her daughter, and the choice editing assignment she'd always dreamed of.

But Janine was not sure it was really enough or could ever be—all things considered.

For what and whom she had sacrificed as a result was even more desirable to her.

Flora insisted on taking Janine out for a drink after work. Janine suspected she wouldn't be very good company for her. Yet she felt she needed a friend's shoulder to cry on. Flora was the closest thing in Manhattan to fit the bill.

They went uptown to a club on Broadway.

"So, you don't look anything like someone who got her man in more ways than one," observed Flora over a glass of pinot grigio.

"It seems that there's no such thing as fairy tales in real life," Janine moaned, feeling as if she had turned from Cinderella into a frog.

"Oh…?" Flora wrinkled her nose. "I was there when Richard came in this morning. He was still as fine as I remembered. I figured his road back to respectability, not to mention his jump-starting of his career in photography and writing, went straight through you."

"It may have," Janine granted, sipping her drink. "Only, there's been a slight detour. No, make that a *major* one."

Flora fluttered her lashes outrageously. "Yeah. He alluded to that, somewhat. So what happened, girl? Or maybe I should ask, what *didn't* happen?" She tasted the wine. "You did remember to tell Richard that you worked for Callister-Reynolds, didn't you?"

Janine took a deep breath, lowering her chin in shame. "I guess not soon enough to suit him."

She wondered if it would ever have been soon enough, and considered that she might have been simply trying to rationalize her own failures in being upfront with Richard from the start, and hold on to him afterward.

Flora mumbled an expletive. "So now he's copped an attitude because of it, huh?"

"More like he doesn't want anything to do with me," Janine muttered with a sense of finality. "I feel sick to my stomach about the whole thing."

Flora stiffened. "Why is it that we sisters seem to always be chasing after brothers who can't see straight for the nose on their faces?"

Janine asked herself the same thing. She had already gone down this road with John. Now she was doing it again with Richard—only, the impact was even more devastating, for she'd never felt so strongly about a man before.

"I suppose it's because we fall in love too easily, and lust for them even more," Flora stated, seemingly reading Janine's mind. "Usually it's fools that we end up giving our hearts and bodies to. Richard is starting to sound like one great big damn fool."

"So what does that make *me?*" Janine voiced sourly.

"Someone who may not be perfect, but has a hell of a lot to offer to anyone who'll just open his eyes." Flora downed her drink and ordered another round. "We'll figure this out together. I'm with you all the way, girl."

Flora's sincere facial expression betrayed that of an older, caring person. It made Janine feel all the more appreciative of her company. She confided in her everything of merit, right down to Richard checking out of the hotel without so much as a goodbye. She didn't tell Flora just how guilt ridden and low she felt in spite of everything else, though Janine suspected Flora understood as much.

"One moment we're on top of the Empire State Building—like having the entire world at our fingertips—talking about living together," Janine recalled sadly. "The next, we're apparently no longer on speaking terms. I really don't know if this is just a bump on the road that we can somehow get past in time or if the damage is irreversible and the relationship over." She suspected the latter but could not bring herself to face up to it.

"Do you love him?" Flora asked point-blank.

Janine felt a little uncomfortable sharing this most private of emotions with Flora. But there was no mistaking what her heart told her, loud and clear.

"Yes," she admitted. "I do love Richard. I've known that for some time now, even if it took me a while to come to terms with it. But I also love Lisa. I have to put her needs before my own. The one thing I do not want to subject her to is more pain and heartbreak. She's only seven and already has seen enough failure in adult relationships to last a lifetime!"

"Children are far more resilient than you think," Flora expressed confidently. "Lisa's not the one I'm worried about. You are." She regarded Janine with intense eyes. "If Richard won't come back to you, girl, you've gotta go to him. You owe yourself that much. It's the only way to find out if there's anything there still worth fighting for. You've both been to hell and back and are still in there, battling. No reason to let a good thing get away. Or in this case, *a good man.* If the man's as smart as I think he is, he'll see that. If not, then to hell with him. At least you'll know you tried and can move on with your life."

Can I? Janine wondered with some skepticism. She feared

that by keeping hope alive she was merely setting herself up for further disappointment. Frustration. Heartache.

She questioned whether Richard was open to trying to somehow work it out between them, based on the way they'd left things. He had seemingly had a complete change of heart about them—and any future they might have.

To Janine this suggested that there was nothing she could do to make Richard believe she truly cared about him over and beyond their connection to Callister-Reynolds.

I can't continue to fight what looks like a losing battle, she thought, even if he was more than worth the effort.

Janine considered how Richard had hurt her, as well. She wasn't sure if she was ever up to hearing again about how she could never measure up to Kassandra. Janine saw it as a no-win situation for her to be compared to the one great love of Richard's life, no matter what else happened.

I couldn't be content always playing second fiddle to Kassandra, Janine told herself with resignation, having already come in second to the women in John's life. *I want to be number one with a man for once,* she thought.

If not with Richard, then with somebody else.

Janine put the wine to her lips while musing sadly as to why love had to be fraught with such complex, stirring and often bitter emotions.

That night Janine called Richard's home. The phone rang three times while she tensely wondered what she would say and how she would say it.

The answering machine came on. "This is Richard. I'm not in. Leave a message at the beep and I'll get back to you."

"It's me, Richard." Janine's voice shook. "If you're there, please pick up the phone...."

She waited for a long moment, expecting him to answer, as the beat of her heart pounded resoundingly in her ears. Instead, the phone disconnected.

Disappointed, yet relieved in a strange way, Janine called information for Henry Lowrey's number in Monterey. She didn't know if it was such a good idea to phone Richard's father. But, as she hadn't spoken to Richard since last night, she wanted to at least know he had made it home safely.

The phone was answered after two rings. "Hello!" Henry's voice boomed.

"Hello, Henry," Janine said somewhat timidly. "This is Janine Henderson...."

Henry paused as if not sure how to respond. "Hi, Janine," he finally said. "How you doing?"

"I'm fine," she said, wishing her quavering body would stay still. "I called Richard's house but his answering machine picked up. Do you know if he arrived home from New York?"

It had never occurred to Janine that he might not have gone home. At least not directly. She realized Richard could still be in the city. Perhaps he had stayed to shoot pictures for his book, she thought, at an undisclosed location.

"Yeah," Henry muttered with a long sigh. "He's here all right."

Janine breathed a sigh of relief for that much at least. Her nerves were working overtime because of the other issues between her and Richard.

After a moment or two, she said simply, "Can you tell him I called?"

Henry paused again. "I'm not really sure I want to get in the middle of this, Janine. You know what I'm sayin'?"

All too well, she feared. He didn't want to be seen as the

messenger when his son obviously did not wish to speak to her. She could not force Richard to do so.

Janine bit her lip, losing her will in trying to reestablish what seemed to be a lost cause. She did have some self-respect left.

"Sorry I bothered you." Her voice cracked. "Goodbye, Henry."

"Wait!" Henry called out at the last moment before Janine could hang up. "What the hell. Don't be sorry. I'm not. I like you, Janine, even if Richard doesn't very much at the moment. Maybe we can change that. I'll tell him you called."

"Thank you, Henry."

"No problem." He coughed away from the phone, cleared his throat and said hoarsely, "Look, Janine—for what it's worth, I hope it can still work out between the two of you."

So do I, she told herself in spite of all else. But she held out little hope of that happening.

Janine clutched the phone for a while after Henry had hung up, as if it was glued to her fingers. She hadn't a clue as to what to do next, if anything.

Would Richard call back? Janine felt agitated at the notion, and then considered where they might go from there even if he did call.

She tried to put herself in his shoes. Now that he'd had a little time for reflection, perhaps Richard had realized the error of his ways, that he had overreacted and made a mistake.

Or maybe he believes more than ever that our relationship was one big mistake. That he should have stayed in his dark hole of self-pity, worshipping a dead woman and child—instead of facing up to the complexities and intricacies of a real bond with a living woman, imperfections and all.

Inside, Janine feared that Richard had retreated to his safe space—living in the past instead of confronting the present and future.

She had to face up to the fact that they may have reached a point of no return....

Or that there was nothing she could do to reverse the course and save their relationship.

Janine hurt just as much for her daughter as for herself. She knew that Lisa had already grown attached to Richard, leaving her deeply disappointed in his absence—just as Janine was.

It was possible, Janine knew, that Lisa, already used to relationship failures, would bounce back and simply give that much more of her youthful affections and exuberance to Bernadette.

Did I get in way too deep with Richard? Janine asked herself, finally clicking the phone off. *I set myself up for far more hurt than I ever realized. What a lovesick fool I've been.*

Janine didn't even pretend to know how she would deal with this latest setback in her life...other than to remember that she had to be there for Lisa, no matter what woes she went through. Even then, the disillusionment rolled through Janine's head like a scroll full of regrets and things that might have been.

Chapter 44

Richard chose Zimbabwe as the setting of his book *Autumn in Zimbabwe*. Its natural and spectacular wonders, array of birds and animals and affable, charming African residents made for the perfect black fine-arts book. Using all the skills afforded him, Richard used his lens to beautifully capture pictures that illustrated the heart and soul of Zimbabwe. These included the magnificent Victoria Falls and its three-hundred-foot drop into a gorge of mystical mist; the great Zambezi River; Lake Kariba and the Hwange National Park, featuring four hundred types of birds and more than one hundred animal species; and the Eastern Highlands, with its rugged mountains, breathtaking waterfalls, clear streams and pine forests.

Accompanying Richard on the trip were Kassandra and Sheena. It was their first and only trip together as a family to Africa. Richard was thirty-five and he and Kassandra were fresh off of celebrating their tenth anniversary. Sheena had just reached her sixth birthday and continued to be the little darling of her father's eye.

Though Richard was mostly preoccupied photographing Zimbabwe for his book, he made a point to spend as much time as possible with his family. Based in Harare, they toured much of the country together, taking in the sights and sounds of game reserves, the incredible Matopos Hills caves, Lake Chivero, and tea and coffee estates.

Richard had never felt so at peace, connected with nature and blessed to have a loving family as on that trip. One night in their hotel suite they talked about having another child. Both Richard and Kassandra felt it would be nice if Sheena had a sibling—something neither of them had experienced.

"If it's a boy, we can name him Richard Edgar Lowrey II," Kassandra cadenced. "If it's a girl, Verhonda Nicole might be nice."

"How about a girl *and* a boy?" added Sheena, her eyes glowing at the prospect.

Kassandra looked at Richard, tossing this one to him. He thought about it for a moment. Admittedly, twins scared him a bit, as competition between them would be inevitable and not always healthy. But what frightened Richard even more was the thought of Sheena growing up an only child, without the love and support of a brother or sister—or both, if it was meant to be.

"It's not always possible, honey," he told his daughter gingerly, putting her on his knee, "to have two at the same time. But I do like the names your mother has picked out. And, who knows? If the forces of nature are on your side, little lady, then there just might be a baby girl *and* boy for you to dote on someday."

Kassandra rolled her eyes. "Uh, excuse me, but I wouldn't

hold my breath on that one if I were you. I can hardly keep up with babying you two." She flashed Richard a wicked smile, then Sheena. "Two more at once might be downright impossible."

Sheena broke into a silly giggle.

Richard laughed mirthfully. He brought Kassandra closer to him, kissed her on the mouth and declared, "You're wonderful, you know that, lady?"

Kassandra kissed him back. "So you keep telling me, mon."

"And I'll keep saying it again and again," he told her unflinchingly. "Because it's true. Isn't that right, Sheena?"

"Yes," she chortled. "Daddy's for real, Momma. I think you're wonderful, too."

Kassandra's face lit up radiantly with pure love. "Well, I feel wonderful having you both in my life. I don't know what I'd do without either of you."

"You'll never have to find out," Richard promised blissfully.

"Oh, Richard…" Kassandra cadenced emotionally, and hugged him tightly. "I love you."

"I love you, too, Daddy," Sheena seconded gleefully.

She joined her parents in a family embrace. Richard wished they could stay that way for eternity, so nothing could ever come between them.

Chapter 45

Richard sat stone-faced across from Henry in the study. Neither man had spoken in some time, content to let what had already been said settle in like pollutants in the air. Henry had done most of the talking—or lecturing, Richard would say—while Richard had done most of the listening and pouting.

For his part, Richard felt there was nothing more to say. At least, nothing more he cared to say that he hadn't already said in New York. He'd been back for over a day and had been unable to return Janine's call. He wasn't sure he ever would. Or that he could. She'd conned him once into letting down his guard and falling for her in a way that had been reserved for Kassandra.

And her memory.

He'd further made an imbecile of himself by actually suggesting he and Janine live together in his house.

In the house of his adored wife and daughter.

In the process, he had betrayed Kassandra by falling in love with another woman, taking away from the love Richard had sworn to give only to his late wife.

Never again, he thought solemnly.

How could I have been so damn gullible that I didn't see through Janine's editor-on-a-business-pleasure-trip charade?

She'd played on his remorse about Kassandra and Sheena's deaths like a trumpet. Gotten him to turn away from his preoccupation with them as if it were a curse. Or worse, an obsession.

All with Dennis DeMetris *and* Callister-Reynolds pulling her strings like a puppet.

Damn you, Janine, for going along with the treachery!

He hadn't realized it would hurt so much. Janine had given him a bona fide reason to live again—to be a man again. The motivation to return to the profession he loved. And she had taken it away after reeling him in under false pretenses.

Henry looked weary studying his son's tortured face. At last he spoke. "Richard, you're making this thing more difficult than it has to be."

Richard scowled at him. "How would *you* make it? I trusted her, for crying out loud. As much as I trust you. But all she was really after were those books I owed the publisher that she works for. Only, she neglected to inform me of that little fact—till there was no other choice."

Henry shook his head. "Think about what you're saying, Richard," he said evenly. "Do you honestly believe for one moment Janine would go to those lengths—including talking about making a life together—just to get you back to work? That don't make sense, son. So maybe she didn't tell you right off why she was in town. Maybe she planned to. But things don't always go according to plan. You should know that as well as anyone. And from what you tell me, she may have tried to tell you the full story at one point, but you wouldn't let her. You can be pretty stubborn when you want to be."

Richard pursed his lips meditatively but said nothing.

Henry sighed. "What I'm trying to say to you, Richard, is I think you jumped the gun in hightailing it out of the Big Apple like your pants were on fire—without even giving Janine the chance to make her case. It's plainly obvious to me that the woman's crazy about you no matter what her game plan may have been from the outset. Hell, she even let you spend time in her home with her child. And you're crazy about her. I know it. You know it. Don't blow a good thing, son, all because of your foolish pride."

Richard listened to his father and, though he tried to reject everything Henry had to say, he knew there was wisdom in his words. Admittedly, he had a stubborn streak ten miles long, as his mother used to always tell him. Maybe he had gone too far, too fast, and was too quick in leaving New York and Janine before they could talk this out properly.

Regardless of what Janine's initial motivations were, Richard felt it was really far-fetched to believe that the way her body reacted to his touch, her mouth to his lips, their passionate lovemaking and their kindred minds was not genuine. It was just as real as the way he had responded to Janine, whether he chose to face it like a man or not.

There really was something there between them, Richard knew from deep within his soul. No escaping that, even if he wished he could.

Maybe we can still somehow recoup what we lost and start over again, Richard told himself, knowing it would be an uphill battle. He had said some pretty hurtful things to Janine. He hadn't meant them in the manner in which they were pre sented, but he'd wanted her to take the words at face value because it made him feel better about himself.

Now it made him feel worse.

He wondered if it was too late to pick up where they left off—or if the damage done both ways was simply too great to overcome.

Richard looked up at his father, fumbling for words. "I don't know what the hell to say to her, Dad. For all I know she won't even want to talk to me at this point. And I couldn't really blame her. I acted like an asshole, plain and simple. I felt betrayed and didn't give a damn about her point of view." He sighed miserably. "Might be too late to undo what's already been done and said...."

"It's *never* too late, Richard," Henry said firmly. "The woman that called me yesterday to find out about you is the same woman that is waiting for your call today. She made a mistake—a big one—and I'm sure she's sorry for it. Now, don't you make one that you'll be even more sorry for. You had no control over losing Kassandra—but you *do* have control over whether you lose Janine."

Richard allowed the words to sink in. As much as he wanted things to get back on track with Janine, he just wasn't sure they could get past this—the deception, the half truths, the misunderstandings, the histories, the regrets, the mistrust.

Richard looked into his own psyche. He wondered if after all that had happened he would mentally be able to move forward again and push Kassandra back into the world they once had. It was a world that Richard knew in his gut he no longer belonged to, even if he found it hard to let go.

Kimble, who had been sitting quietly on the floor listening to the father and son go back and forth, suddenly began to bark and dashed out of the room as if in hot pursuit of a cat.

"Where the hell is he off to?" Henry asked.

Richard cocked a brow. Kimble usually reacted that way when there was a visitor. He could smell the person before he or she ever reached the front door.

"I'd say we have company," Richard said.

His first thought was that it might be someone trying to sell them something. The solicitors were big at this time of year. Then he considered that with tours of 17-Mile Drive on the increase, it could well be someone from the Del Monte Forest Association suggesting ways to avoid the crowds, embrace them or keep their properties safe from crime and opportunists.

Henry stood. "I'll get it. Meanwhile, you think about what I said."

There was little else Richard could think about. The truth was, Janine had remained on his mind from the moment he left New York and ever since. Part of him had wanted to stay and find a way around his frustration and disappointment. But the part of him that wanted to distance himself from it all and retreat to the safety of his own little world had been stronger.

He heard noises in the foyer. Henry was saying something Richard couldn't quite make out. A woman's low voice gave a terse response. Henry seemed to reply with a forced, gravelly chuckle.

Then silence.

Curious, Richard got up and was about to leave the room when Henry reentered.

"You're right," his father said, expressionless. "We do have company. Or should I say *you* do...."

Before Richard could put thoughts into words, Janine walked into the room. Her face was filled with consternation but her voice was calm when she said, "Hello, Richard."

Chapter 46

A look of shock spread across Richard's face like a shadow as Janine stood before him. In truth, Janine was just as stunned that she had summoned the courage to actually fly across the country to be where she was at this moment. But, after giving it much thought, she knew she had to see Richard and talk to him face-to-face—even if it turned out to be all for naught and he flatly rejected her presence and told her where to go. It was a chance she was willing to take.

For both their sakes.

Henry cleared his throat after a moment of uneasy silence had spread across the room like poison gas, and said, "I think I'll just leave you two alone. I need to be getting back home, anyway." He paused, eyeing Richard. "I'll take Kimble. I think he could use some fresh air."

Richard nodded appreciatively, before fixing his gaze squarely on Janine.

Henry favored her, forcing Janine to look his way, and said, like he meant it, "Nice seeing you again, Janine."

He left the room, closing the door behind him. Moments later the front door opened and shut.

Janine felt knots in her stomach now that she and Richard were alone, meaning she had to face the music. She knew there was no turning back. Nor did she have any such intentions. She had to clear the air right here and now. For better or worse.

And let the chips fall where they might.

"What are you doing here?" were the first words to come out of Richard's mouth since she'd arrived. Janine noted that he was wearing the calf-length black robe she had become all too familiar with during her last visit, and black slippers. Thinking about what lay beneath the robe sent a shiver down her spine.

"I came to see you," Janine told him with a catch to her voice. She tried to settle her nerves. "When I called the hotel two days ago they said you'd checked out. Then yesterday, Dennis told me you'd come by the office...."

Richard ran his hand nervously across his chin, which had the outline of a day's hair growth. "I shouldn't have left the way I did," he mumbled sincerely. "I'm sorry."

Janine seized the opening. "When you didn't return my phone calls, I..."

Richard lowered his head forlornly. "I guess I just wasn't in the mood to talk."

The twinge of regret and retrospection nibbled at Janine like mosquitoes. "I should have told you from the very beginning that I worked for Callister-Reynolds," she admitted sorrowfully, knowing that was no justification for not doing so.

He looked at her with cold eyes. "Yeah. That might have been a good idea!"

"People make mistakes, Richard. I certainly made a whopper of one." Janine's lower lip quivered uncontrollably. "But sometimes they're for the right reasons with pure intentions. I was never attempting to deceive you, believe me. I only tried to help you without hurting us. Is that so wrong?"

The hard lines etched across Richard's face softened. "No," he said thoughtfully.

"I love you, Richard," Janine told him straightforwardly, from the bottom of her heart, inching ever closer. "I didn't plan on it, but there's no untruth in that, in spite of everything else." She sucked in a deep breath. "I hope you still love me, as you said you did. Let's not ruin what we started for something I did—or didn't do—that has nothing to do with how I feel about you."

Richard held her gaze and swallowed somberly. "Look, what I said about you not measuring up to Kassandra—"

Janine put a finger to his lips, not allowing him to finish. She suspected he wanted to apologize but felt it went without saying. After thinking about it, she'd come to the conclusion that his outburst was never meant in malice. He had reacted in the heat of the moment to his feelings of hurt, shock and anger.

She, in turn, had felt the sting of his words as much as if she had been stung by a swarm of bees. Even if Richard hadn't meant it in his heart, Janine knew that Kassandra's strong and haunting presence would always be there, like the very air she breathed, and nothing she could do would ever change that. Fate and misfortune had all but assured that reality in the tragic scheme of things.

But Kassandra was gone, thought Janine, with all due respect. *And I am here as a living, breathing human being. And so is Richard.*

Janine felt that they both deserved some happiness in the land of the living, without it being denied by the dead. Or a cheating spouse.

Janine's eyes glazed over with tears while she wondered if she could be enough for Richard. Or vice versa.

There was only one way to be sure. One way to put their demons to rest.

She took Richard by the hand and silently led him from the study. Walking through the house, Janine led him straight to his bedroom, previously off limits, implicitly or otherwise.

Richard made no attempt to resist. Instead, he seemed just as eager to make love in that room as Janine was, as if to free the misgivings of his own mind, once and for all, by giving in to the demands of his body, heart and soul.

The painting of Kassandra remained on the wall in all its dark mystery and enchanting beauty. But her penetrating gaze no longer intimidated Janine. Rather, it encouraged her to fight for *her* man, while facing up to the fears and insecurities standing in the way—as well as the woman who, even in death, stood between Janine and Richard like a ghostly woman scorned.

Janine held Richard's cheeks with trembling hands and brought his mouth to hers. Their lips opened and tongues caressed in a passionate exploration of each other as they stood at the foot of the bed. Her body was pressed against the solid flesh of Richard's torso. His manhood bulged from beneath his robe, threatening to spring free with the slightest movement.

Richard's face went down to Janine's chest and he kissed through her blouse as if it were absent. Janine felt the heat of that kiss like it was red-hot fire. Her need to have him became overpowering and all consuming. She began removing his robe, then his underwear, as fast as she could—reveling in the masculine nakedness before her.

Richard followed Janine's lead with equal abandon, undressing her until she was naked. He admired the magnificence of her slender butterscotch-skinned body before taking her into his arms and to bed.

They made love with more passion and promise than at any other time, forsaking all that had come between them for what ruled their bodies and souls at that exquisite moment in time. Unrestrained cries and sighs flowed unabashedly from their mouths as the ecstasy of their mutual release set them free.

When it ended, neither wanted it to. Not for one moment, given the almost violent and urgent craving each held for the other. Only the command of their spent bodies forced them apart.

It was some time before Janine escaped the firm, comforting grip of Richard's arms. In spite of the rebirth of their lovemaking, intense ardor and ultimate in satisfaction, she knew there were still major issues on the table that needed to be resolved. Questions to be answered. Answers to be questioned. Ghosts to put to rest. Demons to purge. Trust to rebuild.

And, most of all, hope to be restored.

None of these would be easy. But all were possible when two people were of the same mind, heart and spirit.

Janine slipped quietly from the bed, content to allow Richard to sleep while she absorbed all that had happened from a safe yet close distance.

Chapter 47

Richard was dreaming of Kassandra, the beauty of her smiling face making him grin with joy and appreciation. They were making love on a secluded beach, having just had a picnic for two. Then they magically appeared back in their own bed, the passion picking right up where it left off without missing a beat.

Suddenly the images became distorted. Richard fought to refocus on the lips he was kissing, the hair he was caressing, the body he was interlocked with—the face so close to his that he could count every mole peppering the high cheeks.

Only it was no longer Kassandra he was with. Instead, it was Janine who lay beneath him, her eyes filled with happiness, her mouth urging him on, her body yielding to his, moving together with his in perfect harmony as they made love.

Richard did not question where Kassandra had gone, knowing that it somehow felt right being with Janine, as if they now belonged together. His mind told him that Kassandra had ascended to a heavenly place where she could take good care of their daughter. Neither of them needed him anymore, content to watch over him spiritually from afar.

When Richard opened his eyes he saw that he was in his bed. Alone. He'd been dreaming. Caught up in a land where the lines between reality and fantasy were often blurred. Unreal. Surreal.

There was Kassandra. And Janine. He was with both women, as if being given a choice of one over the other.

Or maybe only one.

Instead of the other.

Richard believed he now understood the meaning of the dream. It was Kassandra's way of telling him it was time to let her drift away to that distant land above while giving himself completely to another among the living who could love and cherish him the way she once had.

Janine Henderson.

Richard got out of bed, feeling more content than he could remember, and slipped into his robe. He favored Kassandra's painting for a long moment, smiled and whispered, "Thank you."

With that he took the portrait down, knowing it no longer belonged in his bedroom. He put it in the closet for now, treasuring its memories but glad to be able to give everything he had to the new woman he loved.

Janine.

He found her sitting in the living room with a cup of coffee. She was wearing one of his shirts. He liked the way it looked, oversized on her, and found himself aroused.

Truthfully, Richard knew the lady inside the shirt was more than capable of turning him on all by herself.

Janine looked up cheerfully. "You're *finally* awake," she teased him.

"I was hoping you'd still be there beside me when I opened my eyes," he admitted, feeling a fresh need for her. "Thought we might be able to go another round. Maybe two...."

Janine blushed. "Has anyone ever told you you're an insatiable, sexy-as-hell brother?"

Richard bent his head back and laughed. "Not lately. But then, it's been some time since I've had anyone—especially a drop-dead gorgeous lady like you—that I've had such a powerful appetite for."

Janine regarded him thoughtfully, and Richard wondered if he'd said the wrong thing.

He sat beside her. "What's wrong, baby?"

"Nothing...." She sipped her coffee pensively, looked elsewhere, then back at him. There was worry in Janine's brown eyes. "Where do we go from here, Richard?" she questioned with uncertainty. "Do you still want to go somewhere from here? I'll understand if what happened this evening was...well...something we both needed to comfort one another."

Richard rubbed the tip of his nose. He would have thought it had been obvious that his feelings for her were stronger than ever. He'd assumed the same was true for her.

He wondered if tonight was all about past mistakes...or the future for them.

"I want to move forward," he answered her in earnest, putting his arm around her. "I still love you, Janine. I realized that the moment I saw you again. It was reinforced when we made love. And it's even stronger right now."

Janine flashed him a relieved smile. "I love you, too, Richard, with all my heart. But there's still the little problem of three thousand miles separating us."

And it was killing Richard. Even if they could afford the cross-country travel, he was realistic enough to know that they could only go so far with that and hope to maintain a serious and workable relationship.

"I know," he said solemnly. "I was hoping you and Lisa would want to move here. The offer still stands. I want us to be together, Janine. We could make a good life for ourselves and Lisa."

"And what if we can't move here?" Janine challenged. "What then, Richard? Would you still want us to be together?"

Richard turned away. She'd confronted him with direct questions that got right to the heart of their situation and relationship. It unnerved him. He was just getting comfortable with their being a couple again. He didn't know what the hell to say about it lasting if they weren't even living in the same time zone.

Richard wondered if he was prepared to move to New York, if push came to shove. This would mean abandoning the dream house he and Kassandra had purchased and built their lives around for something and someone on the other side of the country.

He looked at Janine while thinking, *Do I truly care for this woman enough to make the ultimate sacrifice?*

It only took a moment to feel his heart racing at the sight of her to know the answer.

Richard leaned forward and pressed his lips softly into Janine's, then met her eyes honestly. "I want you, baby," he promised, realizing with no more doubt that she meant that much to him, "no matter where you live. Or where I live. I'm willing to do whatever it takes to make this thing work. I almost lost you once, Janine. And I don't want to do it again."

Janine dabbed at her tearstained cheeks. "You won't lose me, baby," she told him reassuringly.

"Is that a promise?" He didn't want to give her the chance to ever renege on the life they could have together.

Her teeth shone and she chuckled tremulously. "Yes, Richard, you have my word on that. We'll find a way to work things—everything—out."

From this, Richard sensed that life was truly beginning to look up again. And he planned to make the most of every precious second of it with her, knowing how short and fragile life could be. One moment, you thought you were on top of the world. The next it was crumbling all around you like an earthquake. He didn't intend to take what he had for granted anymore.

Not with Janine.

Not ever again.

Standing, Janine reached for Richard, pulling him up. She wrapped her arms around his neck and hit him with a look that was arousing and to the point. "I was thinking that maybe we could have a *nightcap*," she uttered. "In there—" She pointed toward the bedroom.

A slow grin crossed Richard's face. It was an offer he could not refuse. Not with this beautiful woman, who gave as much as she received in bed and out. And who was offering him so much more.

In the bedroom, Richard glanced at the empty spot where Kassandra's portrait had once hung with authority. He saw that Janine noticed it, too, and was clearly pleased. It represented a major step forward, he thought. A turning point. Janine deserved to have all his attention as they attempted to carve out a life together with her daughter. This would never diminish what Richard had with Kassandra and Sheena, but rather supplement it as part of the great blessings that he had received in his life.

He was looking at one of them now. He happily scooped Janine into his arms and took her to *their* bed.

They made love well into the night and slept peacefully thereafter, cuddling together. There was suddenly more promise than either could have anticipated for the times ahead.

Chapter 48

Janine had already made the decision to move to California, pending Lisa's approval, which seemed all but certain. She knew Lisa had grown quite fond of Richard and wanted things to work between them. Janine saw this as not just what was best for her life. Her daughter's happiness meant everything to her, too, and she would not have wanted to do anything this momentous if Lisa was not in complete agreement. She thought it only fair to seek John's blessing as well for taking his daughter so far away, even though she doubted it would be a problem.

Janine's job was a different matter altogether in considering whether or not to leave New York. She didn't particularly relish the thought of giving up what she had worked so hard to get and keep—including the opportunity to work with Richard on his next book. But Janine was sure she could get a great recommendation out of Dennis in finding a job with a publisher in the Bay Area. Or even act as an editor-at-large for any publisher in the country, including Callister-Reynolds. She loved what she did and had no intention of going into early retirement.

Of much greater concern to Janine was how she and Lisa might fit into Richard's neat little world, even with the best of intentions of all parties. She mused about the prospects for making the transition to West Coast life successfully. There were the natural fears that living in the house Richard had once shared with another woman and young girl would prove too difficult. Too unmanageable. Too unbearable.

Or downright eerie, Janine contemplated.

Some reservations also persisted in Janine's head as to whether or not Richard would be able to make room in his life for two people, after living alone for three years and becoming set in his ways—perhaps even set in stone.

Moreover, to Janine there were those nagging doubts of whether or not Richard had truly laid Kassandra and Sheena to rest in order to give him, her and Lisa a solid chance at happiness together in the real world.

Janine wondered whether or not marriage was in the cards. Her emotions were mixed on the subject. It was a road both she and Richard had traveled down with disastrous results. She feared that their scarred pasts might make it something to shy away from indefinitely.

For her part, Janine had never given up on the institution of marriage, in spite of her failed one. At the end of the day, she doubted she could ever really be satisfied being in a committed relationship that did not involve the ultimate commitment of love, affection and, most of all, trust—that being marriage.

Whether Richard was of the same mind remained to be seen.

Janine knew these concerns, and very likely many more that she had not even thought of, could not be answered until she and Richard had given it a go in the true sense of the word. It was also clear to Janine that what she felt for this man was not something on the rebound or a short-term, whimsical fling. It was true love, real respect and admiration and a desire to be with him in every way she could. Maybe for a lifetime.

All that was left was taking that all-important next step in moving forward and westward—and, along with it, reinforcing the commitment to make it work for Janine and her daughter.

It had been nearly two weeks since Janine had returned from California the second time around. Lisa had spent much of that time with her father and Bernadette on a cruise ship that set sail for the Caribbean. Janine had reluctantly given her permission to go because she thought it important that Lisa had as much quality time with her father as possible. She wanted her daughter to know that she could be happy with both parents, even if they lived separate lives with separate loves. John seemed grateful that Janine had been so accommodating, even if he knew it wasn't for him but for his daughter.

Lisa had gotten seasick at one point but had weathered the storm and was now back to her old self. Janine wanted to wait until Lisa was feeling better before asking her about moving to Pebble Beach to live with Richard.

Lisa was due to start school in less than a week. The last thing Janine wanted to do was pull her out once she was settled in. But she felt it was better earlier than later in the school session. That would give Lisa the chance to adjust to a new school and friends. As well as to a whole new climate and environment.

And the presence of Richard Lowrey in their lives.

They purchased cheeseburgers and fries at McDonald's that sunny day, eating them in the car as Janine often used to do with her parents.

"So what do you think about moving to California, sweet pea?" Janine tossed out casually after wiping ketchup from a corner of her mouth.

Lisa was between fries when she responded excitedly, "That would be cool."

"Really?"

"Yeah." She looked at Janine with squinty eyes. "Do you want to move there?"

Janine met her gaze. "Richard has asked us to come and live with him."

Lisa lifted a small brow in surprise. "You mean like Daddy and Bernadette?"

Janine wasn't aware that they were actually living together now. How long had that been going on? John had seemingly been more at home keeping his girlfriends at a safe distance. Obviously this one was different. After all, he was going to marry her—or so he claimed.

She couldn't help but wonder if it would last or end up in divorce court. Like her own marriage to John.

She decided not to speculate further, having no desire to get caught up in the romance politics of her ex-husband's life—other than what effect they could have on his daughter. And, right now, Lisa seemed well adjusted to Bernadette. No reason to rock the boat. Especially considering that Janine was set to begin her own voyage that required her utmost attention and steady navigation.

"Yes, honey, just like Daddy and Bernadette," she told Lisa equably, realizing that most kids today understood that sometimes adults who cared for each other chose to simply live together in the same house as partners, without legal strings attached. Or perhaps as a prelude to marriage.

"When?" Lisa asked.

"As soon as we can pack things up and go, honey," Janine answered honestly, the anxiousness in her voice unwavering.

Lisa tilted her head. "Do you love Richard?"

Janine thought about it and what love might mean to a seven-year-old. "Yes, I do," she said feelingly. Janine had never realized just how much till now, when asked candidly by her daughter.

"Are you going to marry him?" Lisa wrinkled her nose.

Janine listened to the innocent but intelligent question. It was one she found herself pondering more and more, but did not have a concrete answer to. Living with a man with no ring on her finger wasn't something she wanted to last forever. She was still old-fashioned and believed in marriage. The last thing she wanted was to set a bad example for Lisa that it was all right to live together with no piece of paper that made it legal.

But she also knew that in this day and age rushing into marriage was foolish by any standard for all concerned. Especially when you had been there, done that, and been unsuccessful.

She wasn't about to put the cart ahead of the horse again— even if she relished the thought of someday marrying again.

"I think there is a good chance we will get married, Lisa," Janine answered optimistically, a soft edge to her voice. "But probably not right away. We'd want to make sure everyone was happy being together. Do you understand what I'm saying?"

Lisa twisted her lips and nodded. "Yeah."

Janine dug her teeth into the cheeseburger, wondering what was going on in her daughter's head in laying all this on her at once. "So how do you feel about all this?" She decided it best to ask.

Lisa played with a fry thoughtfully. "What about Daddy?" she asked worriedly. "Will I still get to see him?"

"Of course you will, sweet pea," Janine assured her. "Anytime you like you can visit your daddy. He can even come to see you in California sometime if he wants."

Janine had already brought up this possibility to Richard. He had agreed it was important for Lisa to feel she could stay connected to both of her parents, though Richard also wanted very much to be a father to Lisa. Janine liked the idea, too, and was sure Lisa would as well.

"Can Murphy come, too?" Lisa's eyes widened with hope.

"We'd never move anywhere without Murphy," promised Janine.

Lisa broke into a broad smile. "Great!"

Janine smiled at her tentatively. "So can I take that as a yes for California?"

Lisa giggled. "Yes! Let's go!" She chewed on a fry. "I can't wait to move there."

Neither could she, Janine thought, elated. Suddenly things seemed to be falling into place for them and Janine sensed that starting over again would come with many rewards, not the least of which was a handsome photographer named Richard Edgar Lowrey.

Janine phoned Richard that night with the good news. He was ecstatic.

"I know you're sacrificing a lot, baby, by moving across the country to my neck of the woods," he said considerately. "I'll do everything in my power to try and make you and Lisa happy here."

Janine sighed wistfully. "I know."

"I love you, Janine," Richard murmured. "More than words can say. More than I was willing to admit to myself before...."

She blinked back tears. "I love you, too, Richard."

It was something Janine never thought she would say to

anyone again. For a time John had poisoned her against love. But Richard had proven to be the antidote. For that alone she felt grateful, as if an angel was sitting on her shoulder, giving her a slice of heaven in the form of one extraordinary man. To be given a second chance at life and love was a blessing Janine would never take for granted.

Not for one second.

Chapter 49

Richard took the *Marjah1* out with Henry on a cool, crisp afternoon at the beginning of September. The Pacific Ocean was calm with only a few ripples on its crystal-blue surface. Janine and Lisa were flying in a week from Monday. Their belongings were arriving a few days later. Richard had never dreamt that this would all come together so perfectly, as if made to order by some force much greater than himself. He had been prepared to do whatever was necessary to have a life with Janine and Lisa, feeling it was the right course to take. He was even willing to move elsewhere, if that was what it took to prove his love for Janine.

But it was Janine who had courageously given up her life to be with him, just as Kassandra had. Richard knew he had been extremely fortunate to meet two remarkable women in his lifetime, falling in love with each. He chose not to compare his love for the two, preferring to keep them as separate loves of his life, but equally close to his heart and spirit.

He had tried to ready the house for its new residents—cleaning, painting, scrubbing, even acquiring some new furnishings he thought they might like. Yet, as much as he wanted to, Richard had been unable to simply pack up and remove Kassandra and Sheena's things as though they didn't belong. They were as much a part of that house as he was, he told himself. While no longer living there, Richard believed he still owed it to their memories to keep them alive, if dormant, through what he could still hold on to.

But Henry thought otherwise, and wasn't afraid to tell his son. "You've got to let them go, Richard." He raised his voice over the roar of the engine and the boat slicing its way through the sea. "You have a new family now."

A new family, Richard thought, gazing over the horizon. *Yeah, Janine and Lisa are my new family.* He liked the sound of that, and considered the future. There had been no talk of marriage as yet. He didn't want to rush into anything neither he nor Janine was ready for. But he believed this to be a mere formality that could be worked out in time. They were right for each other. He knew that without a doubt. It wasn't necessary to have a piece of paper to make it official, even for his role in Lisa's life. He considered her just as much a part of his world as his own daughter had been.

"Are you listening to me?" snapped Henry, a cigarette dangling precariously from his mouth, smoke streaming up into the air.

"Yes, I hear you," Richard muttered, favoring him. "The two families are *not* competing. They are merely coexisting."

"No such thing—unless you're a bigamist." Henry took a drag of the cigarette. "You don't owe Kassandra and Sheena anything more than you've already given them. And I don't think they'd expect anything more. Janine and her daughter deserve a fair shake from you, son. Just as you need to be fair to yourself."

"What exactly are you trying to say, Dad?" Richard tried to keep his voice steady even as he felt his temperature rise.

Henry regarded him squarely. "I'm saying that keeping *everything* that reminds you of Kassandra and Sheena is exactly what you don't want to do. Keeping their belongings inconspicuous in closets ain't going to cut it, son. You need to pack up the stuff and get rid of everything. Keep a few photographs in albums, if you like, but the rest should be donated to the Salvation Army where people can put it to good use. It's the only way you can settle the past, Richard, and move on with the present *and* future."

"Do you realize what the hell you're asking me to do?" Richard shot him a narrow-eyed look, unnerved by the finality of it all.

"I know exactly what the hell I'm asking you to do!" Henry held his ground steadfastly. "I'm asking you to stop living with your guilt for something that wasn't your fault. Holding on to dead memories will only drag you down, son, and maybe Janine and Lisa with you. I don't want to see that happen—not while I'm still alive."

Richard locked glares with Henry before looking away respectfully. It took only a moment for the proper perspective to kick in. Once again his father's insight, often expressed in sharp and candid tones, had managed to cut through his angst like scissors and hit home. As much as he wanted to hoard the belongings of his beloved Kassandra and precious Sheena like priceless gems, Richard knew in his heart that it was time to say goodbye once and for all, for the sake of another woman and girl now depending on him just as much as *they* once had.

Richard turned to his father and sucked in a deep breath. "Maybe it's time we head back in now," he said thoughtfully.

Henry nodded perceptively. "Yeah, son. I think it is."

Chapter 50

It was one of those nights when the wind howled like a freight train and the skies opened up to unleash nature's fury in a blinding rainstorm. The Monterey Peninsula was hit particularly hard by the storm that showed up out of the blue and gave no signs of letting up. A couple of hours earlier it had been a cloudy, cool, dry day with only a mild crosswind, giving no hint of things to come.

Richard's new book, *Autumn in Zimbabwe,* had just been released to rave reviews and impressive preliminary sales. Kassandra seemed to be growing more beautiful with age after eleven years of marriage and Sheena, now seven going on seventeen, gave Richard more to rejoice about than he could have ever imagined. Having talked about and tried unsuccessfully to add to their family for over a year, Richard and Kassandra were hopeful that the coming year would surely bring another daughter or son into the picture to marvel over.

They had even discussed adoption as a viable possibility if another pregnancy was not in the cards. Sheena, eager to have a brother or sister, seemed keen on the idea.

To Richard, life could not get much better. More than one person had told him since meeting Kassandra what a lucky man he was. He didn't need to be convinced. Between his wife, daughter and professional success, he had made a habit of counting his blessings.

He never imagined that one wrong turn of events could shatter that illusion into a million pieces. And, in the process, turn his life and everything in it upside down and spiraling out of control.

That night, Richard, Kassandra and Sheena celebrated the publication of his book by taking in a movie, then having dinner at an elegant coastal restaurant. It sat atop a hill overlooking the ocean and all its wonder. For Richard, the five-course meal seemed a fitting celebration.

In his mind, they would drive home, tuck Sheena into bed and he and Kassandra would go to bed themselves. There they would make love, sharing every part of their bodies with the other, drift off to sleep wrapped in each other's arms like human octopuses and wake up to a new day with endless possibilities—maybe even having conceived a child during one magical night.

But something went horribly wrong that would alter the course of their destiny and be an albatross Richard would carry around his neck forever.

The bad weather had come in before they ever left the restaurant that night.

Sheena, brave as she was, clung to her mother and cried, "I'm scared, Mommy."

"Don't be," Kassandra said to her, sounding unconcerned.

"It's just a bit of nasty weather that likes to rear its ugly head every now and then. It'll pass over, sweetheart, before you know it."

But the wary glint in Kassandra's eyes, favoring Richard with concern, said otherwise. Richard also knew something was strangely wrong out there. The truth was that he had never known the rain and wind to mix with such venom since they'd lived on the Monterey Peninsula. There had been no reports of hurricanes, tornadoes or other natural disasters headed their way. He guessed that it was merely an anomaly that had taken them by surprise just for the sake of it and had no plans to stick around indefinitely.

Further, he chose to believe that there was less bite to the bad weather than it appeared at first glance.

So, half an hour later, when the storm failed to abate, Richard called for the check, deciding to go for it and brave the conditions to get home. All he could think of was sharing a glass of wine with Kassandra before retiring. There seemed no need to wait the rotten weather out all night.

"Maybe we should stay here for a while longer," Kassandra uttered edgily.

"Please, Daddy," Sheena seconded, her small body fidgeting. "It's too scary out there."

Richard thought about it. But not for long.

"We're only about ten minutes from home, honey," he told his daughter, seeking to ease her uneasiness and that of her mother. No more than twenty minutes tops with a slow drive. "I won't let anything happen to my two girls, I promise. In fact, I wouldn't be surprised if the storm has all but disappeared by the time we pull up in our driveway...."

Richard wasn't sure if he really believed the part about the storm disappearing or not, but it seemed to go a long way in convincing them everything would be all right.

He had already convinced himself.

They left the restaurant in Richard's silver Mercedes—a birthday gift a year earlier from Kassandra, courtesy of the interest earned on some sound investments. Up to that point there had been no mechanical problems to speak of with the car.

And no checkup in the past six months.

Though they'd had little need for an umbrella when they'd left home, everyone got soaked and nearly blown away before reaching the Mercedes. The shared family experience of getting drenched seemed to relieve the tension, causing them all to have a good laugh once in the safety and dryness of the car.

Richard pulled his seat belt across his broad chest and latched it. Kassandra put hers on beside him, while Sheena was strapped in her booster chair in the back seat. Right away Richard could see that the visibility was not very good. But he had seen worse. That, along with the stubborn streak he'd inherited from his father, bolstered his courage to finish what he had started.

They began the drive home.

For a while it seemed as if they would weather the worst of the storm as Richard moved down the slick coastal highway at slightly more than a snail's pace, not daring to go any faster. A guardrail separated the road from rugged steep cliffs that hung above the ocean like ghosts and goblins. The radio reported the severe weather pattern as a "freak of nature" that came along once every hundred years or so.

"Damn," Richard muttered to himself, musing about the bad timing.

He found himself wondering what it must have been like for those caught in this "freak of nature" a century ago.

Or what those poor souls might have to look forward to a hundred years from now.

But the immediate concern was to get his family home safely. Instinctively, Richard knew that this desire would be tested in a way he could never have anticipated, when he suddenly swerved to his left to avoid hitting a stalled truck. Its lights were out, making it virtually invisible under these conditions until they were literally right upon it. Only, then it was too late.

In the process, the brakes seemed to lock up as if they had a mind of their own. In spite of his best efforts, Richard could not get them to function properly, causing the first real wave of panic to turn his stomach to jelly. They were headed downhill with no way to prevent it. And the car's speed began to pick up as though being swept forward by a powerful magnet.

"Richard—" gasped Kassandra, the stark fear evident in her voice. "Stop the car!"

"I'm trying to, dammit," Richard blasted, cursing himself for placing them in the precarious situation they now found themselves in. He stomped mightily on the brakes with everything he had, to no avail.

Sheena began crying and screaming in the back, perhaps sensing they were suddenly in a fight for their lives.

And they were losing the battle.

The road was curving left and right and Richard did his best to negotiate it in almost zero visibility at this point and at a speed that seemed to continue to rise by the second, aided by rain-soaked pavement and brakes that had completely abandoned them.

Richard didn't dare look at the anguish in the faces of his

wife and daughter, fearing it would only reflect his own severe feelings of apprehension and helplessness.

Not to mention sheer mortality. He'd never considered that death could be right around the bend for him and his family. Now he had to stare it straight in the face and pray that it wasn't time to meet their maker.

The car almost seemed to slow down, giving all inside pause that they might survive this yet. But it was only a momentary pause. A misperception. A cruel figment of their collective imaginations, borne out of sheer terror.

In fact, Richard had lost control of the Mercedes on a particularly steep curve that came upon them abruptly. Before he could even begin to try and correct it, the car slammed into the railing, ripping it apart like aluminum foil. They plunged down the embankment, unable to avoid it.

Amidst piercing screams by Kassandra and Sheena, the car rolled over several times, windows shattering, metal crunching and twisting, all functions coming to a frightening halt—till the Mercedes settled into the water upside down.

The air bag had slammed into Richard with lightning force, knocking the wind out of him. He was dazed and seeing stars, but somehow still conscious as blood rushed to his head as though in a hurry. The battered and broken car was beginning to take in water.

Fast.

Operating on impulse more than guts or know-how, Richard immediately pushed at the button to release his seat belt. Fearing the worst, he braced himself for a fight to get it off, but was surprised to see that it actually released with no resistance. He dropped onto the roof of the car, wincing from hitting his knee hard. He looked toward Kassandra. She was motionless above him, her head bent sideways at an awkward angle, still strapped in her seat. He tried to get her seatbelt off but the damn latch was jammed. He reached up and felt her limp neck. There was no detectable pulse.

Richard's heart lurched. *Don't die on me, baby,* he pleaded in his head.

There had to be a pulse in there, he tried to convince himself. Somewhere.

Kassandra can't be dead. Richard was panic-stricken, refusing to believe the worst.

Not like this.

Not here and now.

Richard prayed like never before that they would somehow all make it out of this nightmare alive. They had to. He dismissed any other alternative from his mind, as if that would prevent it from happening.

He was starting to have trouble breathing as the icy water crept toward him like a massive, bloodthirsty spider. There was an air pocket.

But for how long?

Every second counted. Richard knew they were passing by faster than he could think.

He looked up at the back seat and saw Sheena. She was hanging upside down, unconscious, her small body twisted like a pretzel. She was still strapped into the seat, which kept her face just out of the reach of the rising water.

Richard could barely believe this terrifying ordeal was happening to him—to them—right before his eyes. One moment they were in the restaurant enjoying each other's company as a family. The next they were trapped in a car somewhere in the ocean and no one was going to come to the rescue. No matter how loud or agonized Richard's prayers were, he recognized that their lives were literally hanging in the balance, with each moment more critical than the last.

It was up to him to save his family.

Or sure as hell die trying, he thought with renewed conviction.

Refusing to panic to the point of breaking, Richard drew on courage and strength he never knew he had. In spite of the damage to the driver's-side door he managed to open it with some effort, letting more water into the car. He turned to Kassandra and yanked at her seat belt, twisting it violently.

"Come on, give, dammit," Richard yelled through clenched teeth, frantically trying to pry the seat belt loose. Finally it snapped open. Once freed, Kassandra sank down to the top of the car, into the murky water now pouring in from all sides with nowhere to go but up. He was able to position her unconscious, limp body into a sitting position to try and save time, before turning his attention to their daughter.

Richard wormed his way into the back seat and, after applying pressure and sheer willpower, unsnapped the belt holding Sheena. She, too, sank down to the roof now at the bottom of the upside-down car, as though a little angel.

Only they were anywhere but in heaven.

Hell was more descriptive of the murky, watery, trapped setting, Richard thought.

He caught Sheena before she could hit the roof. She was still breathing, but barely.

Richard began to feel light-headed, but refused to pass out, ending his own life and any chance of saving theirs. He sucked in a deep breath and held Sheena's limp body close to his chest, while thinking: *Hang in there, honey. I'll get us out of here.*

Bringing Sheena to the front seat, Richard could see that Kassandra had tilted over and was now facedown in the water.

He lifted his wife and somehow, some way, managed to get the three of them out of the car.

Using one arm to hold both Kassandra and Sheena, Richard flailed away with his other arm, desperately seeking to swim toward the surface. Though he hardly qualified as a champion swimmer, he considered himself more than capable of holding his own under normal circumstances. But this didn't qualify as normal.

No, for this Richard had had to reach deep inside and find whatever reserve he could tap into, if they had any chance whatsoever of making it out of the water alive. He could see through the mucky water that the surface was within reach. The car had apparently gotten caught on some underwater logs and had not sunk very deep.

Richard's body felt the weight of water along with carrying Kassandra's and Sheena's lifeless bodies. But they were still moving upward.

Managing to get his head above water, Richard gaspingly brought air into his lungs, which felt as if they were on fire. He used every ounce of strength to pull his wife and daughter up and then half swam and half stumbled to the shore. He dragged Kassandra and Sheena to some nearby rocks where he laid their motionless bodies. The rain continued to come down in buckets, disregarding their life-and-death struggle as if it simply came with the territory.

Immediately, desperation fueling him, Richard tried mouth-to-mouth resuscitation on Kassandra. She was not breathing, as far as he could tell. He suspected she had a broken neck, by the look of the unnatural tilt of her head.

"Please hold on, baby," he cried out. "We're back on land again. Everything is going to be all right."

Richard fought off the urge to believe otherwise, continuing to try to bring Kassandra back, praying and hoping to get a hand from the man upstairs. Richard did not want to lose this person he'd promised to protect always.

There was still no sign of life.

He tried resuscitating her again. Harder this time, using every breath he had, frenetic in his determination to save the only woman he'd ever loved.

Nothing.

Kassandra would not respond, no matter how much he wanted her to. It was as if all life had been drained out of her and she wanted only to be left alone to peacefully make the transition to the next world.

But Richard was not prepared to let her go, even when something inside told him Kassandra was already outside of his grasp and en route to the heavens. Not yet able to come to terms with his wife's death, he went to Sheena. Her wave-splashed, injured body lay still and stiff. Richard put his hand to her neck and again detected the slightest pulse, causing his own heart to skip a beat. It gave him hope that his baby girl might somehow pull through this.

But he couldn't save her alone. He had to get help.

Richard managed to climb the steep rocks that they had gone over and through, ignoring the cuts and bruises his hands and body endured and the twinge of fear that he might not make it back in time.

At the top of the cliff, on rain-soaked ground, Richard ran blindly through the downpour, determined not to be defeated. He found a tavern that was open, stumbling, then falling in.

"What the hell happened to you?" asked the oversize woman with a blond bouffant hairdo behind the bar, chomping on tobacco as if her life depended on it.

"My wife...my daughter—" Richard gasped, his head

spinning. "Lost control of the car. Went over the embankment. You have to help me…help them…please, right away!"

Whether it was the stark realization of what had happened that hit him like a sledgehammer, sheer exhaustion or injuries he didn't know he had, the woman shuffling toward him was the last thing Richard remembered before passing out.

When he came to, Richard was in the emergency room of a hospital with people standing around him as if looking at an exhibit in a museum. Or animals at the zoo. His lips hurt and felt as if they were glued together. He pried them open to speak of the only thing on his mind: his family. He wouldn't allow himself to think that they weren't going to be all right. They had to be.

"Kassandra—Sheena—?" Richard tried to sit up but his aching body would not let him.

A tall, wiry man wearing a doctor's smock and resembling *Star Trek*'s Mr. Spock stepped forward. "I'm Dr. Ronald Carpenter," he said, then furrowed his brow and paused for what seemed an eternity. "Your wife and daughter… I'm sorry, but I'm afraid they didn't make it."

As if in suspended animation, it took Richard a moment or two to digest in his mind what he'd just heard. He wanted to dismiss it like he would a pesky salesman. Shut out what he didn't want to be true, not in his most terrifying of nightmares.

Nor would he have wished it on his worst enemy.

But reality kicked in and Richard began to comprehend the magnitude of what had happened to his little girl and his loving wife. It was more than he could stand.

"Dammit, noooo—!" Richard screamed from the top of his lungs, as if it would somehow right this horrible wrong. The mere thought of life without his beautiful Kassandra and their remarkable daughter, Sheena, was something he wasn't prepared to deal with. And never would be.

How could fate be so cruel as to deliver such a fatal blow? Richard could only ponder in his hysterical state of mind as the doctor and others held him down.

He had to wonder if he'd done something so wrong to deserve this. Or if Kassandra or Sheena had.

Richard quickly dismissed the latter, knowing full well they didn't deserve to have their lives snuffed out so suddenly and cruelly.

He wanted to be dead, too. He was overcome with enormous guilt that he couldn't save them. He didn't deserve to live—not without the two people he loved most in the whole world. It would be forever empty were he forced to go it alone.

But Richard would live with the terrible consequences of that stormy night. Officially, they were listed as weather-related fatalities, the failure of the brakes an unfortunate result.

For months afterward, Richard woke up bawling like a baby, wondering what he could or should have done differently to change the outcome. He replayed that night over and over in his mind again and again like a broken record. But nothing he did or thought could alter the fact that two precious lives were lost forever. And his life had been inexplicably spared. He came to believe that it was punishment—his own private hell—for the ill-advised decision to put his family in harm's way.

Richard sank into a deep depression, one that caused him to shut out the outside world in virtually every way. He blamed himself for Kassandra and Sheena's deaths and had no desire to live his life, as a result. At least, not as it had once been lived. He didn't feel like a man now that his precious woman was no longer with him. Nor did he feel like a father with his only child dead.

This left Richard as only a shell of his former self. His career as a successful photographer, which had once been his lifeblood, came to a crashing halt. He saw this as too painful a reminder of a life that had been good. One that included his beautiful wife and daughter.

In his mind, Richard didn't ever want to feel good again. His all-consuming guilt wouldn't allow such a luxury.

But then things changed inexplicably.

A new woman entered his life just when Richard thought the flame had been snuffed out of it forever. Janine Henderson, like an amazing gift from God, taught him how to forgive himself and others. They taught each other how to live and love again. She had a daughter who warmed Richard's heart and gave him pleasant memories of his own daughter.

He was sure that Kassandra and Sheena would approve of his new family, encouraging him to be happy and make Janine and Lisa as happy as they had been.

Richard found himself at peace again and welcomed a second chance at love, tenderness, devotion and a family he could call his own.

He had found this in Janine and Lisa.

Just as surely as he had with his first family.

Chapter 51

The gulls and cormorants nuzzled lazily along the shoreline as if they had not a care in the world. Farther offshore, herds of seals and sea lions gathered on rocks, content to be amongst one another as if one big, happy family. Miles of marine-blue water extended as far as the eye could see. Above, chalky white clouds looked like painted, billowy images on a canvas of powder-blue skies with a bright yellow sun full of zest and energy.

Richard stood on the beach, gazing into the water pensively. Kimble ran around him as though he'd lost his sense of direction.

"It's all right, boy," Richard said, his voice a calming influence that got the dog to settle down and stare solemnly at the ocean. "I miss them, too."

He wiped a solitary tear from his face as he held a silent memorial for his wife and daughter. They had been buried at sea, their cremated remains dispersed so that their spirits would always be free as part of the community they'd enlivened so with their presence, if only for a short while.

Even Kimble could feel their essence, Richard sensed. Just as surely as if Kassandra and Sheena were still alive. But now the time had come to say goodbye. To release their souls from the bondage he had kept them in by refusing to relinquish what they once were as a family. He knew now this was wrong for them and him. Even for Kimble, who Richard suspected was feeding off his own guilt and grief in keeping them alive.

"I'll never stop loving you, Kass, baby," Richard cried. "Or you, Sheena, sweetheart. You'll always be a part of me, wherever I go, whatever I do, for the rest of my life." He wiped away more tears. "But I won't let you rule my life anymore. You see, I finally understand that it's time for me to move on. And to let you move on to that place where you can be at peace eternally."

Richard reached down and grabbed a handful of golden sand. Flinging it toward the ocean, he watched it disperse with the wind, just as Kassandra and Sheena had three years ago. This was, in effect, their final send-off.

And his own, as well.

"I've found a most precious woman," he told Kassandra, certain she could hear him in heaven. "One who's as sweet and loving as you were. She's filled a void in my life that had been there following me everywhere I went like a tall, gloomy shadow ever since you left. I'm in love with Janine, Kass, and I intend to make a life with her and her daughter, Lisa. I just wanted you to know that you won't have to worry about me anymore. I'll be fine. So will Kimble. Be good to yourself, baby, and take care of Sheena for me. Both of you rest in peace."

Richard took one final long look into the ocean, almost imagining he could see their spirits rise up, lighting the sky with a heavenly smile, then disappearing into a dimension of spiritual contentment. Peace. Freedom.

It was done. Kassandra and Sheena were now at peace. It was time to welcome his new family and let them know that he would be there for them as long as they wanted him to be.

And he fully intended for that to be many, many years.

Hopefully a lifetime.

Richard began to walk away. The tears were still in his eyes. Only, this time they were tears of love, happiness and life.

"Come on, boy," he called out to Kimble. "Time to go home."

The dog barked once or twice—still looking out at the water, as if saying his final goodbye—then dashed toward Richard, who sensed that he, too, knew they had made their peace and could now get on with their lives.

With so much to look forward to.

Chapter 52

That September they began the rest of their lives. Janine and Lisa left New York for the tranquil scenic beauty of Pebble Beach, California, and the welcoming arms of Richard Edgar Lowrey. It was a match made not only in heaven but also on earth, where good things happened to good people.

Though John had initially resisted the notion of his daughter being taken across the country, he warmed up to it when he realized it was what she wanted and that Janine and Richard were committed to making sure Lisa remained an important part of his life.

Using contacts she'd made at Callister-Reynolds, Janine was able to find work as a part-time senior editor with a distinguished San Francisco publishing house. She also agreed to stay on with Callister-Reynolds temporarily as an editor-at-large to work with Richard on his next two books. Dennis promised her there would be an in-house job waiting if they ever moved back to the Big Apple. She told him politely not to hold his breath.

Her first and foremost obligations were to Lisa and Richard and making what they had set into motion work. There were some adjustments to be made all around, but they were committed to doing so as a group, with everyone having an equal vote.

Janine was ever conscious of the ghosts of Kassandra and Sheena in the house, even though Richard had tried hard to rid it of their spirits, removing everything that was theirs or reminded him of them in a sad way. Eventually Janine began to regard her predecessors as allies rather than enemies.

Friends instead of foes.

Heavenly angels watching over all of them rather than up-to-no-good spirits.

With their unspoken but important celestial support and encouragement, Richard was successfully able to resume his photography career with no sign of erosion of his skills. In the years ahead, he would go on to complete his books with Callister-Reynolds, both becoming wild bestsellers with critical acclaim, and to sign on to do three more. In between books, he kept busy on assignments to take pictures for several prominent African-American magazines and newspapers.

Richard asked Janine to marry him one sunny evening while they were walking barefoot on the beach. Henry was sauntering ahead of them, a cigarette stuck lazily between his lips. Off to the side, Lisa and Kimble were playfully running circles around each other.

"I think we should get married." Richard had said it almost out of the blue. It was six months after they had started living together.

Nearly floored, as he had not hinted about marriage, Janine

quickly gathered herself and responded with fluttering lashes, "Are you proposing, Richard?"

He stopped walking and gazed earnestly into her eyes. "Yes, Janine, I'm asking you to marry me. I know we've dodged the issue so neither would risk stepping on the other's toes, but I love you and want you to be my wife. It's time for us to make it official. That is, if we're on the same wavelength here...."

Janine was trembling as she said, "We are, sweetheart. But...are you sure?" She didn't want any second-guessing later.

"I've never been more sure." Richard took her shaking hands, brought them to his lips and kissed them. "Baby, I know what you're thinking. You're wondering if I am over Kassandra. Or if this is some kind of impulsive thing that I'll only end up regretting later. Or you will." He paused. "Well, I can put your mind to rest. Yes, Kass was my wife and life, but she's gone. So is Sheena. I accept that. Now I want to marry you and spend the rest of my life with you. And I want Lisa to be our daughter, even if she has another father, too. I love you, Janine."

She caught her breath, her heart threatening to burst with joy. Marriage was something she had always hoped for, for it spoke of a commitment of love and togetherness as husband and wife. Nothing could be more sacred. But only if both parties were of the same mind.

Janine knew Richard had made his peace with Kassandra and Sheena and was ready to move on. She, too, was ready for a life as *Mrs.* Richard Edgar Lowrey, wanting it more than anything she could imagine at this point in her life.

Janine's eyes welled with tears as she gazed at the man who had brought her such happiness and continued to, and murmured, "I love you, too, Richard. Yes, I'll marry you, baby!"

A broad grin lit Richard's face and he hugged Janine tightly. "You've made me one happy fellow!"

She kissed him on the mouth. "And you've made me one happy girl." She beamed.

"Oh, yeah?" he asked, as if in doubt.

"Yeah." She tapped him on the nose and, tiptoeing, kissed it.

Richard looked down the beach. "So why don't we let the rest of the family in on our little secret?"

"Yes, why don't we?" responded Janine effervescently.

They held hands and gazed at Henry, who was like a child and grandfather at the same time as he played lovingly with Lisa and Kimble in the sand.

As they approached, Janine snuck one more sweet and tasty kiss of her fiancé, before beginning the next exhilarating chapter of their life together.

Shortly after marrying Janine, Richard adopted Lisa. A year later the family moved to Santa Monica, feeling it was time for a fresh start in their own place. Henry came with them, staying in the guest cottage that was remodeled to his specifications.

The main house itself was big enough to make room for a new addition to the family. Verhonda Nicole Lowrey was both a tribute to the past and the gateway to a promising and loving future.

Dear Reader,

After a highly successful first Arabesque romance novel, *Dark and Dashing*, featured in the bestselling two-in-one book, *Slow Motion*, I am excited to be back with my second contemporary romance, *Love Once Again*.

As Arabesque has now joined Harlequin and its terrific line of romances, it will allow even more readers to discover my writing and passion for creating wonderful love stories that warm the heart and soul.

~~Being~~ a male romance author in the tradition of Nicholas Sparks and similar novelists, it is especially gratifying to write romances alongside female authors in allowing readers a broader perspective on the magic of love, romance and passion.

Love Once Again is sure to please those who love a heartwarming romance with plenty of sizzle and spice. It will take you from the busy streets of the Big Apple to the breathtaking beauty of the Monterey Peninsula and Pebble Beach.

I hope to meet many of you here and there at book signings, conferences, conventions or wherever I travel across the country and abroad.

I welcome reviews on *Love Once Again*, that can be posted at online booksellers, such as Amazon.com and BN.com.

Also, feel free to share your thoughts on this book with me through the Harlequin Web site.

Stay tuned for future contemporary romance novels by this author.

All the best,

Devon Vaughn Archer

Slow Motion—Four and a half stars and Top Pick from *Romantic Times BOOKclub*